KISSPROOF
WORLD

a novel

WILLIAM WEST

Relax. Read. Repeat.

KISSPROOF WORLD
By William West
Published by TouchPoint Press
Brookland, AR 72417
www.touchpointpress.com

Softcover ISBN: 978-1-956851-35-9

Editor: Kimberly Coghlan
Cover Design: Colbie Myles

Visit the author's website at williamwest.net

First Edition

Printed in the United States of America.

This book is for the victims.

Kissproof World is a work of fiction and all the characters are of my own creation. It was inspired by my work many years ago as a child protective social worker with Harris County Child Welfare which is responsible for investigating reports of child abuse in Houston, Texas and surrounding areas, including Deer Park and Clear Lake. The story came to me after reading a poem by Dylan Thomas titled *When Like a Running Grave*. I also wish to acknowledge my wife, Amber, for her patience and guiding thoughts; and Kimberly Coghlan for her exceptional editing.

All, men my madmen, the unwholesome wind
With whistler's cough contages, time on track
Shapes in a cinder death; love for his trick,
Happy Cadaver's hunger as you take
The kissproof world

—Dylan Thomas
excerpt from *When, Like a Running Grave*

Part One: Summer Feather

Chapter One

Alec arrived at Morning House during the early summer, when tropical storms out of the Gulf of Mexico took turns slashing at the Texas coast. The old, sturdy house shivered under the threat of an approaching squall as darkness descended over the windows like the closing of a heavy, tomb door. Only moments before, the sky was clear, but now, the heaviness of unforgiving rain tapped incessantly at the walls and roof.

Neva and Warren faced the window, their backs to the bookcase filled with Neva's dog-eared and spine-cracked books on child development, adolescent behavior, cognitive therapy, and behavior modification. Dr. Mueller sat at Neva's desk, quietly thumbing through pages of a file in front of him. Across the desk, Alec waited. A sofa, a small table, and a floor lamp in the corner occupied the only other space in the office. Pretending not to watch Alec, Neva delicately dusted the lap of her skirt with slender fingers. Alec sat motionless, with what Neva perceived as calm indifference—just one more time waiting for someone to decide about his life. She knew he was about the same age as the others, old enough to have his own beliefs and biases, his own history, but too young to be so relaxed, so unruffled. That frightened her, and she wondered if it indicated something deeper, a personal aberration that might make him dangerous.

"Ah, here it is," Dr. Mueller said. He held his finger on a passage in the file. "Dr. Edelstein noted that you frequently exhibited hostility toward the hospital staff. I want to address that because your time here will be very different from the hospital. You'll find Morning House more like a family. This is a halfway house, not a hospital. Your time here depends on how well you do, so we want you to get along with the other residents. We expect it. Ms. Bell and Mr. McKinny are your counselors, and they are here to help you with that. If you can't, well, you won't be here long. It's that simple."

Neva tilted her head and pushed her hair behind her ears, sweeping her hand through her dark waves. If Alec looked her way, she could smile to comfort him, see if it had any effect. He turned his head toward the window instead but quickly adjusted his gaze to the desktop, scanning the objects in front of him as if searching for answers. His eyes fixed on the framed bird. She wanted to believe it provided him comfort.

"I know that sounds harsh," Dr. Mueller continued. "But it's necessary to have an understanding about that rule. Actually, I think you will find rewards here if you just give it a fair shake." Dr. Mueller leaned back in the chair, his long fingers shaping a church, its steeple gently touching his lips. Without a word, he lowered the steeple away from his mouth and smiled at Alec, who didn't move. Dr. Mueller shifted his gaze to Neva and sent her a self-assured wink.

Neva turned away and noticed Warren rolling his eyes. Warren had once told Neva that Dr. Mueller seemed to be acting out a part in a play. Neva was amused by Warren's cynical nature, but she was his supervisor, and she didn't want to jeopardize that relationship by being too familiar.

"I think everything is going to work out just fine," Dr. Mueller said. "Dr. Edelstein has assured me that you are ready for this."

Alec was silent.

"Does the rain bother you?" Dr. Mueller asked.

"No," Alec said as he lowered his eyes to the photograph of the bird on the desk.

Neva could see his lips reading the words silently.

Here on the earth's brink
I have for a time
Miraculously settled my life.

3

The words had given *her* hope. She saw them on a card in a drugstore and framed the card to put on her desk. Neva wanted to reach out and tell Alec that everything was going to be all right. The sky rumbled long and low as another door closed, and Alec drew back, sitting upright in his chair.

"The streets will be flooding soon," Warren said.

Dr. Mueller looked to the rain-blurred window. "I have always been fascinated by the powerful force of nature. You get used to the rain, I suppose, living here. Especially along the Gulf Coast. But you already know that, don't you, Alec?"

"I haven't lived here in a long time," Alec said.

"Four years can seem like a long time," Dr. Mueller said. There was a moment of silence, but the pause in Dr. Mueller's smile indicated that he did not want it broken. "You can forget a lot in four years. But it is not really forgotten, Alec. Somewhere inside your mind, your past lies hidden. You may not need it, or you may not want to remember it, so you repress it. You store it away, sometimes so far away that no one can get to it, not even you. But it's still there, and it can bother you. It can affect the way you behave. Like nature, the mind is also a powerful force."

Neva could see Alec's grip tightening around the armrests of the chair. She wanted to tell Dr. Mueller that he could leave and they would be fine.

Suddenly, a flash of light ignited the sky, exploded into the room, and shook the house on its foundation. With a shriek, Neva leaped in her chair and grabbed for her heart. "My God," she said, taking in a deep breath. "I thought the house was coming down on top of us."

Alec watched her with a pleasant grin on his face, as if Neva's shock and fear had extinguished his own apprehension. She didn't know why she was so unnerved by the storm. When she laughed, he laughed with her, and she watched his searching eyes. Then, she heard in his voice something strangely familiar, something that made her uneasy, and she looked away.

"Maybe we should reschedule this conference for a time when the weather is not so dramatic," she said.

"Or *traumatic*," Dr. Mueller interjected with a sharp laugh. It was more of a scuff in the atmosphere than a true laugh.

"I'm sorry," she said. "I didn't mean to . . ."

"Oh, that's quite all right, Ms. Bell," Dr. Mueller said, a smile still trapping his handsome features. "The interruption might not have been planned, but it was certainly necessary. I had better leave before I get flooded in." For a moment, Dr. Mueller gazed at Neva as if he had forgotten the urgency in his own words.

Warren interrupted, "We'll need to be checking with the school to make sure the others get back safely."

"Good idea," Neva said, suspecting Dr. Mueller was waiting for an invitation to remain until the rain subsided. "We also need to get Alec settled in."

"Yes, of course," Dr. Mueller said. He collected his papers and addressed Alec with a strange sincerity. "Morning House will be your home for a while, Alec. At least until you are ready to make it on your own. Anytime you have a problem, you can talk to Ms. Bell or Mr. McKinny." Dr. Mueller walked around the desk to where Alec was sitting, stood over him, and extended his neck so his eyes could capture Alec's through the underbrush of their shared unfamiliarity. Alec watched Dr. Mueller cautiously but remained still, prepared and undetected. With an avuncular display of affection, Dr. Mueller patted Alec on the shoulder. "In the meantime, I look forward to getting to know you better."

Neva motioned for Warren to wait with Alec as she hurried after Dr. Mueller, who was already moving past the dayroom. He had a refined way of walking, which made him appear taller than he was. His sharp, slender features gave him an intimidating air of confidence. He was still a young man, considering his position as psychiatrist in charge at Morning House, and the premature gray might have made him look older if not for the vulnerability in his eyes. What stood in the way of any quality she might have admired in him was his constant use of the title 'Miss' in such a demeaning fashion when addressing her. Whether a barrier between them, or a control mechanism, she didn't care. It was impolite.

Dr. Mueller stopped short of the front door and turned abruptly. "We will need to have a talk about this one," he whispered.

"What about the group?" Neva asked quickly, knowing he would be out the door and into the darkness of the rain if she didn't get to the point. "We didn't get a chance to discuss it."

"I haven't forgotten about your request, and I'm convinced that you won't *let* me forget it. But when things aren't broken, why do you want to fix them? I'm happy with your work, Neva. Why do you want to take on more than is necessary?"

"These kids won't be here long. When they turn eighteen, they'll be gone, or the court will send them back to their homes before then. In any case, we don't have much time, and I feel they could benefit from therapy."

"They can benefit from behavior modification too. That's why the program is set up the way it is."

"I just feel we can do more. Therapy can get at *why* these kids behave the way they do, something behavior mod couldn't possibly touch. Do we just want to alter their behavior or cure them?"

"What if I told you I didn't want you curing them, at least not too fast? I know that may sound callous, but we have to think about funding. We get money to run this program based upon our needs."

"That sounds like a lot of political hogwash."

"It is. I agree. But it still exists, and there's nothing I can do about it. There's also another danger. If these kids gain intellectual insight on their problems, they could feel cured when their basic problems remain hidden, just waiting for the next crisis to occur. Behavior modification is designed to give them exactly what they need, the tools to deal with every crisis. If I feel it is necessary, then I will use psychotherapy." He pulled a thick, yellow folder from his leather briefcase and handed it to Neva. "Here, if you want to read about problems, sit down with this when you get a chance. When you're done, we'll discuss it, perhaps over dinner some night."

Neva focused on the large red letters stamped across the top of the folder: CONFIDENTIAL. Below this word, typed letters sat neatly in the center of the folder:

Texas Children's Psychiatric Hospital
Patient: Alec Gogarty
Status: Discharged

It slowly occurred to Neva that she was not making any progress, and this was Dr. Mueller's peace offering, his compromise, his polite way of saying no. Then, like the repercussive echo of sudden thunder, it struck her. She tensed at his impudence, the suggestion that he could buy her off with some confidential information and a dinner invitation disguised as a business meeting, which she might be reluctant to refuse. Or perhaps this was his way of shutting her up for good.

When Neva returned to her office, she was in a mood as sullen and dark as the sky. She tried to shrug off the irritating feeling that she and Warren were not ready to handle whatever might come out of the folder that Dr. Mueller had given her.

Warren glanced toward Alec and said something, but another crack of thunder swallowed his words. In the remnants of light, Alec's eyes sparkled, and suddenly Neva saw what was so familiar before, and it reminded her that this was the anniversary of her brother's death.

Jim and I could see the big, anvil-shaped cloud from twenty miles away, moving toward us with the low rumble of a herd of mustangs. We didn't pull the blanket off the beach until the wind filled with sand and stung our legs.

I clung to Jim's back as he raced the motorcycle toward the highway, just ahead of the rain. We were late getting home, but we didn't care—we laughed at the rain galloping behind us. It was the first time either of us had laughed, I mean really laughed, since our father died.

The rain overtook us when we had to stop for the drawbridge in Kemah. Jim looked back at me, his face glistening with the rain that streamed over his dark hair. "I could have made it," he said.

"You've gotta be kidding." I started laughing so hard my laughter sounded more like hiccups because I was shivering from the cold rain.

"No, really," Jim said, and he was getting mad now. He stared with determination at the upright arm of the bridge. "If you hadn't been with me, Neva, I could have made it."

• • •

The others were coming back. Neva heard them downstairs, clamoring through the house. She waited, watching Alec, expecting the inevitable. The rain had subsided, and Alec had relaxed until he heard the footsteps, the doors slamming, and the chatter of Spinner's harmless vilifications toward the girls. Alec turned to see where Neva was, then remained frozen, a fawn in the underbrush.

Warren watched them both, his tall frame a protective shadow in the

7

emerging light from the window. Alec's eyes moved like a hummingbird, flitting from Neva to the door and back again. Warren watched for Neva's reaction, but there was none. She appeared to be lost in thought.

After Jim decided he would jump the Kemah drawbridge, he took me to our secret place. He wanted to show me something. We sat on a sandy bank beneath the hull of a dry-docked skiff, and he pulled a folded piece of paper out of his pocket. It looked like an old, weathered treasure map. He insisted that I read it, but when I saw what it was, I told him that I had never known anyone who had written poetry.

"I know it's not cool," he said.

"I think it is," I said.

I was shocked by what I read, his words, his voice, his feelings. Reading them was like looking into his soul.

"I'm not crazy," Alec said, looking at Neva.

"I know," Neva said.

Spinner came through the door with a rhythmic stride, purposeful and acquired. He held his books in the crook of one arm. He saw Neva sitting and Warren standing nearby. Then, he saw Alec's silhouette in the broken shafts of weakening yellow light, and his head turned like a Baptist preacher. "What did you go and do now, Ms. Bell? You know I need my space. He can take one of the extra rooms, can't he?" Spinner moved closer where he could see Alec better, where the glare from the window didn't hide him. Then, he stopped, slumped, and rose again with a lamenting cry. "Oh no! You brought me a white boy? What am I supposed to do with this here white boy?"

"You're quite an actor, Spinner," Warren said.

"I ain't acting, Mr. Mac. I just can't hang with no more of this lily-white world. Next thing you know, we'll be dressing for dinner and wearing name tags and all kinds of white folk shit."

"And I thought white people were prejudiced," Alec said.

Spinner froze, like he was playing a child's game. His back was to Alec, and he stared at the wall above Warren's head. Then, only his lips moved. "Say what?" Spinner turned to face Alec. "Was someone talking to you, white boy?" They were face to face now, Spinner's lankiness looming over Alec like an impatient vulture.

That was when Neva noticed the others at the door, trying to get a look at the new guinea pig.

Alec stared right back into Spinner's eyes, almost pleasantly, as if he somehow knew that Spinner was harmless. "White folks hate people because they're different," Alec said. "White folks who have never known what it's like to be different and hated for it. They need a scapegoat for their anger and fear. They're afraid of what they don't understand. What are you afraid of?"

"I ain't afraid of you, Mr. Philosopher." Spinner's anger was mounting. He turned away and ambled back across the room. Now, he talked to the wall. "Shit. You had to go and bring me a white boy who thinks he's smart."

"I don't like this any more than you do," Alec said.

Spinner turned back quickly like he was going to start something. When he moved out of the glare, he noticed Alec's boots and half-smiled. The girls nudged each other. Then, Spinner's voice got twangy. "Well, gosh durn, we got us a cowboy. I tell you what, cowboy, maybe you got shit on your boots, or maybe you got shit for brains, 'cause the way I see it, we ain't the same. No way, no how, ya hear?"

"That's enough, Spinner," Neva said.

Alec grinned and said, "If you want to hate me so much, at least let me give you a good reason first."

"You're working on it, cowboy. You're working on it real hard," Spinner said.

The girls giggled as Alec and Spinner both turned toward the doorway.

"You might as well come on in girls," Neva said. "I want you to meet someone. Alec, this is Krista and Janeen. Girls, this is Alec Gogarty. He'll be staying with us a while."

Krista didn't take her eyes off Alec as she moved into the room. Janeen stayed a few steps behind, her silence almost making her invisible.

"We couldn't help but hear the commotion," Krista said. "I hope we're not interrupting." She pushed her plumpness provocatively into the light and moved slowly about the room, exploring as if it were her first venture into the realm of the teenage boy. "You go to school here in Clear Lake?" Krista asked.

"No. I mean, I don't know if I will or not." Alec watched her warily. "They haven't told me yet."

"I didn't think I had seen you before. We all have to go, though, even though it's summer, whether we like it or not. Isn't that dumb? I guess they have to do something with us. We're problem kids, you know, all of us, even you. I mean, I guess you are, or you wouldn't be *here*." She pursed her lips almost into the shape of a strawberry, and with both hands, she scooped her thick hair into a bundle behind her neck, pulled it all to one side, and let it swing in a thick mane that came almost to her waist. Her head tilted to expose the curve of her neck, and she watched him, her eyes like aqua crystals, coaxing him.

Alec stepped back stiffly, the heel of his boot catching in a groove between the floor planks.

"Give the cowboy room to breathe, Krista," Spinner said. "This ain't no barn dance."

"I wasn't doing anything," she said, defensively. "I was just getting to know him. Are you shy, Alec?"

He glanced over at Neva, and she just shrugged, hoping he wouldn't take any of this too seriously.

"Yeah," he said with a breezy laugh. "I guess so."

"Well, then, come on," she said, and she took him by the hand quickly. "I'll show you around, and we can get to know each other. Then, you won't be shy anymore." Krista nearly dragged Alec out of the room.

Spinner tilted his head toward Neva with a smirk. "What just happened here? I feel like I'm on some kind of dating show."

• • •

It was Sunday, and no one was in the garage but Jim and me. I was waiting for him to finish. He was so far under the hood, his feet were off the ground, and as he wrestled with a frozen bolt, his groans echoed off the ceiling. I walked around between the cars; one was perched on a pedestal like a large, metallic sculpture. The air smelled of oil and rubber.

"I know you're stalling," I said, trying to sound perceptive. "But you're gonna have to talk to me sooner or later because I'm not leaving."

"If she sent you here, you can forget it." He spoke without looking up, and I was perturbed that his perception was clearer than mine.

"Mom had nothing to do with this," I insisted. "I swear. It's me. I'm worried about you."

"I don't want to hear this."

"I'll talk to your backside then, if I have to, but you're gonna hear me because I'm not leaving."

I stopped because I was upset at myself. I heard my mother's voice coming from my mouth. I had lost all self-conceptualization.

I stood in front of the workbench, gazing up at a poster-sized calendar. The actual calendar was only a small square of fine print in the lower left corner. The poster itself was a photograph of a sporty convertible the color of a red delicious apple, and leaning under the raised hood, a young woman's blond hair flowed over the fender. She wore overalls cut into shorts that exposed most of her buttocks, and the bib barely restrained her ample breasts. I thought of my own metamorphosis.

"Is this why you quit school?" I asked. "Because you think that fast cars and beautiful girls go together?"

"You're just jealous," he said and continued working.

"Right. I really want my picture on a wall where every beer-guzzling slob can drool all over himself while thinking God only knows what."

"Nobody asked you for your picture."

"And what if they did? Would you object?"

"You're nuts."

"No. I want to know. Would you care?"

"Okay, okay. I get the point."

"Well, then, has it ever occurred to you that you're doing something I don't think is right for you?"

He was leaning against the car now, his legs and arms crossed in casual defiance. "I'm doing what I want to do, and I feel good about it. That's what matters. Not what you think."

"How come you stayed in school while Dad was alive? He wanted you to finish school. He wanted more from you because he believed in you. So how come you quit now . . . now that he's not around to make you go back? Are you telling me that what he thought doesn't matter either? You know, if you ask me, I don't think it has anything to do with you defying the world and living out your dreams. I think you're trying to escape. You don't want to face the fact that our father is dead."

He didn't say a word, not until he had washed all the grease off his hands, not until he had locked up the garage and motioned for me to get on the back of his motorcycle, not until we had reached a little sandbar in Seabrook where the yellow light from the setting sun was lying on the wet sand like broken glass. We climbed under a skiff embedded in the dunes, and he pulled out this piece of paper and gave it to me. "I've never shown this to anyone before," he said.

I unfolded the dampened creases, amazed. "It's a poem," I said softly, startled that I discovered a new side to my twin brother. He had always been the hero, the athlete, and now the rebel, leaving his education behind to become a mechanic—and one day, he hoped, a racecar driver. That same defiance motivated him to believe he could jump the Kemah drawbridge, but somewhere underneath, he mistook his sensitive nature for weakness. I read the poem while he waited patiently.

> The dance and music play to my deaf heart.
> The crowds, no longer laughing, now depart.
> Like smoke,
> I drift through empty halls of gallery walls
> Where portraits with disfigured faces hang
> In rock,
> And spy with dead eyes blurred by rain that falls
> Through storm-ripped roof where weathered cock once sang.
> I run, pursued by fears that grab and stall
> The clock,
> And chase a virgin kiss through mist and haze
> Of blood red roses in a latticed maze.
> Atoned,
> My hands grasp hidden thorns that cut the bone.
> My numb hands feel no pain, and still I'm left
> Alone
> To find my way through all mistakes I've known
> With questions slated clean from lips bereft
> By news, like thunder's slow and distant moan,
> He's gone. . . .
> . . . He's gone. . . .
> . . . He's gone.

I read the poem several times, the last time through tears. He held me in his arms and tried to quiet my sobs.

"I'm sorry," I sobbed.

"You don't have to be."

"I thought I knew you better than anyone. I thought I could tell what you were feeling, like we shared the same consciousness through some invisible embryonic bridge. I knew that you were hurt by Dad's death. I just didn't know how deep."

"Do you feel guilty about the past, Neva?"

"No, I don't think we should. We've done nothing wrong. We've always been close. We've never kept any secrets. Whatever we did was just a part of that. A part of growing up, of sharing."

"What do you think Dad would have said?"

"That's not important. If he were still alive, it wouldn't be important. What matters is how we feel."

"I'm pretty mixed-up, Neva. I have so many questions I didn't even know I had until he died, and now, I'll never know the answers."

"Sometimes the answers to our questions are inside of us. You seem to have found a beautiful way of expressing that part of you. Perhaps the answers will come to you one day if you keep looking there. I think that maybe Dad is still talking to you. He might be telling you not to give up on yourself. Not to give up on your talent before you've developed it. Oh Jim, you can't just quit now. You can't just run away from what might have been to chase this dream that may never be. Society values poets more than racecar drivers."

"Society values money. It doesn't matter anyway. I want to do what I want, before it's too late. Dad lived as if there would always be a tomorrow, always planning for something in the future, and now, there is no future for him. I don't want that to happen to me. I want my future now."

Jim died trying to jump the Kemah drawbridge just two weeks after he showed me his poem—and exactly one month after our father's fatal heart attack while jogging one evening after work. Jim was just seventeen.

Then, it hit me. *Alec—his eyes, his laugh, his introspection driving a cautious will—was so much like Jim.*

Chapter Two

In Deer Park, not far from Morning House, Emily English lay on the bed in her room, waiting for the inevitable. When she heard the car enter the driveway and saw the lights swing through the blur of rain, she turned onto her side, away from the door, away from that space where all ensuing evil dwelled. She pulled her knees up to her chest until she was almost in a ball. If only she could make herself small enough to disappear altogether. It wasn't long before her mother was moving inside the house.

Then, the door swung back and slammed against the wall. Her mother, who wasn't her mother, occupied the evil space. Marion English stood in the doorway for a long time without speaking. Emily sensed her presence commanding the doorway, her gray-brown hair tied back in a bun, her skin so tight it shined, her usual straight skirt and loose blouse adding more weight to her already broad shoulders. Marion English had a man's frame, thick waist and shoulders, slender hips, no buttocks to speak of, and thin legs. Her breathing was slow and viscous, a smoker's breathing, and with each breath, her agitation grew.

Marion English spoke to Emily's back. "I want you to know that today I had the most humiliating experience of my life. I thought our talk had settled things, had changed things. I had to be called into the principal's office and hear it from him that my daughter was caught with one of the teachers. Are you listening to me?"

Emily remained still as a bead of sweat trickled over her forehead to the pillow. She thought she had answered yes. She felt the word form in her mouth, but it seemed to escape and dissolve into the shadows.

Marion English thought she was being ignored. "You little tramp! You know I was almost fired because of you? Mr. Woodruff holds *me* responsible. He said it should never happen again, that I should do something about you, find you some help. Well, I hold *you* responsible." She paused as if reconsidering where her thoughts were taking her. "You know what I feel like doing? I feel like taking you back to that agency."

Another bead of sweat drifted over Emily's cheek. She wiped it away, and it brushed against her lips, tasting salty.

Marion English threw up her hands. "I can't believe this has happened. You don't even seem to care what you do to other people. Well, you've ruined Bill Clifford's life. He was dismissed. He'll be lucky if he doesn't have to face criminal charges. I won't let you ruin my life. I won't let you do it. I've given you everything, and this is what you do to me." Her voice grew weak and pleading, the voice of a person lost and delirious. "My God, why did you have to do this? Right there at school, where you should have known you would get caught. I have to go back there. I have to face the other teachers . . . and the students. They all know by now. It's humiliating. It's disgraceful. My God, what am I supposed to do?" She started forward, half out of anger, half out of fear. Tears formed in her eyes. She stopped. "Don't you have anything to say for yourself?"

Emily sat up in bed, clutching her ankles, her chin on her knees. Her face was wet and red. She wanted to bury it in her nightgown. She wished Marion English were someone else, someone she could talk to. She wished her real mother would just come back, and everything would be better, just like she had dreamed countless times. Emily stared straight ahead. "I'm sorry, mother," she said softly.

Marion English approached the bed nervously. She sat down and placed one arm around Emily's shoulders. She felt Emily's soft sobs against her breast. "When God gave you to me, I felt he gave me the responsibility to *help* you, to lead you down the right path. I've taught you the best I can, but now the burden's getting heavy. You know the time I have is too short. I can't waste it. Even the chemotherapy makes me sick.

I can't take anymore, Emily. What you've done is wrong, and you must promise me that you won't let it happen again."

"I promise," Emily said, her voice muffled in her mother's blouse.

Marion English patted Emily on the back, stood up, and left the room. Emily waited until the darkness fell over her window, and when her mother came back, Emily said that she wasn't hungry.

"Why is it we can never talk?" her mother asked.

Emily remained silent, and her mother left. The rain stopped, the darkness grew darker, and Emily's window became a mirror in a tomb, holding only the faint reflections of what was inside.

Emily could control it no longer. As she got dressed, she saw her image moving about in the mirror, watching her every movement, her soul freed from its body, watching the dead attempting to translate life. When Marion English finished grading her students' papers and went to bed, Emily climbed out of the window and walked down the street, away from Deer Park.

When she reached the main drag, Emily continued to walk until she saw the street signs change. She stopped under a streetlamp and thumbed the oncoming traffic. She had walked a long way. She had escaped, and she felt good. Overhead, a swarm of moths darted about the yellow globe in a dramatic, aerial dogfight. Occasionally, one would dash itself against the droning bulb with a popping sound that made Emily jump. Pasadena was a yellow town, soured by the smoke that drifted from the oil refineries. At night, it took on a jaundiced glow, with the odor of a dead man's clothes, a smell that could never be washed away.

Most of the people who passed just looked away, but Emily was in no hurry. Sooner or later, someone would come by on his way to Gilley's, someone who could get her in without having to show an ID. Across the street, a rat tightroped a telephone wire toward an apartment building, then scurried into an open vent. Emily shuddered and reached into her purse for a hairbrush. She brushed her hair briskly, leaning into it so her hair would stand fuller.

A van approached quickly, bumping the curb and stopping just ahead of the light. A bristle of yellow hair came out of the side window. "You need a ride?" he asked.

From inside the van, another voice shouted impatiently, "No, fool, she was just exercising her thumb. Let her in."

The door swung open, and the boy, as if attached, swung out with it. Standing in the shadows just outside the fading reach of the lamplight, he appeared to be Emily's age. She wondered if he knew her, if this would get back to her mother.

She put the brush back into her purse. "Where are you headed?" she asked.

"Where are you going?" he returned.

"Gilley's," she said.

The voice inside the van came again, "Ain't this Friday night? You tell her we're headed any direction she wants to go." Then, there was another voice, but Emily couldn't make it out.

The boy at the curb shrugged and motioned toward the open door. "Hop in."

When the boy slipped in beside her, there wasn't enough room. Emily shifted her weight. The boy driving looked at Emily and motioned toward the back of the van. "You can sit back there if you want." Then, he spoke to the back. "Hey, get her a beer, and pass around some of that shit."

Emily moved between the seats to the back of the van, where another boy sat in the dark with his back against an ice chest. She sat down across from him as the van started up again. Beneath her, she felt a dirty, matted carpet. The boy smiled as they swayed with the movement of the van. "Take it easy," he said to the boy driving. Then, he smiled again at Emily. "You want a beer?" he asked.

Emily shrugged. "Sure."

The boy reached into the cooler and pulled out a can of beer. Without rising, he moved over next to Emily, opened the beer, and handed it to her. He took a cigarette from his shirt pocket and lit it, taking a long drag before holding it out for Emily. She immediately knew that it was weed. She took a drag, and he motioned for her to pass it to the front.

The van skidded around a corner, pushing Emily forward and then back against the side of the van, spilling some of the beer on her blouse. The yellow-haired boy reached over the seat. "Let me have some of that, Toad."

"He just call you a toad?" Emily asked.

The boy laughed. "No. They call me Toad because I have these here big eyes, like a toad."

"If the cops stop us, we won't get there at all," the boy with the yellow hair said, his laugh stuttered with gasps for air.

Emily laughed nervously.

"Do you go to Gilley's often?" Toad asked.

"I've been there before," she said.

"You don't look old enough."

"It doesn't matter," she said, taking the cigarette back from the boy with the yellow hair. "You don't have to go if you don't want."

"I didn't mean anything," Toad said. "In fact, I'd like to go with you if you don't mind. I think you're . . ."

The van screeched to a stop, pressing them together toward the front. Emily grabbed the boy's leg to keep from being thrown against the back of the front seats. They laughed it off.

"Fucking red lights," the driver muttered.

"What were you going to say?" Emily asked, once she had regained her balance. She tossed her head back and combed her hair out of her eyes with her fingers.

"You have pretty eyes. Even in the dark, I can tell."

"You really think so?" Emily sounded surprised.

"Yeah." Toad took the cigarette, inhaled, and handed it back. As Emily took another drag, she closed her eyes and thought about how good it was going to make her feel, how it was going to make her forget about her loneliness—and her mother who wasn't her real mother anyway. When she opened her eyes, the boy with the hair that looked like straw was now sitting on her other side. She handed him the cigarette, and he smiled anxiously as he took it. She finished her beer and leaned back against the wall of the van.

There was something behind her neck. Emily felt a hand on her shoulder and realized that the other boy had put his arm around her. She made no effort to move away. She closed her eyes again. Someone was stroking her hair, and she thought she felt a kiss on her neck. The rocking of the van stopped, and the darkness seemed to get even darker. The boy who was driving had moved to the back, and now they were all close, telling jokes and laughing, and giving her more beer. It was hot. She must have said so because they were clawing at her blouse and then her bra. She tried to get out, to crawl to the door, but her arms and legs were sluggish, and she couldn't tell which way to go.

Something pulled her back and held her down, something dark and close. . . .

"Do you think we should be doing this?" she heard one of them say.

"Jesus, we're just having some fun. Anyway, she don't seem to mind."

"Yeah, chicken boy, you gonna play or not?"

So close now, she felt smothered by the laughter and something warm blowing against her face.

• • •

When Alec left the hospital for Morning House, he didn't think about what put him there—what he had done. He didn't even think about where he was going. It was just another place with different people, and he had learned to protect himself from the hurt or the indifference of others. He *had* thought about the dream that had bothered him for the last four years—how the doctors analyzed it and made each part a symbol for what happened. To Alec, it still didn't make any sense, but it was the only dream he ever remembered.

It always started the same way, in a place he had never been—but it felt familiar. Lulled by the undulations of the lake and the swaying pine trees, he wanted to drift asleep, but something was wrong—something in the light, or on the water, or in the whistling wind. He was not alone. There were others with him, although he didn't know who they were, and they sensed the menace too.

What they feared was an invisible force that came at them from the edge of the forest. It sped toward them, skimming swiftly over the surface. There was no time to waste. Turning in unison, they pushed about for room, a cacophony of trumpeting and wing slapping that rose to a thunderous din, drowning out his cries. Panic fell on their efforts to escape. Their eyes bulged, and their necks stretched for buoyancy. With flat, heavy feet, they slapped at the surface, churning up a froth of water. He struggled to keep up. Suddenly, the heaviness fell away, and they lifted off, a graceful squadron. He was carried up with them, unencumbered, flapping his arms in a desperate attempt to sustain the air that kept him aloft. He wanted to stay in the center of them as they pushed up through the canyon toward that blue refuge above. Distance was their salvation.

Curiosity overwhelmed him, and he looked back toward the fringe of the fluid plate, that juxtaposition of light and dark where the bristling tall pines met the clear lake. A disturbing, faceless figure stood on the shore, obscured by shadows. When it moved, sunlight glinted off something that was a part of it, like a spark in the brush, and then was swallowed up. A small puff of smoke billowed out over the rippled surface.

He felt a sharp pain in his cheek, just below his right eye. He looked around and finally saw his companions—they were geese.

The pain seared in his cheek. At first, he thought one of the geese had struck him with its wing. He had come too close in his awkward attempt at flying. He looked over at the one next to him and saw that the bird was too far away to have struck him. The goose slowly turned toward him and laughed. That was when he noticed it wasn't completely a goose. It had a goose's body, and Bubba's face, and it stopped laughing only to say, "Go back to your mother, Alec. You always were a wimp." It started laughing again and getting farther and farther away. Alec realized he was falling. He tried harder to fly, but his hands only clawed at the empty air. Suddenly, he was plunging quickly through the coldness that numbed his face. He landed in shallow water, his face in the mud, gasping for air, until he lurched awake.

The first time Alec had the dream, his bed was wet when he woke up. He could feel the dampness, but he didn't get up until he was sure his father was gone. The right side of his face throbbed. Alec blinked several times, but nothing came into focus. He turned back toward the ceiling. Gray, undulating forms swept by like ripples on the water. He closed his right eye, and his vision cleared, but the pain was still there. His dream had been so real.

Alec didn't remember every detail of the dream at first. It was only later that he remembered, when he had to tell Dr. Edelstein about the dream. In the dream, somewhere, in the symbols of the canyon, and in the blue sky and the comforting lake, was what Dr. Edelstein had referred to as the Uterine Sea of our dreams. It was in the rocking cradle of trees and their phallic irony, leading down to the shadowy, faceless figure—whom Alec could never identify.

Dr. Edelstein said it was his father, always there at the edge of his life, threatening to harm him, making his mother's comfort even more appealing. Alec had the dream many times and always woke up as he was falling. Actually landing for the first time was a day he would never forget.

• • •

His father's footsteps passed his bedroom door. Alec felt his arms and legs tighten. A bitter, swirling sickness rose from his stomach into his throat. It settled only as the footsteps faded away down the hall into the kitchen. Alec knew he had to get ready for school, but he couldn't face his father. He lay quietly, listening to the sounds emanating from the kitchen. The refrigerator door opened and closed, water ran through the faucet, footsteps thumped heavily back and forth. They were not his mother's footsteps, with the scraping sound of sandpaper that her slippers made as they scuffed across the linoleum. A pot rattled on the stove as water came to a boil—the sound of pouring, then silence.

Alec sat on the edge of the bed. The willow tree outside his window glowed in the morning light. He guessed it was about seven o'clock. His father would have to leave soon.

A clatter of dishes, more water running into the sink, then the footsteps started toward the front door. When the door closed, Alec waited a moment. His mother was not up yet. He didn't want to face his mother either. He crept through the house to the front window and peered out a small opening in the curtains. Alec's father was already in his truck, his rough, thick fingers gripping the steering wheel as if they would snap it in two. As the truck pulled away, the low morning light glinted off a rifle hanging in the back window.

Alec went into the kitchen and opened the refrigerator. There was a can of beer, a wrinkled half of a tomato, two heels of bread in a twisted wrapper, and one egg next to an empty mayonnaise jar. Alec took the bread and went to the bathroom. His stomach was tight and knotted. He set the bread next to the sink and swallowed hard until the sickness went away. His image in the mirror was liquid and pale, except for the small purple bruise below his right eye. He touched the skin and flinched when pain darted into his eye. It brought back the piercing image of his father and mother shouting at each other from opposite sides of the kitchen.

"You have no right to blame me for all of this," she said. "I just wanted us to be together."

"I planned this huntin' trip for a long time, and I ain't gonna cancel it."

"Fine. You never cared about what I wanted anyways, so I shouldn't expect you to start now."

"Don't start with me."

"What?"

"Always throwing everything back on me."

"Well, ain't it true. You're never around enough to know what I want . . ."

Alec was sitting on the sofa watching television, trying to ignore them, but he couldn't shut it out. . . .

". . . maybe he ain't even yours."

That's when Alec spilled his glass of milk. His father stormed into the room, grabbed him, and dragged him to the kitchen. When his mother tried to intervene, his father grabbed her throat and hit her across the face with the back of his hand. Alec tried to stand in the way. He was crying and holding on to his mother's arm when his father pulled him loose and flung him against the chair. As the chair went over, his arms flailed about, unable to grasp anything to stop his momentum before he hit the edge of the table. Alec could remember nothing after that, except the nightmare.

He brushed his teeth quickly and slipped into his clothes, which were on the floor next to his bed. He folded the bread wrapper around the two heels and set it inside his jacket. Through the wall, his mother's voice called out weakly. Alec waited as she called several more times.

Then, he went to her room and stood in the doorway. Slowly, she pushed herself up on one elbow and reached out to him. Alec moved to the edge of the bed, just out of reach. The thin strap of her nightgown slipped off her shoulder, but she didn't attempt to correct it. She saw him looking at the two yellow bruises on her cheek and pulled her hair over the side of her face.

"Are you all right?" she asked.

"Yes." He backed away as she reached out to touch his cheek.

"Oh, Alec, I'm so sorry. I just . . ."

"I'm all right, Ma," he insisted.

"Can you ever forgive me?"

Alec looked down at the floor. "Is Dad going away?"

"I don't know, Alec. I didn't talk to him this morning. He might."

Alec looked away as if he had just remembered something. "I'm going to be late, Ma."

"Alec, I wish I could change things, but I just don't know how. I'm scared."

Alec remained silent, and when his mother put her head back on the pillow, he backed out of the room quietly. Then, he ran outside and kept running until he reached the end of the street. He felt a lingering mist on his face. The chill in the air brought tears to Alec's eyes and burned in his throat as he tried to catch his breath.

When he reached the schoolyard, Alec sat on a bench and waited while other children emerged from buses and cars. He heard his name and saw Bubba Harris, a big boy who was repeating the eighth grade, and Davy Richards, who always hung around Bubba. Davy was thin, had hair like straw, and always did whatever Bubba told him to.

"G-G-G-Gogarty," Bubba said, then pretended to toss a rock and laughed when Alec flinched. "You still waiting for that dumb dog?"

"He's not a dumb dog," Alec said, pulling the bread closer to his leg.

"He ain't much of nothin' no more," Bubba said, grinning at Davy and pushing his shoulder to throw him off balance. Davy laughed as he stumbled backward. "You wait here every day for that dumb dog," Bubba said, "just to feed him them bread crumbs. Why don't you bring him a steak? Don't you have money for no steak?"

Davy came back next to Alec, who glared up at him. "Hey, look at that shiner," Davy said.

"Yeah, where did you get the black eye, wimp?"

"I fell," Alec said.

"Yeah, sure," Bubba said. "Or maybe a seventh grader beat you up."

Davy laughed again, too hard this time, and started coughing.

"Look, I got something that will make you feel better. You want some?" Bubba held out his hand to display two cigarettes, which were twisted at both ends.

"What is it?" Alec asked.

"Ah come on, ain't you never seen weed before?"

"Of course, I have," Alec lied.

"I don't think he has," Davy said.

"He can't afford it anyway," Bubba said. "If he can't afford steak for a dumb dog, then he can't afford weed." The bell rang, and Bubba started toward the building with Davy, turning back as if he forgot something. "Oh, by the way," Bubba said, "you better teach that dumb dog of yours not to play in the street." Then, they disappeared, their laughter dissipating to the edges of the schoolyard.

Alec waited, but the dog never appeared. He left the bread on the bench and went into the building. Alec's teacher was addressing the class from behind her desk when he entered the room. She was a short, barrel-shaped woman who sprayed spittle into the air when she talked, and she had bags under her arms that shook when she wrote on the chalkboard.

"Alec, you're late again," she said, stopping him before he could make it to his seat.

"Yes ma'am, I'm sorry," Alec said.

"Why can't you ever get here on time?"

"I'm not always late, ma'am."

"Don't talk back to me, Alec. I don't like troublemakers. Could it be that you're late because you've been fighting again?"

"No, ma'am." Alec looked down at the floor.

"Don't lie to me, Alec. I can see your eye. And look at me when I'm talking to you."

Alec looked up but still could not see clearly. His teacher was facing the class now. Someone in the back of the room snickered. Alec felt her take him by the arm, and then, he was waiting outside the principal's office. Soon afterward, he was sent home with a note. He knew he would have to wait until school let out before he went home.

The schoolyard looked big and empty. Alec heard the chain on the flagpole clanging in the wind, a menacing reminder of another whipping he would have to face. Several birds gathered around the bench where he left the bread. As he walked, he noticed the chain faded into the chime of a distant church bell.

Alec walked for a long time before he saw it. At first, he thought it was a folded rug bumped off a passing truck. As he got closer, he noticed broken pieces, and he drew in his breath. Several cars passed by and swerved in the street, becoming one long blur. Alec stood at the curb and stared at the dog's blank eyes, those once beautiful, trusting eyes.

Alec ran down the street and up the block toward his house. The wind left his skin chapped and numb. When he reached the house, he saw his father's truck in the driveway. A feeling of sickness filled his stomach. Alec followed his own fearful thoughts to the front door and stopped to listen. Had the school called his father? Were they both waiting inside, waiting for him to turn the knob and enter, waiting to see if he was big enough to take the punishment he deserved? Alec didn't care anymore. A pressure mounted in his head, and his thoughts swam about inside, struggling against a stormy sea. He turned to leave when he heard a crash and a scream, quickly muffled by his father's angry voice. He was unaware that he had stepped inside until he felt his father's hand grab his arm.

His father's voice drummed inside Alec's head. "What are you doing home?"

Alec looked around the room. His mother sat on the edge of a chair near the sofa with her forehead in the palm of one hand and the other arm wrapped around her waist as if she were going to be sick. On the floor, he saw a shattered lamp. His father's rifle leaned against the kitchen door.

"Can't you answer me when I'm talking to you?" his father shouted.

The room suddenly exploded. Alec felt something slam into the side of his face and push him to the floor. His head throbbed with voices stretched to unrecognizable limits, pushing and pulling at the same time until his eyes felt like they were being squeezed from the inside.

Alec curled up on the floor with his hands over his head. Through his fingers, he saw a shadow walk back across the room to where his mother sat. His father stepped within a few feet of her when suddenly she lurched forward and pushed him backward over the table in front of the sofa.

"Get out!" she screamed. "I don't want you here anymore!"

Before she could continue, Alec's father came off the floor and brought his fist across her face, pushing her back onto the sofa as blood spurted from her nose. He jumped at her again and grabbed her neck with both hands, drawing from her lips several weak groans.

Alec groped his way across the floor, his head pounding. Unable to think, he only wanted it to end. He reached out for it, not wanting to define it or know what it could do. It was just a means to an end. He pulled it down into his lap, feeling the heaviness and the cold grip. He pointed it toward his father's hunched figure and pulled the trigger. The sound was deafening. His mother's mouth was open in a silent scream. His father was suspended like a marionette held up by strings until they broke, and he collapsed onto the sofa.

When Alec left the hospital, he knew he had killed his father to protect his mother.

Chapter Three

Neva placed Alec's folder on the desk and let out a long, frustrated sigh. The notes from the doctor at the hospital had given her a clear picture of what Alec had been through. Breakfast chores were done, and the house was momentarily quiet. This was her designated conference time with Warren, and outside of a crisis, any conference time was respected. House rule.

"You shouldn't let it get to you," Warren said. "I know this job is twenty-four hours a day, but you can't let it consume you."

"It's not the kids," Neva said. "It's not even these tragic life histories." She half picked up Alec's folder and gave it a modest shove, enough to spread the loose pages out like a Chinese fan. Before going on, she leaned back, scrutinizing Warren. Her eyes became fixed, focused on one thought, a lioness stalking her prey, all her sensory images merged into one. "You are on my side, aren't you, Warren?"

"Of course," he said. It was the truth, and yet, he was afraid to move, afraid that even a twitch of the finger would show fear, triggering her instincts to attack. Though there couldn't be more than a year or two between their ages, Neva was more serious about her work. Warren had never seen her play. She spent her spare time on her Doctorate, and this uncanny devotion and passion only increased his attraction to her.

"Sometimes I feel that Dr. Mueller thinks I'd be dangerous with too much information," she said.

"Is he holding something back?"

"No, not really. It's more what he's making *me* hold back."

"You don't have to tell me if you . . ."

"It's not that serious. I want to start a group with the guineas, and Dr. Mueller feels we should just stick to the program. It's frustrating. I'm tired of feeling like part of a giant Skinner box. Behavior modification is fine, but I want to do something deeper here, not just monitor their adolescent mood swings. There's more to them than that, and I feel group therapy is the best way to get at it."

"Why would he be against it?"

"Funding. He's protecting his job. And he has a power complex, and he wants to maintain control. If there is any breakthrough, any success at all, he wants it to be *his*." Neva wanted to tell Warren about Dr. Mueller asking her for a date, but she decided that would be taking his confidence too far.

"Call it a planning conference," he said. "Dr. Mueller will never know. We'll be discussing chores or planning a picnic for all he knows."

"Just one big, happy family." Neva laughed.

Warren realized that his idea sounded weak, more like pick-up conversation in a bar. *You sound very intelligent. Your sign must be cancer.* "I know it sounds trite," he said, "but it just might work, and if any discussions during these conferences proved to be therapeutic, then it would be purely coincidental of course."

"If I'm going to do this, I want to do it the right way. I want to find out what makes these guineas tick. You've seen them when they get together, the games they play with each other—and with themselves. There isn't an honest feeling in the whole bunch. They can only manipulate or attack each other or set up defenses to protect themselves because they've been hurt too many times. Somewhere, they've got to learn what is causing this reactive behavior."

"Aren't we all pretty much the same way to some degree?"

"Yes. I know that's true, but somehow, some of us, the lucky ones, survive, and we manage to maintain some order in our lives—or at least what appears to be order. Somewhere, these guineas stepped over the line. It might just be the product of generations of bad parenting."

"Would it help to bring the parents in on this?"

"I don't know. I've always made it a general rule to stay away from parents, at least until a cause and effect can be established. With Alec, however, some pieces seem to be missing. His mother might be able to supply them for us, so he just might be the exception."

• • •

Anna Gogarty was still an attractive woman. Even through the screen door, Neva could tell that she had the type of face that remained youthful, almost cherubic, even when lines set in around her mouth and eyes.

"We wanted to talk to you about Alec," Neva said.

"Where did you say you were from?" she asked. Her voice was sleepy and distant.

"Morning House," Warren repeated. "It's a home for teenagers. Alec lives there now."

"He does? He's not at the hospital anymore?"

"No. He's not."

"When did this happen? Why wasn't I notified?"

"That's what we're doing now, Ms. Gogarty." Neva's voice remained calm and pleasant. "Can we come in and talk to you?"

The room was surprisingly cool for June, when the pavement outside sizzled beneath a visible curtain of heat. Anna Gogarty left the door open, which became the only source of light. It drew the air, heavy with a pungent aroma. Warren detected a dizzying amount of spiced fruit. He suspected that Anna had just made some herbal tea, but then, he noticed a thin stream of smoke rising from a glass cup across the room. A tiny light flickered inside like a trapped fairy, barely illuminating the assortment of ornamental dishes and boxes on the cabinet and the Indian tapestry hanging on the wall above. Warren concluded that Anna Gogarty had fixated on the sixties.

"I'm sorry if we interrupted something," Neva said.

Before answering, Anna Gogarty glanced behind her toward a door caught in the reach of reflected sunlight. "No. You didn't." She paused and then motioned toward the sofa against the wall. She took a chair facing them, her hands cupped on her knees. She seemed to be waiting for an explanation. A darker tapestry covered the sofa.

Anna Gogarty looked up nervously as another woman entered the room from the illuminated door. She was younger than Anna with hair in a short, masculine cut.

"I didn't know we had guests, Anna," she said. "Why didn't you call me?"

Neva glanced at Warren, as he appeared to be staring. The woman was statuesque and noticeably in control. She wiped her hands on her jeans and gave Anna's shoulders a supportive squeeze. Anna instinctively reached up for one of her hands.

"I'm sorry," she said. "This is my friend April."

April took a chair next to Anna, crossing her legs comfortably. After glancing at Warren, April fixed her gaze on Neva, smiling confidently. Neva sensed that April resented Warren's presence.

"They're here about Alec," Anna said.

"I would have called first," Neva said. "But I couldn't find a number."

"I don't have one," Anna said.

"You learn to live without some things when you're on assistance," April said.

Anna lowered her eyes for a moment as if to apologize for her situation. Her hair flowed loosely like a dark river whose ripples emitted glimmering flecks of light. When she looked up, she seemed confused, her eyes soporific. "Where is this place? You called it Morning House?"

"Yes. It's in Clear Lake," Neva said.

Suddenly, Anna lit up with the enthusiasm of a child who had just received a surprise gift. "I knew this was going to happen soon. I could feel it. My horoscope was right. He's closer to me now. He's going to be coming home soon, isn't he?"

"I don't know," Neva said. "That would be a decision for the court to make. It will all depend upon how well he does. We're going to help him with the transition as much as we can. Of course, when Alec becomes an adult, that decision will be up to him."

April leaned over the space between their two chairs and placed her hand tenderly on Anna's arm. "Oh, Anna, that's wonderful news!"

Neva wondered if April was her real name.

"When can I visit with Alec?" Anna asked. "I want to see him."

"Soon," Neva said. "He just arrived, and we'd like to let him get settled first."

"You can't deny his mother," April said, still smiling.

Warren sensed Neva's bristling. "We're not," he interjected. "Keep in mind that Ms. Gogarty's parental rights were terminated by the court. We're taking a big step to keep her informed about Alec because we feel that she might be able to aid us in helping him. We're just taking one step at a time . . . to make sure Alec can handle all the changes in his life right now."

"Will he be going to school?" Anna asked. "It was all those kids that upset him before, you know. When they found out what he had done, things were so difficult. Kids can be so mean, you know."

"He's attending a school in Clear Lake," Neva said. "I can assure you that it's a good school. They have a good summer program, and he'll be well supervised."

In the corner of her eye, she saw movement on the fireplace mantel, and just as Neva looked up, a cat leaped from the mantel to the floor. Neva straightened up quickly and placed a hand to her throat to stifle any audible surprise. The cat arched its back along the leg of Anna's chair with an air of self-gratification.

"Oh, that's just Samantha," Anna said, reaching down for the cat. "Come here, silly girl. You want Mommy to scratch your head?"

Another cat appeared from around the corner of the sofa and rubbed up against Warren's leg. Warren jerked away at first, feeling the cat before he saw it. He attempted to pet it, but the cat drew back with a hiss.

"Oh, Tabatha, leave the poor man alone," April said, getting up to retrieve the cat. "You naughty girl. She's quite jealous when the other cats get any attention." April crouched near Warren's leg, pulling the cat to her lap. It pressed against the cushion of her breasts, exposing at the open collar an abundance of cleavage. "Here, go ahead and pet her. She won't scratch you."

"How many do you have?" Warren asked, petting Tabatha cautiously.

"Just seven."

As if on cue, they all appeared, emerging from the shadows, flying from the tops of bookshelves, bounding, sauntering, until the whole room seemed alive with cats. Neva was still in her chair, as each cat purred up against her leg. She had worn a dress to appear more professional. Now, she was reciting a silent prayer that the cats would not use her leg as a scratching post. Her irritation had started as she and Warren were coming up the walk to the house. Warren had commented how nice she looked, and Neva snapped at him. "This is not the time for personal remarks, Warren."

"It was just a compliment," he said. His voice held a tone of contrition. "I didn't mean anything by it."

Neva wondered if she would have received his comment as a compliment if he had been a woman. She had not offered any apology.

Anna Gogarty was nice enough to shoo away the cats after she had taken the time to introduce each of them, commenting on their personalities as if they were her children.

"Ms. Gogarty," Neva interjected. "April mentioned you were receiving assistance. Do you have other children besides Alec?"

"Yes, I had a child since they took Alec away from me. But I'm also on disability because I can't work."

"Where is the child's father?" Neva asked.

"Do you really need to know all this?" April asked.

This time, Warren was unable to circumvent Neva's irritation. "Exactly how are you involved?" she asked April.

April and Anna briefly exchanged glances, and Warren only caught April's consoling shrug. "I'm just a very concerned friend," she answered.

"Ms. Gogarty," Warren said. "We're not checking up on you to see if you're doing anything illegal. We just need to know your situation in the event that Alec returns to your home. We would like to know what his family life will be like."

Anna Gogarty sighed before answering. "Josh's father left. I haven't seen him since before Josh was born."

"So there is just you and Josh?" Neva asked.

"Yes."

"You might as well tell them everything, Anna," April said.

"I thought she was asking about my family," Anna said.

April turned back to Neva. "I live here too," she said. "We've created a good home for Josh, and we can do the same for Alec."

"Alec will be an adult soon," Neva said. "He doesn't need the same type of care as Josh. The support he needs is more of an emotional nature."

"I just don't want to see Anna hurt anymore," April said.

"I can appreciate that," Neva said. "And I don't want to see Alec hurt anymore, either." She turned her attention to Anna again. "Before we go, I was hoping you could clear up something that has been puzzling me."

"I'll try," Anna said.

"In Alec's hospital record, the doctor stated that Alec appeared to have a hatred of men and a fear of women, and this was why he was hard to work with."

"The doctor just said that to cover his own failure," April said.

Neva smiled at April before turning back to Anna. "I'm curious how the doctor came to that conclusion? Did the doctor talk to you about Alec?"

"Only once," Anna said.

"Why do you think the doctor would say something like that?"

"I don't know. I'm afraid I agree with April."

"In the record, there is mention of a boy named Bubba. Do you remember him? Alec would have known him before he went to the hospital."

"No," Anna said, pausing. "Wait. Yes, I do. He was a big kid. A neighborhood bully type."

"Do you remember if Alec mentioned him in connection with anything that might have bothered him?"

"No. In fact, I think it's a mistake to bring up the past. Alec is better off forgetting. That was a bad time in his life. A bad time for all of us."

"Do you feel that Alec is still disturbed?" Neva asked.

"No! I never did." Anna jolted, drawing out a spark of emotion which was not there before. "He just needs to be at home again, not living with strangers in a hospital."

"Why was he taken away, Ms. Gogarty?" Neva asked.

Anna looked surprised. "Don't you know?"

"I know what I've read in the record," Neva said. "I know what the doctors say, but I want to know what *you* know. The record doesn't say much about you."

"None of what happened was Alec's fault, you know."

"You mean how Alec's father was killed? I think he understands that he was just protecting you."

"It was more than that, though. You see, I *willed* him to do it. I didn't mean to; it just happened."

Neva frowned. "I don't understand."

"Anna has certain abilities," April said.

33

"I've been called a witch, but I'm not a murderer. I couldn't kill my own husband, even though he was a cruel man who hurt Alec and me. I mean he hit us both. I was afraid of him. I wanted him to die, so I *willed* his death. But I didn't realize that Alec would become my agent. The judge didn't think that Alec belonged with me, that I couldn't take care of my own son. That's why he was taken away from me."

Suddenly, the incense, the tapestries, and all the cats fit into Anna Gogarty's profile. Warren looked around again with a scrutinizing squint. He observed candlesticks, wands, a silver-handled knife, beads, a chalice, and other ornaments, which he suspected were all used for concocting spells. The room appeared to be the general headquarters for Anna Gogarty's coven.

Neva cued Warren by rolling her eyes toward the door as she stood to leave. She offered her hand to Anna in a cautiously cordial gesture. "Ms. Gogarty, we're going to do our best for Alec. I promise."

"I do hope so," Anna said, as she took Neva's hand. Her smile faded as if she had seen a ghost. She stared into Neva's eyes and tightened her grip. Anna's composure turned cold. "I fear there is something terribly wrong with all this."

"What do you mean?" Neva asked, a puzzled wrinkle appearing on her brow.

April stepped closer and placed her arm around Anna's waist as if to support her. "Anna, are you all right?"

"It may already be too late," Anna said. "Too late to turn it around."

"Too late to turn what around?" Neva asked.

"Fate," Anna replied. "I felt it just now, in your hand. A terrible fate."

As they hurried down the walk to the car, Neva tugged at the collar of her blouse, stirring the warm air. "We're not dealing with someone who is tuned in to the same radio station we're listening to," she said.

"Let's just hope she's on our side," Warren said.

• • •

"Jim and I are a dioscurian pair, imperfect—I am the castorated mortal, forever in the shadow of his polluxed brightness."

That's what I told everyone. Whenever our father introduced us at the parties our mother gave for Dad's associates at NASA, the usual comment was that we didn't look a thing like twins. I would give that explanation, which was inevitably received by the most puzzled look. We would run into the bedroom, laughing, and mimicking the expression until we were about to burst.

We experimented. It was nothing to be ashamed of. We were young. One night after a bath, he surprised me. I had a towel around me, with water dripping from the ends of my hair. He was hiding behind the bedroom door. When I passed, he leaped out and surprised me. We circled each other, playing a game as he teased, tugging at the towel. When I pulled away, the twisted ends loosened, exposing my breasts. Those were secret, stolen moments of time, our furtive fondling, our souls forever seeking to be reunited. We were so young. We didn't know where that dangerous point was—or if we had gone beyond it. We thought we were safe. In a way, we spoiled each other for the real thing.

His death, the accident, which took away his smile forever, that comfort, will always haunt me.

Neva started visualizing these vignettes from her past on the day Alec arrived at Morning House. After her visit with Anna Gogarty, she suffered the memory of Jim with the vividness of an epiphany that left her with the strangest urge to reconcile with her mother.

Warren had asked Neva if she thought Anna Gogarty and April were lovers. She should have said yes and left it at that.

"Don't you ever think of anything but sex?" she asked.

"Yes, of course," Warren said. "There's always money and power."

"Jesus."

"I was just kidding."

"You really expect me to believe that? I saw you staring at April, gaping at her breasts with your jaw on the floor. You men are all alike. And I suppose you were just kidding with that sexual innuendo about the way I look." Neva was getting irrational. She could see it in the look of bewilderment on Warren's face. And neither one of them understood why.

"I'm sorry," he said. "But I really think you've misjudged me. If I was staring at April, it was because she looked a lot like my girlfriend, my former girlfriend. Honestly, I was only asking out of professional curiosity."

"Asking what?" Neva said. She had completely forgotten how the conversation began.

"I asked you about Anna and April's relationship. I thought it might have some bearing on Alec's emotional stability, depending upon how he perceived it—and certainly his self-esteem if he is experiencing an identity crisis of sorts."

"I'm sorry," she said. "I misunderstood."

They left it at that, and the silence grew. When they reached Morning House, the chattering and bickering of the guineas was comforting. Neva entered her office and closed the door. Her heart was pounding. Her behavior was becoming so impulsive that she never stopped to question her rationality. She picked up the telephone and watched her trembling fingers press the numbers with anxious anticipation. When her mother finally answered, Neva's next impulse was to hang up, but she resisted the urge and stayed on the line. When she sensed her mother was about to hang up, she said, "It's me . . . Neva."

There was more silence.

"Mother," she pleaded.

Her voice came through the receiver as firm and distant as a stranger. "I don't know who you are, so please leave me alone."

"Mother," Neva pleaded louder. "I want to talk with you."

"I am not your mother. I have no daughter. Please leave me alone."

Then, her mother hung up.

● ● ●

Neva had not been to her mother's house in more than six years. When she reached the house, she noticed it had changed, had taken on a new life. She expected it to look withered from lack of care, neglected by an angry and resentful hermit who still blamed Neva for all the misery in her life. Instead, the house was freshly painted, and a new garden gleamed beneath the front windows. Azaleas bloomed vigorously in a blur of peach and lavender, a fragmented canvas. Camille Pissarro. Woman in an enclosure.

Neva knocked at the door and heard her mother's voice call out. "Hang on. I'll be right there."

She was expecting someone else. When she answered, for a moment, her face shone radiantly with joy and optimism. Her mother was dressed for an evening out, hair brushed back in wispy waves, a conservative amount of make-up highlighting her eyes, a turquoise dress as soft as the azaleas in the front garden. She was beautiful.

When she saw Neva, the radiance vanished.

"Mother?" Neva said.

"I told you to leave me alone," she said.

"Why won't you talk to me?"

"I have nothing to say to you. You are a stranger . . ."

"Mother, please," Neva pleaded. "This is crazy."

"You have no right to come back here."

"What happened was not my fault."

"I lost everyone I loved because of you. You could have stayed. You could have repented. Spencer wanted to help you."

"Uncle Spencer was not the man you thought he was."

"Don't you talk that way! Your uncle was a good man—a man of God. When you left, he changed. He couldn't live here any longer because he believed he failed you. It was like he accepted the blame for what *you* did. He moved away a broken man."

"I didn't do anything, mother. You have to let me explain."

"Spencer had his heart attack because of you, and he died with a broken heart. I have buried my husband, my son, and my brother. And now, I've buried the past. You must stop coming to me for forgiveness. I cannot give it to you. You must turn to God for your forgiveness."

"I don't believe in God that way, Mother."

Neva's mother stared with a destructive gaze, incinerating flesh and extinguishing the spirit. Neva became invisible. "You are more evil than I thought," she said, then closed the door.

Neva waited in the car, unable to drive away, unable to stop trembling. Before long, a car pulled into the driveway, and a tall, gray-haired man stepped out. He could have been a banker or an insurance adjuster, someone who had stepped into the picture after Neva's father had died. He had taken her father's place. Neva watched as they drove away, and she knew that the past was truly dead for her. Her mother had another life now, and there was no place in it for a child she still blamed. Neva's mother had settled her life. In that instant, Neva realized that she was more unsettled and hollow than her mother.

Alec had opened the door, and Warren had pushed her through.

Chapter Four

The foyer at Morning House always captured the afternoon light in a translucent glow. It passed through the frosted glass in the front door and lingered as it swirled about and changed those it touched. Standing in this diffusion of ethereal light and shadow, Neva and Emily looked as if they could be sisters. They were doll-like and porcelain, with small features and an earthy, farm-fresh radiance. Their hair emitted the same rich, reddish-brown of mahogany or chestnut, but unpolished, as if you could take a handful of thick waves and smell the natural wood. Even the way their faces accepted a smile—the crinkle at the corners of bright eyes, an elfish turn of the nose, the eager curve of warm lips—it was uncanny.

It was a Sunday afternoon, and the caseworker was in a hurry. She had introduced the two new placements and was already moving toward the door. Neva had come out of her lengthy gloominess, which had lasted a full day, and as always, she greeted the newcomers with the warmth of welcoming family home for the holidays. This quickly drew an eager smile from Emily. However, her anxiety resurfaced as Neva greeted the boy. Emily's eyes darted about, and Neva knew that the boy's presence troubled her.

His name was Randy. He had remained silent and unaffected by Neva's introduction, and when Warren took his belongings, which he had been holding in a large plastic bag, he quickly crossed his arms defiantly. The caseworker had explained on the telephone that Randy had spent the

38

past week in Juvenile Hall after a fight with his father. His parents had discovered some drugs in Randy's bedroom and thrown them away. Randy had gone into a rage. The police had to break up the fight, and Randy left in his father's car after the police were gone. Randy's parents had left his clothes on the doorstep for the caseworker to pick up.

At Morning House, the caseworker apologized a second time for being delayed. She didn't think either teen would be at Morning House beyond the crisis period. It was just a matter of working out things with the parents. When the caseworker left, Emily seemed somewhat relieved.

The others had passed through the hallway quietly, joining Alec in the dayroom. Alec was reading the first of the Tolkien trilogy, a habit of voracious reading he had developed at the hospital. They asked if he had seen the new guineas and needled him to go and look. He continued to read, acting disinterested.

When Neva, Emily, and Randy finally entered the dayroom, the others grew silent—all but Spinner, who was drumming two knitting needles on the arm of the chair where Alec was sitting. When Alec saw the boy who had come with Emily, he dropped his book and stood.

"Well, if it ain't Go-Go-Gogarty," the boy said. "Is this where you've been hiding out?"

"I thought I recognized you," Alec said.

"I thought you was in some psycho hospital." Randy turned to Neva. "Hey, I ain't crazy," he said. "Is this a place for crazy people?"

"No one here is crazy, Randy," Neva said.

"What are you doing here?" Alec asked.

Randy grinned. "My ol' man said I stole his car, so I left home, but the pigs picked me up and handed me over to these do-good welfare workers."

"You mean your father kicked you out, finally," Alec said.

"Well, at least I have an ol' man," Randy said. "Of course, if I ever want to get rid of him, I could give you a call, couldn't I?"

Alec took a step forward, and Randy shifted his weight back, raising his right hand into a fist. Warren dropped Randy's bag and instinctively stepped between them. Warren was taller than both of them, but he wasn't as big as Randy and probably didn't stand a chance if Randy decided to throw a punch. They pressed against him like two rutting bucks, audibly expelling their breaths, making the air around them humid.

Neva's voice pried them apart. "I think we've had enough of this." The firmness that cut between them made both boys back away slightly. "This is neither the time nor the place to settle any past differences." She had somehow worked her way between Warren and Randy and was looking up directly into Randy's eyes, which he quickly averted. "Do I look like a preacher to you, Randy?"

He looked back. "No," he said, glaring down at her.

"Well, if you think we are do-gooders here, you are sadly mistaken. We have nothing to do with religion here. I only help those who are willing to help themselves, and if you are not willing to do that, then you can go right back to Juvenile Hall. Maybe it's no big deal to you. Maybe you think you can go back to stealing, or using drugs, or whatever it is you do, but one day, you'll end up in some slimy hole, or shot in a robbery, or you'll get hepatitis or something worse from using the wrong needle, and only then will you remember that I gave you a chance. The choice is yours. If you stay here, you obey the rules just like everyone else because that is what life is all about."

She was a translucent rock, standing there, defying everything physical, telling Randy how icy fate would take his hand to a cold grave if he made the wrong choice. A sparkle entered her eyes, a tiny reflection of a fire that suddenly burned inside her.

"Everyone, sit down," Neva said. She moved about the room, waving her arms to motion everyone toward a seat. "It's time we laid down the law here so there are no doubts about what we expect and how that fits into your expectations of me and Warren—I mean Mr. McKinny."

"Mr. Mac," Spinner said.

"You can call me whatever you want," Warren said. "As long as it's nothing obscene." He glanced around the room and noticed Janeen smiling. When he smiled back, she lowered her eyes and returned to that safe place within herself.

"*I* would like to call you Warren," Krista said.

Spinner let out a low howl, like the wind in the trees, and Krista scowled at him for thinking she was flirting.

"Does that mean we can call you Neva?" Alec asked.

"I don't know," Spinner said. "Ms. Bell sort of has a ring to it."

There was a chorus of groans, then laughter, and Krista threw one of the sofa pillows across the room at Spinner.

"I'm trying to be serious here," Neva said, rolling her eyes at Spinner. "And Neva would be fine," she said to Alec.

Warren was a little surprised, but he thought he understood her intent. Getting close to them was the first step, and she had probably already lost Randy, who didn't share in any of the laughter. He sat with his arms crossed, a clear message to stay away.

Neva pushed her hair back in the rake of her hand, clearing her thoughts. She sighed and said, "I want to talk to all of you about what we are doing here. We are here for you because we are interested in you. Now, I realize that a statement like that will probably evoke a certain amount of suspicion on your part—suspicion that Warren and I will have to wear down as we prove to you that we can be trusted. But we cannot be the only ones to do all the work around here. Ultimately, we can only be responsible for ourselves, and each of you must learn to be responsible for yourself.

"The world is not going to protect you—or wait for you to catch up if you are lagging. The world is full of teachers, principals, policemen, and employers who aren't going to bother a great deal about why you screw up. If you're caught stealing or taking drugs, you're going to be arrested or fired. No one is going to care about your reasons, no matter how right they might appear to be in your mind. We want to help you become responsible for your own behavior so that you can fulfill your needs without infringing on someone else and so you don't become a victim because of irresponsible behavior. What I said to Randy earlier goes for all of you. It's all about choices. You just need to learn to make the right ones."

Neva paused and looked around the room. She didn't know what she was hoping to find. There was no sign of acknowledgement or eagerness in their eyes, which were all averted toward the floor or at the idle activity of their hands. For a moment, Neva diverted her own attention to brush away a thread on the knee of her jeans, and as she did, something happened.

In that moment of silence, Alec looked up, which drew Krista's attention first to him, then toward the direction he was looking. Warren realized that Alec's gaze was directed at Emily, who had been glancing at Alec off and on since she saw him. Her face lit up like a shooting star emerging in the darkness with a bright light that faded as she turned away, crossing her legs to reveal an ample view of thigh beneath billowy waves of skirt.

Emily didn't see Alec turn away to bury his thoughts in the pages of his book, nor did she see Krista's startled surprise, which narrowed into a glare of vengeance. When Emily did return her gaze, she found Alec disinterested, and with a jolt of retribution, she lowered the hem of her skirt.

"I won't keep you here forever," Neva said, looking up. "I just wanted you to know that we don't blame you for what happened to you in the past. It's the here and now that's important. And, also, your futures." The luster in her eyes faded, became glazed with a patina of sadness, and her lower lip pouted with what seemed to be a thought that carried her far away.

Warren suddenly had the urge to take her in his arms and hold her close. He repressed his thoughts as quickly as they appeared. Randy's bag seemed heavier when Warren picked it up to escort Randy to his room.

• • • •

At the top of the stairs, Emily's room was clean and whitewashed as if its past had been bleached away. She thought it felt like the inside of a coma. Neva told her that she was free to put up posters or photographs and give the room her own personality. Emily had never thought about her personality before. Was it how she felt or how others felt about her? The other girls were next door—the one who looked like a corpse and avoided eye contact and the pretty one who just glared at her and stood in her way so that she had to walk around her. Emily imagined that they were talking about her, but even so, all she could think about was the mess she was in— and that haunting pressure she felt deeper than any personality.

Emily sat alone in her room thinking that the blank walls *were* her personality. She remembered seeing a cartoon once with little ponies that talked, and she considered painting a rainbow in one of the corners. That would be enough. She would not be here long enough to get comfortable, and Emily didn't want to be anywhere she wasn't welcome. She would not allow herself to get attached. She was tired of getting comfortable, only to find it all taken away.

Emily looked around, thinking that this was the worst of all the places she had stayed. The floor was polished planks of blond wood. There were two beds with a small table between them, a wobbly dresser with stubborn drawers, and a desk with a linoleum top like the ones at school. She didn't bother to rearrange the furniture because it didn't suit her. One bed sagged, and the other one squeaked. Emily chose the one that squeaked. She didn't care. It was closest to the window.

Shadows crept through the slats, feeling their way across the room, embracing her legs and belly with searching fingers. Emily lay in her bed, steeped in the heat that rose about her, making the air thick and humid. A bead of sweat rolled off her brow and over her temple. She closed her eyes and sensed soft hands caressing her legs, her pelvis, her breasts. Instinctively she opened her mouth and moaned softly—a low, wistful cry. Her muscles ached from the tension of trying to hold herself together as every part of her began to pull away, as if she were being torn apart. Her legs quivered, and she heard the bedsprings squeak. Her fingers dug deeply into the mattress until her knuckles whitened. Emily thought she would cry.

She felt nothing. . . .

A cool breeze quickly brushed across her body and was gone. For a moment, Emily relaxed, but then, the heat came back, and she could hear that same lonely cry coming from somewhere in the walls. Or was it deep inside, somewhere in her past?

Emily had heard the popular girls at school talking in the locker room during gym class, when they didn't know she was listening, when they thought it was safe to talk about their beer parties and letting their boyfriends feel under their blouses, or jacking them off because they had to be pleased somehow. There was the one girl who made the other one promise never ever to tell anyone how she had put it in her mouth once, but they all said how they wouldn't go all the way yet, and they giggled because it was a lie. Emily wondered what made her so different from the others, why it was all so right, so socially acceptable when they did it. She was the bad girl, and that made her feel so dirty. Her life had been good for a while, with Marion English, and now she had to go through it all again.

Emily waited for that feeling inside her to get so bad that she couldn't control it, and she waited for it to take over as it had so many times before.

● ● ●

Neva stared at herself in the mirror, amazed at how much she resembled Emily. If she etched away the years in her mind, she could have been Emily. It was uncanny. Except for their eyes, they could be sisters. The color and texture of their hair, the shape of their faces, their mouths, all seemed the same, except the eyes. Emily's eyes were a Bahaman blue, as liquid and clear as the shallow, coastal waters of a tropical island. Neva looked at her own eyes in the mirror, and they were void of color except in harsh light, when they achieved the muddy brown of Galveston Bay.

When Neva heard the noise on the stairs, it took her a minute before she realized it was not the movement of the house. She went to look but found no one there. The house was quiet except for its own life. Neva stood in the doorway, listening to the creaks and groans. The darkness enveloped her. For a moment, she was lost in a murky sense of consciousness. She sensed that Jim was nearby, and she remembered.

I heard a noise in the house and went to look. Jim was in the hallway, dressed, ready to leave. I knew it was too early for him to be up. "What are you doing?" I whispered, so as not to wake Mother.

"I'm going to make history," he said. Jim saw that I didn't understand, so he came back and took my arm. "I'm going to jump the Kemah drawbridge. I'm going to do it this morning. I've planned it out. There won't be any traffic, so I'll just sit and wait for that first ship to sail up the bay. Right when the sun hits the horizon, the bridge will open up like a whole new life for me."

I could tell that I could say nothing to talk him out of it, so I said simply, "I'm going too. You'll need help, or at least a witness."

And he knew from my fierce glow that he couldn't talk me out of it either.

● ● ●

The night Emily arrived was sleepless. Warren lay in his bed, staring at the ceiling, unable to take his mind off Neva. His head was full of doubts and questions, which came to him like ocean waves, each mounting on top of the last, holding him under a current of confusion.

Warren's first day at Morning House had been a portent to the frustration that stalked him in every relationship. He was stranded on the side of the road, staring at the broken-down van he had purchased with what little money he had left. The voice inside his head became a lazy, lilting accompaniment to the beads of sweat that rolled over his temples. Warren stopped on the gravel shoulder of the road and watched the water run under the bridge. Armand Bayou. He wanted to walk into its gurgling banks and disappear in the cool, sweet water that flowed down to Clear Lake and on into the Gulf. The song of the bayou sang in his head deliriously.

> Girl gal Babylon in sweet and lovely song
> As stars rise in your eyes
> To dance the shore of silken sighs
> 'til dreams awake at dawn,
> And gently flow toward lake and see
> My love does ebb and flood for thee,
> Our hearts so full of moon and fire,
> Complete in no sense of desire,
> We journey from despair,
> We leave without a care,
> And pray we stay fair well,
> With waving arm and bye oh.

Warren wiped his brow on the sleeve of his shirt and looked to the sky as he exhaled a little too dramatically. Armand Bayou. *From Deer Park, follow the road that runs parallel to its banks.* He had no trouble with the instructions, and he made good time, despite having to walk the last few miles after his van overheated. Warren was still encouraged, despite the heat and the dust from passing cars that settled in the creases of his neck. He refused to hitch a ride. When he finally arrived at Morning House, Warren stopped in the shade of a large magnolia and raised his arms as if praying for a cool breeze. He saw her on the porch and thought he was hallucinating.

Neva stood atop a ladder, her hair in a ponytail with short, loose strands tripping into her eyes. He eyed her diminutive figure in jeans and a t-shirt, the ticklish part of her middle exposed as she stretched to paint the porch trim under the eaves. A lyrical tune filled the air. A little afternoon music. Like a conductor, she stirred the music with her free hand. Warren came up the walk unnoticed and stopped just short of the porch. Silently, he watched her graceful efforts to extend the reach of her arms. Entranced, he lingered too long. He blinked almost forcefully, pulling himself back.

Neva turned toward him. She was smiling, and immediately, he felt embarrassed. Warren climbed the steps to the porch as Neva descended the ladder. She shook his hand eagerly. Her strength surprised him, and yet, her hand was like a rose in his. Warren was reluctant to let it go, fearing its petals would be lost in the breeze swirling about on the porch.

From his job interview, he knew that she was opinionated and goal-oriented. Her expectations made him realize that she was serious about her job—and his.

"I'm glad you're finally here," she said with urgency in her voice.

Warren checked his watch. "I'm sorry. My car broke down, and . . ."

"Oh no, your timing is perfect. I just got to this spot under the eaves, and I'm having trouble reaching it." Neva pointed up to where she had been painting and then offered him the nearly dripping paintbrush. "Do you mind?"

He laughed and took the paintbrush.

While Warren got the unreachable spot, Neva told him, "The counselor you're replacing was tall enough to get those spots. I don't miss her so much anymore. She quit to get married and work on her doctorate. A disconcerting compromise, don't you think?"

"How's that?"

"Well," Neva explained, "if a woman wants the best of both worlds, a relationship and a career, that is, she shouldn't give up the freedom that allows her to choose which is more important at any given moment. If she is forced to compromise, then she will only end up with regrets for the loss of one, which in turn, will spoil the other."

Warren came down from the ladder. "Do you think it's any different for men?" he asked, handing back the brush.

"Certainly not. Men have rights too, you know."

That breeze swept across his face again. She had captured him with her dark, Italian eyes and bright smile, the inescapable gravity of a black hole, and now he was lost forever.

"Anyway, men are less emotional," she added. "Or at least they are better at hiding their emotions."

Warren felt several beads of sweat slide down the middle of his back. Pulling at his shirt, he asked, "Is it always this hot?"

"Oh no," Neva said. "Sometimes it's even hotter. It's the humidity. It can make you feel like a damp sponge. That's why I keep that fan out here." She was cleaning the brush and didn't look up at him, so she didn't see his look, his Hardy to her Laurel, his Abbott to her Costello. "Where did you say you were from?"

"California," Warren said, moving into the breeze from the fan.

"Good God. What brought you to Texas?"

"A girlfriend. It didn't work out, but I had already started on my masters, so I decided to stay."

Neva turned her head and smiled. "Freedom of choice," she said.

As they climbed the stairs to Warren's room, Neva explained about the house. "This was once a lovely home, in another time. I would like to restore that feeling again—a place anyone would be happy to call home—a real home, of course, for the placements here. It's sad that the house can't be more than just a temporary shelter. Most of the placements are here because they have nowhere else to go—or the only other place is worse."

Morning House had high ceilings with fretwork molding, cherry doors with beveled glass, walnut banisters, window seats, porcelain tubs with claw feet, and a hidden room under the staircase—all the personal touches that give a house charm and character. A veranda covered the entire front of the house, guarded by gables that spied out over the alluvial plains. For miles along the drive between Houston and Galveston, there were only whispering patches of reed and grass and occasionally a glimpse of the prehistoric marshes that once covered the vastness of the Texas coast. Morning House sat on the shore of Mud Lake, amid a small grove of oak trees that dated back a hundred years. It provided a pleasant break to the emptiness.

"I like to think of the name as a symbol for a new beginning of renewed hope." Neva stood at the top of the stairs and smiled at Warren as she swept her arms about, as if completing her tour. "I am very connected to this place," Neva said. "Before the foundation took over, Morning House was a Bed and Breakfast. It lapsed into disrepair, never making ends meet, even after NASA was built and took over most of the land. Before that, it belonged to a wealthy family of generations who fought with Sam Houston at San Jacinto and Hood's Brigade in the Civil War. They've long since disappeared. Restoring the old house into a historic landmark is one of my pet projects. I think the kids can be proud of what they achieve here, and it gives them a sense of responsibility too, which of course is a part of their therapy. We're in a low period right now. There are only three kids living in the house. We didn't want to take on more until we got another counselor, but now that you're here, I expect we'll be getting more very soon."

In his room, Warren followed Neva to the window, where he could see three teenagers painting the side of the house.

"We get most of our kids from Child Protective Services," Neva said. "Krista is the dark-haired one trying to supervise the others. She was caught shoplifting. She was removed from her home when she reported that her grandfather was molesting her. Her grandfather still lives with the family. Janeen is the other one. She was picked up after two boys reported that she gave them gonorrhea. She was prostituting in a trailer when the police arrested her—and her pimp. Then, there's Spinner. He came to us from Gatesville on a probationary program that placed him here prior to his permanent release. It's the State's way of assimilating non-violent delinquents back into society. Next week, we're getting a boy from the State Hospital in Austin. He has been in psychiatric care for four years. I don't know much more about him. So what do you think so far?"

"Quite a variety," Warren said and laughed at his understated evaluation.

"They're our little guinea pigs. Guineas, they call themselves. Spinner came up with that one. He thinks we're using them as test cases, that all we care about is reconditioning them. I suppose we do play our share of Pavlovian games."

"This is just what I was looking for," Warren said, thinking his reply was a bit too fervent.

"Well, if you wanted reality, this is it. They will keep you on your toes—that's for sure. But don't worry, they're harmless. They have their dreams and fears just like everyone else. Just don't play their games, and you'll do fine."

Warren noticed that the three teenagers were arguing with one another, and he wondered what he had gotten himself into. They were here for his teaching and guidance, and yet, they probably had experienced more in their lives already than Warren ever would, and they had survived. What could he possibly say that would impress them?

Warren sat up in bed with his longing, tired of this haunting feeling. He left his room and made his way through the house. The upstairs landing circumvented the stairway with wide, wooden planks like the deck of an old sailing ship surrounding an open hatch.

Warren descended the stairs toward a sliver of light emerging beneath Neva's door. Several boards creaked underfoot, warning that he was treading on forbidden ground. He hurried out the back, circling through the garden to the gravel drive that led to the main road.

Outside, the air was warm and briny, a sea smell that drifted with the onshore breeze. A foghorn droned in the distance. Headlights from passing cars blinked through the trees and played tricks with his mind as he began to see chimerical soldiers marching toward him. The tall oaks with their crusty cloaks and mossy beards murmured low. Warren walked up to the main road. Across from the property, Campbell's Market convened in a smoky yellow haze that came from the lights strung around the vacant parking lot. He decided to stop in on his way back to get a beer, but first, Warren headed away from NASA, toward the bridge over Mud Lake and the boatyards and fish markets, where the road darkened as it wound its way toward El Lago, and Seabrook, and finally Kemah. He wanted to be alone in the world outside Morning House.

Even though Warren was thinking about Neva, he wanted forget her. Somehow, he knew he had no chance of a relationship with her. She was too involved with Morning House. Warren envied her commitment. He was even jealous of it. Cruelly, he thought how unimportant their jobs were. There was no Nobel Prize for enabling a teenager to return to his or her family. In fact, it was a job with little or no positive stroking. Dr. Mueller had warned him of this during his interview for the job, and Neva had mentioned it during their first conference.

"These guineas might stop in the doorway to extend a grateful smile or give you a quick hug before leaving," she said, "but the realization that they will soon forget you is all too clear. Whatever you achieve in self-esteem has to be wrenched out of your own conception of success."

Before arriving at Morning House, Warren had only been able to think about surviving. Success was the farthest thing from his mind. Neva, however, was motivated by something he did not understand.

In one rare moment, Warren caught Neva watching a soap opera ironically titled *All My Children* during lunch, when none of the guineas were around. She had shushed him when he tried to talk, so he sat down and watched with her as Erica Kane, a raven-haired seductress, charmed her way melodramatically into the arms of her lover. Stubbornly, Warren fantasized that Neva's real needs were just as dramatic, yet merely repressed, and he longed to be the one to fill what he deemed was that void in her life.

Warren stopped at the bridge and looked back up the bank that ran along the back of Morning House. The water glistened with moonlight. On the surface, long shadows reflected from a dilapidated pier jutting out from the remains of an old boathouse. A mournful howl broke the lapping current. A hollow sound followed like a question.

Whooooooo?

Warren looked back toward the pier. A large white owl perched on a solitary piling in the water. It remained still for a long time, waiting for an answer, which Warren was unable to give. With a sudden lunge, the owl spread its slow, swooping wings that carried it into the darkness around Mud Lake.

Warren continued to walk, realizing that his own personal void had been bothering him. He had not told Neva the real reason he took the job at Morning House—the decision to part with his girlfriend, a decision which had left him unable to afford a place to live, a decision which had not been all his own. The choice had been made *for* him—or at least taken away from him. All along, Warren wanted the plans he had made with her—their future.

Those plans changed when she invited a work friend to dinner—a photographer at her ad agency who had convinced her that her future lay in modeling for ads, not writing copy for them. When Warren was not around, she posed for the photographer, first with clothes, then without. She repaid him for all his kindness one night when Warren found them in the bedroom. They didn't notice him at first, they were so involved, and for a few agonizing moments, as if viewing a private screening, he watched her passionate consumption of this stranger.

What hurt even more was the coldness in her reply to his final, anguished plea as he left with bags in hand, the empty victim of cuckoldry. Warren turned in the doorway and asked simply, "Why?"

"You couldn't give me what I needed, Warren," she had said. "You just weren't enough."

He had sought solace in art museums but had found more questions than answers. He had stared at the Broken Obelisk outside the Rothko Chapel and felt the emptiness of Martin Luther King's unfinished life. Taking the job at Morning House was necessary because Warren needed a place to live. He also needed people around him, people to take his mind off his depression, off the desolation he found in the dark depths of the Rothko paintings, off the decision he had almost made to put an end to his questioning, to break his own obelisk.

This void Warren felt was his need for human warmth and touch and sexual energy, and it was drowning him. He realized he needed that beer, at least as a symbolic gesture. Warren was returning, rounding the last curve, when he saw a shadowy figure scurry through the moonlight in front of Morning House. It took Warren a minute to walk back to the entrance, and by then, the phantom was gone and probably tucked away safely in bed. He decided to try his luck with the clerk in Campbell's Market.

The clerk was a young man, not much older than Warren. He was speaking angrily into the telephone when Warren entered the store. All Warren overheard was, "You're damn right I want to press charges. I've got one of them right here. Good, I'll hold her until you get here."

The clerk finished and hung up the telephone as Warren approached the counter. Almost simultaneously, Warren saw the empty cash drawer hanging open like a gaping jaw in front of the clerk and Emily sitting behind the counter in front of the magazines, which were too pornographic to put in the rack for public viewing. She was startled when she looked up and saw Warren, and with the back of her hands, she tried to wipe away the tears from her already reddened eyes.

"Emily?" Warren asked, addressing her as if his eyes might have deceived him. "What's going on?"

"You know her?" the clerk interrupted.

"Yes," Warren said. "I'm a counselor at Morning House. She lives there." Warren pointed across the street.

"I know the place," the clerk said with a tone of scorn, as if he were discussing a neighborhood eyesore. "The other one must be from there too, then."

"What other one?" Warren asked, remembering the figure that darted across the road.

"The one who stole the money from my cash drawer. I always figured those little maggots you're harboring over there were thieves. Now, these two are going to jail, where they belong."

"Wait a minute, there's no need to . . ."

"He thinks I'm in on it." Emily sobbed.

The clerk turned quickly to Emily and pointed a finger at her. If he had intended to strike her, Warren would not have been able to prevent it. "You shut up!" he demanded.

"Please try to control yourself," Warren said.

The clerk wheeled around with his finger now pointing at Warren. "Listen, buddy, you better stay out of this if you know what's good for you." He aimed his finger back at Emily, who now had her face in the palm of her hands. "This girl here helped her friend steal my money. The cops are going to be here in a minute, and I hope they take your whole little gang of delinquents to jail." The finger came back around to Warren as if the clerk were now using it to hold them both at bay. "And you can go with them for all I care, or maybe I'll just take care of you myself."

This man is a moron, Warren thought. He wanted to tell him that juveniles don't go to jail, but he suspected that this bit of information would turn the clerk's finger into a lethal weapon. "How did they steal the money when you were here in the store?" Warren asked instead. "Did you even see the other one?"

The clerk started to speak, then stopped. He had to think about it. "She was talking to me. She diverted my attention so the other one could sneak in here when I wasn't looking."

"Is that true, Emily?"

"No, Mr. McKinny." She sniffed. "I didn't do anything. I didn't know anything about it."

"She's lying!" the clerk shouted.

Warren looked at Emily and the tears streaming down her cheeks. "I don't think so," he said. He was getting angry now. "She'd practically have to tie you down for you to miss someone stealing money from the cash register. You're a big man. You mean to tell me you couldn't control this little girl? Where were you anyway?"

"I don't have to tell you anything, asshole!" The clerk continued to shout, but now he sounded more defensive than angry.

"Emily, where were you?" Warren asked. "You must tell me now." He was getting frantic. He felt his heart trying to pound its way out of his chest. He needed an answer before the clerk became uncontrollable.

Emily started to cry again. "In the back," she said, through the tears. "We were in the back."

"Look, I didn't take her back there," the clerk said. "She asked me. She wanted it." The clerk continued, stuttering out words as if he had wanted a way that cultured people might talk about it, to make it more acceptable. "She propositioned me. I never forced her to do anything."

"You moron!" Warren shouted. "She's a juvenile. That means it's still rape, even if you didn't force her." He knew he had lost control and probably would regret it, as the clerk was starting to come over the counter, when suddenly the police car pulled up in front of the store.

"Good," Warren said, pointing to the headlights outside, so the clerk would see. "The police are here. We'll let them straighten this out. I'm sure they'll be interested in everything that happened here tonight."

"I didn't know she was underage," the clerk pleaded, gripping the edge of the counter with white knuckles. He was off balance, still leaning toward Warren with a red face that made him look like a young, country preacher.

"You could be mistaken about a lot of things," Warren said.

As the two policemen entered Campbell's Market, the clerk quietly closed the cash register drawer. "Maybe the money was stolen before she came in," he said. "I think I might have left the drawer open."

Chapter Five

The next morning, Neva invited Emily into the office and asked if she knew anything about the stolen money. She didn't. Did she want to talk about what happened? Emily shook her head, avoiding eye contact.

"Can we talk about why you were placed here at Morning House?" Neva asked.

Emily looked up at the wall behind Neva. She drew in a breath and sighed, long and anguished, as if she were clawing about in quicksand; then, she rose out of it, a flower laying open its petals, tears like morning dew clinging to her cheeks. "No one knows what to do with me, Ms. Bell," she said.

"I thought you were going to call me Neva."

Emily sniffled as she smeared away the tears on her cheeks and managed a smile. "I guess I could someday. Right now, I just feel kind of funny about it."

"Fair enough," Neva said. Watching Emily now reminded Neva of a little bird. She was so small and fragile. "Would you like everyone to leave you alone, let you control your own life?" Neva asked.

"Yes."

"How would that make you feel?"

"Good."

"You made the decision to go out last night. You made it all on your own. Did you feel good about that?"

"Yes. Well, I thought I was doing the right thing."

"What made you feel good about it?"

"I don't know. I felt I *had* to do it. It just felt good, like doing it made the pain and loneliness go away."

"Can you describe the pain to me?"

"I can't explain it. It's just something that comes over me. It's like it controls me. I can't help it."

"I'm trying to understand. Did the pain make you want to be with that man last night, or did you choose to be with him to remove the pain?"

"No. I don't know. When you put it that way, no matter how I answer, it makes what I did sound bad. What does it matter, anyway?"

"Because I would like to see you fly out on your own."

"What?"

"Never mind. I don't want you to think about what you did. That's not important. It's how you *feel* about it—not only before but afterward too, before the trouble in the store but after you were with that man. How did you feel then?"

"I felt bad, okay? I knew I had done something wrong. But it felt good too, him wanting to be with me and all."

"How do you feel about yourself right now, Emily?"

"I don't know!" Emily blurted out. She was angry but not quite ready to express it. She apologized. "I feel like no one really likes me very much. I don't blame anyone because I don't like myself much. Are you going to send me back, Ms. Bell?"

"No, Emily. I realize that is a real fear for someone who has been in foster care."

"I was adopted the last time."

"Oh. I didn't know. I thought the social worker brought you from the county . . ."

"She did. My mother, Ms. English, I mean, she sent me back."

"I'm sorry. Do you want to talk about it?"

"I was too much trouble for her. It was much easier than trying to understand. We were always fighting." Suddenly, Emily started to cry again, this time uncontrollably.

"Is there anything I can do?" Neva asked.

At first, the words didn't come. Emily held her hands over her chest, trying to push the words out. "Yes, you can get me out of here."

"But I didn't think you wanted to leave just yet."

Emily pounded her chest, trying to grasp something that Neva couldn't see. "I want you to get me out of here," she repeated.

After Emily left the office, Neva remained at her desk, unable to move from her chair, unable to turn away from the chair where Emily had been sitting, that space now occupied by the ghost of someone she had known before. What happened to the girl who loved life, loved her twin brother, and loved her family—the girl who cherished the smell of the ocean and the rain? The ghost, before it faded, was the mirror Neva refused to see until now; then, it was Emily again—because they were the same, only different in a way.

Neva opened Emily's file and saw a copy of a police report near the bottom. Though she hadn't volunteered the information, Emily had been raped. The deduction was made after she had been examined in the emergency room. That was Friday night, the same Friday Alec arrived at Morning House—the night Emily left home after a fight with Marion English and walked from Deer Park to Pasadena. Someone found her dazed in the parking lot at Gilley's and called the police. Three boys had given her a ride in their van. Emily couldn't describe them or remember any details for the police to go on, just sensations of light and sound and touch. Marion English didn't believe her. She only knew that Emily had run away, and that was the last straw.

Straws were all Neva had to go on.

● ● ●

Dr. Edelstein had made a note in Alec's record at the time of his release from the Texas Children's Psychiatric Hospital.

> Alec remains generally withdrawn, with a depressive affect, but he no longer is acting out with what has been found to be brief and sporadic episodes of aggressive behavior toward the staff and older patients, mostly male. He seems to have a fear of females, withdrawing

from any physical or emotional contact. As yet, these episodes are unexplained. The change, however, appears to be due to a sublimation of his hostility into a learned skill, which may someday provide him with a means of support, specifically automotive mechanics. Alec is no longer a threat or a danger to himself or society.

Alec got into a fight his first week at school. Neva originally was afraid of this, expecting some acting out due to a change in his environment. The way he reacted to Randy confirmed that. However, because Alec spent most of his time reading alone, and because he had not displayed any abnormal emotional reaction to the news of Neva's visit with his mother, Neva was confident that the doctor's evaluation was correct. When she asked Alec about his mother being a witch, he said he didn't remember anything about it. Neva didn't mention April.

"She was very excited about your being here and would like to see you come back to live with her," Neva said.

Alec remained silent.

"I'm a little worried about this witchcraft business, though. She may have to undergo an evaluation so we can determine what it all means, how it affects her ability to provide for you. It won't weigh a great deal. Since you're so near to being an adult yourself, you'll be on your own soon. We can't be too concerned about your mother."

"Do I have to see her right away?" Alec asked.

"Well, no—not if you don't want to." Neva was hoping for another response, but she understood his concern about being with the one person who could have kept him out of the hospital. Perhaps Alec blamed her for what he had to go through. Neva changed the subject. "How are you and Spinner getting along?"

"We manage. Don't expect any miracles."

"Don't expect any from me, either."

"Is there anything else?" Alec asked.

"I noticed you were looking at the picture on my desk." Neva picked up the picture and handed it to Alec. "I'd like you to have it."

"Thanks," was all he said.

• • •

Neva received a call from the principal that Alec and Spinner had been in a fight with some other boys. When Neva arrived at the school, Krista met her in the hallway. "You're here about Alec, aren't you?" Krista walked closely beside Neva, almost guiding her.

Neva noticed an overpowering scent of perfume, a drugstore scent. Krista's nearness was intimidating. Neva sought control by slowing her pace. "Is there something you know about this, Krista?"

"I was there. I saw it all. Really, I can't believe this whole thing is so blown out of proportion. I mean, the teacher who stopped the fight got so bent out of shape. It's ridiculous."

"What exactly did you see?"

"It's silly. Alec didn't mean to start anything. Jarrett was just jealous because Alec was showing me some attention. Jarrett came on kind of strong, and Alec just didn't understand. It was really gallant the way Alec defended me."

"Who is Jarrett?"

"My boyfriend. I thought you knew."

Neva stopped at the door to the office, thinking that she needed to be better prepared. She turned back to Krista. "Did anyone get hurt?"

"No, of course not. I told you the teacher broke it up. Do you think Alec is in trouble?"

Alec and Spinner were waiting in the outer office. Shortly after Neva arrived, the principal joined them. He was a large man with a Cheshire-cat smile and a circle of dark, neat beard. He invited them into his office as if they were going to discuss awards for the boys instead of punishment.

Before they even sat down, Spinner blurted out, "It's my fault because I'm black. As soon as I change the color of my skin, there won't be any more problems at school."

The principal chuckled.

"Do you really think that's the problem, Spinner?" Neva asked.

"It's always the problem," he said. "Some white folks ain't got nothing better to do than make trouble. It's the only way they can make themselves feel big."

"This guy was just a punk," Alec added. "That's why he said what he did. He just wanted to start something."

Neva asked Alec what the boy said, and Alec just looked at Spinner.

"Nigger," Spinner said. "It's all right now. I ain't mad no more."

"Well, Spinner," the principal said, "Jarrett claims that Alec started this whole ordeal."

Spinner laughed. "Yeah, right. Look, we know we're outsiders here. We're not stupid enough to go around looking for trouble. This guy just got his ya-yas out because we were talking to Krista—or rather, she was talking to Alec. Krista has the hots for this guy because he's a jock. So what else is new, right? Anyway, when Krista sees him walking down the hall, she waves at him, almost as if she were setting up the whole thing. So he comes up to us with his two friends, and he looks at Alec and says, 'Beat it, and take your nigger with you.' Well, Alec just lays this guy out with one punch; then, his two friends jump in, and I do a little dance with them."

"You could have used a little more diplomacy," Neva said, "considering you knew you had the advantage."

"It all happened too fast," Spinner said, knowing what she meant, knowing his code of ethics was more important. A sentimental flutter crept into his voice. "I couldn't just stand there, anyway. I have to fight my own fights."

"Wait a minute," Alec said. "We were outnumbered. I don't exactly call that an advantage."

"Those three boys didn't realize that Spinner was a boxing champion at Gatesville," Neva said. "He's been working out at the local gym ever since he came to Morning House. He hopes to compete in the Golden Gloves in the fall. I thought he would've told you."

Alec laughed as if the whole incident suddenly struck him as funny. "I wouldn't have stepped in if I had known that."

"I didn't need your help anyhow, cowboy. In fact, the next time, you can just stay clean out of it."

"Hey, no problem," Alec said, leaning askew and smiling so big now that his eyes sparkled, capturing the overhead fluorescent light.

"There won't be a next time, though, will there?" the principal asked, standing up and taking a place between them with fatherly arms around their shoulders. "I don't think there will be a need for any strong discipline here. What do you think, Ms. Bell?"

"I think they've learned their lesson," Neva agreed.

The principal escorted everyone to the outer office, where he released the boys, and then, he took Neva commandingly by the arm. "There is something I think you should know," he said, as he escorted her back into his office and closed the door behind them.

Suddenly, the principal's nearness irritated Neva. She stopped and pulled her arm away, forcing him to release his grip. "I don't have a lot of time," she said.

The principal smiled and said calmly, "Neither do I, Ms. Bell, so I'll get right to the point. I thought it was significant that Alec's mother visited him today."

"I'm sorry," Neva said, embarrassed that she had considered his intentions to be unprofessional. "Of course, that *is* significant. I had no idea she would try to see him here."

"Neither did I. In fact, I wasn't even aware of it until Alec's teacher called me. She realized the visit wasn't going well. I politely intervened. I wouldn't say that Alec was upset. He was quite distant, though, possibly even holding back some resentment . . . toward his mother, that is. I'm just guessing though, so don't hold it up to any unbiased scrutiny. It may not hold water."

"No. I trust your opinion," Neva said.

"In any case, I didn't make a big deal about her being here. No need to cause a scene. She left, and there appeared to be no harm done. However, it could be why he struck that boy, releasing his frustrations on a third party, someone he didn't care about hurting."

"You have very good psychological instincts," Neva said.

"It comes with the job, Ms. Bell. I recognize problems and pass them on. In this case, I leave the untangling to your expertise."

"Well, if you ever leave this job, you can always run for public office."

That afternoon, Neva got Alec a job, hoping that by fulfilling Dr. Edelstein's diagnosis, this sublimation of Alec's aggression would keep him out of trouble. Alec said he would rather work on cars than go to school anyway. She offered him a deal—go to school half a day, then to work. The principal agreed, and it was all set up.

Johnny Rodriquez, who owned the garage in Seabrook, said he didn't need anyone, but as a favor to Neva, he gave Alec a job.

• • •

After days of silence, Warren brought up the store incident at dinner. Everyone stopped eating, and Neva and Warren looked at each other across the table, straight-faced.

Warren studied their faces. Emily lowered her head, but he already knew that she didn't steal the money. Janeen looped a frayed and oily rope of hair back behind her ear. Chewing her fingernails, she watched Krista with eyes flitting back and forth, like a base runner waiting for the signal to steal. She knew something, but it wasn't her own guilt she was hiding.

Krista sat slack-mouthed with disbelief, expelling a sigh of exasperation strong enough to blow out a candle. "You've got to be kidding," she said. "That happened like a year ago. Now, you bring it up like we're all under suspicion because someone stole some money from that filthy little store?"

Warren raised his eyebrows.

"I expected this sooner or later," Spinner said. "The cops think I did it, don't they? Pin it on the black guy. I'm sure the word got out that I did time in Gatesville, so naturally, they think I stole the money."

"You're being a little hasty, Spinner," Neva said. "I don't think anyone is assuming anything in this case."

"Yeah? Then, why don't you just say who it is?" Spinner asked.

"We don't know who it is," Neva said.

"See? Just as I thought. If you knew, you wouldn't have brought it up here, in front of all of us. You would have done it all in secret, and maybe one of us would have just disappeared," Spinner spat out.

"The fact is," Warren said, looking a bit like Hercule Poirot with his hands folded across his stomach, "the clerk said he saw the guilty party run from the store, across the street, to Morning House."

Krista sighed, this time with relief. "Then, it's simple. Why don't they just arrest whoever did it? Then, the rest of us can stop feeling like you think we're guilty of something."

"I don't think they want that," Warren said. "I think the owner of the store is willing to forget the whole thing if he just gets his money back."

"Well, then, cough it up, Spinner, so the rest of us can get out of here," Randy said.

"Say what?" Spinner asked, narrowing his eyes at Randy.

"You're the thief, right? If the shoe fits . . ."

"I'll tell you where I'll stick my shoe . . ."

"Please, let's not start anything," Neva said quickly. "Nothing will be resolved by pointing fingers at each other. It's more important to talk about how we feel. From the comments that have been made, it seems that guilt is a strong motivating factor. Money was stolen from the store across the street, and *someone* was to blame. But beyond that, why should we react to that news as if we were guilty, even if we weren't?"

"No one likes to be accused of doing something she didn't do," Krista said.

"No one accused anyone of doing anything," said Warren.

"Sounded like Randy just did," Alec said.

"I do believe the cowboy's right," Spinner said.

"Do you have any facts, Randy?" Warren asked.

A smirk fell across Randy's face as he sat back in his chair defiantly.

"House rule," Neva said. "Stick to the facts. No low blows, and don't talk about your feelings unless they are strictly your own, unless you state positively that they were created by some fact. For example, I am disappointed when one of you breaks a rule because I believe you are all capable of following the rules. They are not set up to hurt anyone. They only exist to establish fairness and order. I also feel that Spinner is afraid of going back to Gatesville, and *that* is why he is worried about being accused of stealing the money."

"You got your facts wrong, Ms. Bell. I ain't afraid of nothin'," Spinner said.

Neva smiled at her bait being taken. "You're right, and I'm sorry. I used you to demonstrate a point. My statement just got Spinner upset with me because I didn't stick to the facts. Even though I said I felt a certain way, I didn't describe *my* feelings; I just accused Spinner of feeling a certain way. Before, when I said I was disappointed, *that* was my own feeling."

"How about this fact," Krista said. "I saw Emily sneak out of her room that night. Maybe she went over to the store and stole the money."

Emily pushed herself back from the table and rose with a radiance of despair. She didn't look at anyone, least of all Krista. "I didn't steal anything," she said, as tears started to come. "I went over to that store, just like Krista said, but I didn't steal anything, and someone here knows that." And then, Emily was gone. They could hear her footsteps on the stairs and the door to her room closing.

"Talk about your low blows," Spinner said.

"I wasn't lying," Krista squealed. "You heard her. Why shouldn't she be a suspect?"

"Did you see her steal the money?" Alec asked.

"Alec, please don't defend her," Krista pleaded. "It's not right that she comes here and takes over."

"You should know about taking over," Spinner said.

Krista's jaw tightened. "Just what is that supposed to mean?" she asked.

Spinner leaned into his words. "You pull Janeen's strings like she's some kind of puppet, and you've been trying to do the same with Alec ever since he got here."

"I'm tired of you always harassing me, Spinner. You're always so free with your cute little remarks. Why can't you just leave me alone?"

"'Cause I see right through your games, girl."

"Oh, and you're so perfect," Krista said, tilting her head with a provoking smirk. "You can sit there and . . ."

"You smother people, Krista," Spinner interrupted. "You don't let them breathe, and you don't know what it's like not to be able to breathe, or you wouldn't do it. You've never had to wake up with nothing to eat and try to sleep with rats crawling under your bed. You've never had to experience having no hope except that your prayers could be answered and take you out of the shithole you were born in. You don't know what it's like to have to fight to survive and to lay awake at night and wonder why your world is closing in on you. And when you try to break out of it, you end up making a mistake and trading that world for one that's just as bad—or worse, and more closed in, where all you own can fit into a cigar box, and people are always telling you what to do, so you even gotta ask permission to take a piss."

"You don't know anything about me, Spinner."

"I know enough. I know you always got what you wanted, just by asking, not by working for it or being forced to take it because there was no other way. Your world was always full of new shoes and clean sheets and no hand-me-downs or thrift stores. Your future was always full of things you wanted, not needed. You've never known what it's like to need anything—or to have people look at you like you was supposed to be happy with someone else's old shit. You're crazy, girl, and it's because you ain't got the sense to know when you got it good."

"Ease up, man," Alec said, trying to calm him. "She made a mistake, okay, but you're just making it worse. It's not her fault where she was born—or where you were born."

"Oh, man! Now, you on her side? You white folks stick together no matter what, is that it?"

"That's not it at all," Alec said.

"You people just don't see the point," Spinner said, throwing his napkin on the table.

"Maybe 'cause there ain't no point," Randy said. "There's no point to nothing. None of us even matter. You ain't had it no worse than any of us," he said to Spinner. "Maybe you had it bad in your own way, but not worse."

Suddenly, the conversation stopped. Warren glanced across the table at Neva. She quickly signaled him with a finger to her mouth. She wanted to wait. She wanted the argument to play itself out even though the rules had obviously been broken. Janeen asked softly if she could start clearing the table. Neva waited before answering, but the others were silent, exhausted. Neva nodded to Janeen as she got up to go check on Emily, and the others followed Janeen to the kitchen.

Alec finally broke the silence. After he put his dishes on the counter next to where Janeen was starting the water in the sink, he spoke to no one in particular.

"We're not all that different, you know," he said.

"Who asked you," Spinner said.

"No one. No one had to ask me. I'm just as much a part of this as you are, as any one of us is."

"Okay, you tell me how I'm like Randy, mister smart Alec."

Krista giggled.

"Cute," Alec said, then turned to Krista. "And look at you. You think it's funny when he teases someone else, but you get angry when it's you."

"I'm waiting," Spinner said, impatiently.

"We're all here, aren't we, in this place," Alec said. "Society's misfits.

And I don't know one of us who chose to be here. That must say something."

"We're guinea pigs," Krista said.

"Exactly," Alec agreed.

"You're all nuts; that's what you are," said Randy, throwing down his towel. "I ain't no guinea pig, and I ain't doing no dishes." He started to leave the kitchen.

"Hey, wait a minute," Krista said. "You can't just leave. We all have to help with the chores around here."

Randy turned around and looked at Krista as if she had just asked him to hold his breath until he passed out. "Why?" he asked, then left.

Spinner started to move toward the door.

"Let him go," Alec said. "If he breaks the rules, let them deal with him."

"What's the matter with you?" Spinner asked. "You suddenly get chicken?"

"You know, you're just as stupid as he is," Alec said.

"That does it," Spinner said. Then, without warning, he jabbed Alec with a punch so quick and precise that Alec didn't even see it coming. Suddenly, Alec was falling backward, and he couldn't control his legs enough to gain his balance.

When Alec hit the floor, Krista screamed. She watched blood run from his nose and knelt beside him, holding her towel to his nose as Warren ran into the kitchen. Then, Janeen fell. No one noticed until they heard her hit the floor, when they saw her lying on her side, twitching as if she were having a nightmare, with her eyes rolled inside her head.

• • •

"You all right, cowboy?"

"Yeah."

"What you did, not tellin', not snitchin' on me, you didn't have to do that."

"I know."

"Only thing is. Don't go thinkin' that maybe I'll be returning the favor anytime soon."

"I won't, and you don't need to. That's up to you. The way I look at it, it's hard enough just keeping it together around here. It never hurts to have a little help."

"Just so you know, I didn't ask for it."

"I know that. I did it because I know you really like me and you just don't know how to say it."

Spinner let out a howl that could have awoken the dead if there were any still lingering in the old walls of Morning House. "You something else, cowboy. I gotta hand it to you. You really something else."

"I know," Alec said and tucked his hands behind his head.

"Anyway, I'm sorry I hit you. I shouldn't a done that. Times I just kinda lose control, 'specially when I feel cornered. My trainer's always telling me it's gonna get me in trouble. He's always telling me I gotta stay cool. Imagine, someone telling me about cool. Maybe I'm just not used to someone being straight with me."

"Forget it."

"Can't. That's twice now you went out on a limb for me. And after I punch you in the nose too. It don't figure."

"There's nothing to figure. It's just that they wouldn't understand—that's all."

"I hear that. Guess it took Janeen getting sick to turn us all around. Put our heads on straight."

"I heard the doctor say it was just her nerves. She needs rest."

"I don't know, man. She looked like more than just a case of nerves. She looked like something got her from the inside and was trying to get out. I saw this guy once coming down off smack, looked just like that."

"She just looked sick to me. Of course, I've only seen the stuff that nurses pass out at the hospital to keep all the patients sedated. The new ones usually came in ranting and raving like rabid dogs. They always got strapped down until the medication took over. That place was a trip, a city of zombies, the walking dead."

"Too much, man. Sound like a weird place. You know, in the joint, you can get all the drugs you want, whatever kind. Nothing else to do there but get stoned or pump iron. The joint was a trip too. I guess I was lucky to get into this boxing thing. It got me away from all the bullshit. I just hope I can stay away. This State shrink told me once I needed some way to vent my anger before it built up in me and made me do something stupid. I guess that's what my trainer was getting at. He wants me to focus my anger, long as I do it before the other poor sucker focuses on me."

"Psychiatrists aren't so smart. They pick your brain. Then, they take everything you've told them and screw it all around and give it right back to you in some language that makes it sound like they've discovered what's wrong with you. They think that just because they've learned all this stuff about you that they've cured you. People who are crazy don't want to be cured. They just want a safe place to hide, and being crazy is about the safest place there is."

"Randy seems to think you're straight-up crazy. Why is that?"

"Randy's a dick, and he doesn't know what he's talking about. He knew me four years ago, and that's when people thought I was crazy. There just wasn't any rulebook for my kind of problems, so they sent me to a hospital. One thing I learned there was that people who are really crazy aren't dumb. They know how to use the system, and they know how to get back in when they need to, when they need that safe place with real walls. I saw plenty of them while I was there. Revolving doors they called them."

"You must be pretty smart. You talk funny, but I can tell you ain't dumb. Some folks think they smart, but on the street, they don't have what it takes. That's when they're dangerous, like Randy. Me, I'm smart. I just ain't very lucky. Always had to work for everything I got. But you, you just spit right in its face. I can't figure that."

"You think I'm lucky? What am I doing here then?"

"Luck is where you find it, cowboy, and Krista is willing to give herself to you, but you won't have none of it. And Emily too."

"Now, *you're* crazy."

"No, I seen her looking at you. They don't want none of my action, but then, that's their loss. They don't know what they're missing."

"Yeah?"

"Say, you ain't . . ."

"You're wrong, there. I just haven't seen it, that's all."

"Then, you better open your eyes, cowboy, 'cause you're the man as far as they know. And you just might be missing something good."

"Yeah?"

"You think Emily stole that money, like Krista said?"

"I don't know. Sneaking out is a whole lot different than stealing. I think maybe Krista was just being Krista."

"She sure don't cut Emily no slack. I guess that's what got me going. Emily didn't do nothin' to deserve what Krista said."

"No."

"What you looking at?"

"Stars. The sky is full of them, like it's raining stars."

"I wouldn't know about that, cowboy. Those stars are for dreamers, anyway. You wanna see a real star, you come down to the gym sometime and watch me fight."

"Right."

"No foolin', cowboy. Spinner is a winner."

"Where did you get a name like Spinner anyway?"

"I was born with it. Jerome Spinner. Never liked Jerome much. I need to find a good boxing name. All the big stars have one."

"A big star, huh?"

"Ain't no one gonna stop me, cowboy. I'm going to rocket right up to those stars you're looking at. Soon as I win the Golden Gloves, then I'll be ready for some real fights. I'll be shinin' brighter than any of those stars you been wishin' on every night."

"Rocketman."

"Say what?"

"Your boxing name."

"Rocketman. I like that. Yeah. I'll make 'em see stars. I feel like this is a real beginning for me, you know what I'm saying? I think I'm finally gonna turn things around."

"Yeah, that's good. At least one of us will get out of here."

"You know there's got to be more for you too. You don't want to be a grease monkey all your life, do you?"

"I don't know. It's not a bad job, and Johnny Rodriguez is a good boss and all, but I can't see doing that forever."

"There must be something."

"No, nothing. Maybe someday though."

"That's a shame. A real shame."

"Yeah."

Chapter Six

Replacing the money was the only way Neva knew of to resolve the incident. She couldn't have everyone at odds. When everyone was gone, she looked in on Janeen, who was still in bed, too ill to attend school. Then, Neva walked out toward the highway.

When she came out of the grove of oak trees that lined the drive near the house, Neva felt the warm, fresh air from the bay against her face. Overhead, a clear, vast, blue expanse reflected a sudden, pure joy flowing from her heart. Even as she walked toward Campbell's Market clutching the envelope filled with money, ready to give away most of what she had been able to save over the past six months, Neva knew that deep inside, she was happier than she had been in a long time. She'd never be able to leave this place again—especially not now.

After getting her master's degree in Houston, Neva had come back feeling a need to be near her past, near a place where she would always be sweetly haunted by familiar, secret places. And she wanted to make amends with her mother, though that aspiration seemed impossible.

Until Alec arrived, she thought she only came back to revive memories of her past. Now, Neva felt like her destiny was bright again. This time, she knew it was right, and this time, she would not be hurt. That was part of the reason for returning the money. Neva had to take steps to protect herself. Never again would she let something slip from her hands because she failed to act on it. Everything happening now seemed to be part of a plan, and yet, Neva still questioned the possibility of divine intervention. Was Alec's arrival at Morning House more than an accident? Was Emily's arrival somehow predestined? Neva had yet to figure out the significance of her part in this plan. She would not lose the opportunity.

Last night, she had gone to Emily's room, expecting tears and a plea for an explanation to all the meaningless frustration over never fitting in. Instead, Emily was sitting on the edge of the bed, humming a song to a stuffed bear in her lap. The tears had already dried. She didn't even look up.

"My sister gave me this bear when I was fourteen. She said he would always comfort me when she couldn't, when she wasn't around."

"He looks like he has had lots of hugs."

"I haven't seen my sister in a long time. Now, she's sick."

"I'm sorry."

"She needs me, but my mother, Ms. English that is, she wouldn't let me do anything to help. She wouldn't even let me see my sister."

"I don't understand."

"You wanted to know why she sent me away."

"You had an argument about your sister?"

"Yes, that was part of it."

"Why won't she allow you to see your sister?"

"My sister needs a bone marrow transplant, and they say I'm the only one who can help her. Ms. English didn't want me to have the operation. She said it could kill me. I don't care, though. My sister will die for sure without it."

"Oh, Emily, I'm so sorry. I don't know what to say. Is this what has been bothering you, not Krista or what happened at the store?"

"Yes." Emily was nearly choking the bear in her embrace.

"Do you want me to talk with Marion English?"

"I don't know. I guess that's over. There doesn't seem to be any point in talking with her now."

It doesn't have to be over, Neva was thinking as she entered the store. Why is love so easily lost when one life doesn't fit so neatly into another? A faint ringing above her head brought her out of her reverie.

Duffy Campbell leaned around a display of Coca-Cola bottles and waved to Neva. Perched atop a throne of cream corn like an elfin king, his short, strong legs straddled a box of collard greens as he stamped out prices like edicts, then stacked the cans carefully on the shelf in front of him. Duffy was an old seadog who had sailed out of ports Neva had never heard of. Neva had found an instant friendship with Duffy, a relationship based on good-natured teasing, a challenging game that always helped to relieve Neva's stress.

"Does anybody really eat that stuff?" Neva asked. "I mean, except maybe you and Popeye."

"You betcha." His eyes glistened over the top of half-rimmed reading glasses. "Nothing more healthy for you. These greens will put more color in your skin than those hamburgers and cokes you call a meal."

"I can't eat anything that looks like seaweed, Duffy."

Duffy pointed to the coke display, despite his own good advice. "I got your favorite on special this week. Diet."

"I'll have to take a raincheck. Here." Neva handed him the envelope. "I just came by to give you this."

Duffy put down the price stamp and took the envelope. When he saw the money, he looked up at her, his eyes narrowed to quarter moons in his large face. "What's all this for?"

"One of my kids took it. I'm giving it back."

"The heck you are," he said, shoving it back at her. "This is nonsense. Even if one of them did steal it, I wouldn't take it from you."

"What do you mean, even if . . . I thought . . ."?"

"You thought wrong. You've got a good heart, Neva. Maybe too good."

"Are you saying that one of my kids didn't take the money?"

"I am. My clerk told the police that he left the register open, but that was just to cover up the fact that he took the money himself. If he was in the stockroom, he still could have heard the bell that rings when someone enters the store. He could have been out here long before anyone had a chance to take the money out of the register. I think he took it, and that's why he disappeared."

"He quit

"Left town, as far as I know. That wasn't the first time he stole from me, either. God knows Mimi and I don't have much, but if he needed money, I would have helped him out, if only he asked. He took advantage of me, though, and I can't tolerate that."

The pieces just didn't fit. As Neva walked back to Morning House, she thought about the loose ends to the stolen money. She didn't doubt that Warren had seen someone cross the road that night. She just wished he had been able to see who it was. There would be no way to find out now unless the guilt became overbearing—if there *was* any guilt. It could have been any one of them. No one had even attempted to establish an alibi. The most logical choice was Krista just because she had seen Emily leave, and she might have followed out of curiosity. The only one Neva was sure about was Emily. She was the part of the story that Duffy Campbell was not aware of—the part the clerk lied about, and he deserved to be punished for what he did. She decided not to tell the others what Duffy told her.

● ● ●

The house was quiet, so Neva went to her office and pulled the case files on Emily, Janeen, and Krista. She noticed on her calendar that Friday was the date for court hearings on Alec's and Emily's temporary custody with the County Protective Services. Usually a formality, Neva thought, unless someone contested the action. If Marion English changed her mind, then Neva would have to talk with her about Emily's sister. And the call from Alec's caseworker bothered her. She wanted Neva to bring Alec to the hearing because he might have to testify. Apparently, there was to be a review of his status because Anna Gogarty objected to his placement at Morning House. This sounded more like April's doing. Neva knew that fretting about it would not help. She would find out on Friday.

As Neva was making notes, she heard the television go on in the dayroom. She found Janeen nearly buried under a blanket in the large armchair everyone fought over. As Neva approached, Janeen looked up apologetically. In the corner of her mouth clung the wet end of a twisted strand of hair.

"I couldn't sleep," Janeen said. Her voice was soft and shallow. "I was going crazy up there."

Neva sat down on the arm of the chair and pulled the strand of hair from Janeen's mouth. "You must be feeling better then. That's a good sign."

"I'm sorry if I made everyone worry about me."

"Don't be silly, Janeen. You don't need to apologize." Neva continued to run her fingers through Janeen's hair.

"I'm just so embarrassed about fainting and everything. I don't know what happened to me."

"You've been through a lot, and you're still weak. It may take some time to recover. Would it make you feel better if I washed your hair and helped you fix it up nice?"

"I guess I wouldn't mind that, if you think I really need it."

Neva was astounded, and yet she felt a vague attachment to Janeen's ignorance of her own condition. As the soap lather discolored in Janeen's hair and fell into the basin, a sense of déjà vu overwhelmed her. Neva could not erase the look of uncertainty and vulnerability in Janeen's eyes when the doctor examined her in the emergency room. Now, as she rinsed the soap from Janeen's hair, turning her head from side to side, Neva saw the restless energy pulsing beneath Janeen's tight shut eyes, her lashes darting like a pair of butterflies avoiding the net.

The shampoo worked a miracle, giving her hair a silky radiance. Neva watched this beginning of Janeen's metamorphosis with an odd awareness of changes going on inside herself, a confusion created by ambivalent feelings that kept rising in her.

She dried Janeen's hair briskly with a towel, leaving it damp, then combed it out, and trimmed the ends. Then, she combed it all back out of her face. Neva applied a small amount of mascara to Janeen's eyelashes, added blush to her cheeks and eyelids, and darkened her eyebrows, all to give just a slight color to her otherwise pallid complexion. As a finishing touch, Neva stroked on a peach lip gloss to Janeen's dried lips. Janeen watched her in the mirror.

"That doesn't even look like me." Janeen giggled.

"Of course, it does. You're very pretty, Janeen, and you shouldn't hide it."

Neva used a blow dryer to remove the dampness from Janeen's hair, and as she brushed it out, the hair fell in gentle waves broken only where the color changed. That simple break allowed Neva to escape the alarming presence of Janeen's vulnerability.

"You should let your natural color grow out. I think it would be much prettier."

"No one liked me until I bleached it. You know what they say about blondes."

"You should please yourself, not others."

Janeen smiled at Neva in the mirror. "I know you mean well, Ms. Bell, but you don't know what my life has been like."

"Are you and Krista getting on okay?" Neva asked.

"Oh, yeah, she's all right. I don't mind her ways so much as everyone thinks. It's just me. Sometimes I feel like crying, and I don't even know why."

"We're going to work on that. Making you look better on the outside was just the beginning. Feeling good about yourself is important too."

"You might be taking on the impossible."

"Oh, I don't know. I think we've done all right so far." Neva fluffed the wispy waves of hair about Janeen's face; then, they both stared at the reflection in the mirror. Janeen modestly placed her hands over her mouth and giggled. "What really happened the other night?" Neva asked.

"What do you mean?"

"When Krista saw Emily leaving her room."

"Krista already told you."

"I know, but I just thought maybe there was more."

"Is that what this is all about? You just want information from me?"

"No. It's not that, at all. I just thought you might have seen something, but maybe you didn't say anything because you didn't want the others to get mad at you."

"I didn't see anything. You'll have to talk to Krista if you want to know about what she saw."

"Will Krista tell me the truth?"

"There's really nothing else to tell. Krista and I were in our room all night. That's it. We didn't steal the money."

"Krista didn't follow Emily when she saw her leave?"

"No. There was someone else. She heard someone, so she closed the door."

"She didn't see who it was?"

"No. Please, I don't want to be a part of this. I don't want any more trouble."

Neva tried to brush over a part of Janeen's hair that had fallen out of place, but Janeen pulled away. Neva didn't speak. She started to leave. At the door, she turned back. "I didn't set you up, Janeen. My feelings were honest, and I believe what you tell me. I just hope you can do the same. If we can't trust each other, then I will have lost you, and I don't think I will be able to endure another loss."

• • •

Neva nervously moved a hair out of her face as she headed to her office, knowing that Dr. Mueller was waiting for her inside. She was more convinced than ever that a therapy group was necessary, but just with the girls. The dinner group wasn't working, not the way she wanted, not with the boys. There was no control. They were too disruptive, always wanting to fight. And she was having serious doubts about her evaluation of Alec, since his behavior seemed to be nothing more than childish acting-out. She knew she would have to monitor his progress at his job.

When Neva entered the office, she was still thinking about Alec. In her preoccupation, she fumbled with the top button of her summer dress. It was light blue and sleeveless, with a low neckline.

As she entered the office, the button popped open, and her inner voice spoke to her. *You fought all these years to be recognized as an intelligent person who could achieve success on her own productive merits, and look at you now, stooping to sexual wiles just to get a little therapy group of your own. You don't even normally wear a dress.* Neva made no effort to re-button her dress. Instead, she tugged at the hemline of her skirt, crossing her legs, and let it rest several inches above her knee.

"You look particularly charming this evening," Dr. Mueller said.

Neva thanked him pleasantly, feeling a glow of selfish pride blush her cheeks.

"I thought we could go to Jimmy Walker's," Dr. Mueller said. "It's just on the other side of the Kemah drawbridge."

"I'm familiar with it," Neva said.

"Oh, have you eaten there before?"

Neva hesitated and then said, "A long time ago."

Dr. Mueller's little smile was almost pleasant, but his lips would not stretch over his fangs. He pretended to look into her eyes, but she could feel the heat from his peering laser-eyes move under her skirt and up the back of her leg.

Jim warned me about those feelings, those desires. He told me it was like steam that had to release, or it would explode. We had a long talk after I tried to get even with him.

Early one morning, I was pouring myself a glass of orange juice from the container our mother always kept neatly labeled in the refrigerator. I was standing in front of the refrigerator, thinking about how meticulous our mother was, when I realized that my hands had turned almost white with cold. That was when I conceived a plan to get even with Jim for all the times he had surprised me. I hurried to his door and listened. He wasn't up yet. Quietly, I opened the door and crept up to the bed. I ran my hands under the sheet and placed them on his back.

"Jesus!" he hollered and nearly came up off the bed.

I ran my hands over his stomach and started to tickle him, but he was able to grab me and find ticklish spots I didn't even realize I had. Suddenly, we were rolling in the bed, laughing and trying not to make too much noise so we wouldn't wake our parents.

Jim pulled me and I felt him between my legs, and I realized he was different. Our tussling had pushed the sheet back, and I could see that he was naked. I was startled because I was able to feel him through the teddy I wore. I tried to pull away, but the more I pulled, the more he held me down. I got angry, and he apologized, but I said it wasn't that. I knew he didn't mean to hurt me. I had never seen him like that, and I guess I was curious, and that is what got me angry.

Neva cleared the thought from her head and smiled at Dr. Mueller. She didn't feel guilty. She felt powerful. "Did you want to go over any of my progress notes before we go?" Neva asked.

"Uh, no," he said. "I think we can talk as we eat."

He was practically thrusting his heel in front of her. As they walked, Neva noticed how quiet the house was. Emily was preparing dinner in the kitchen, so Neva told her they were leaving. They walked out to the car, and as Dr. Mueller opened the door, Neva glanced up to see a corner of the curtains in the front window quickly close.

Dr. Mueller drove a Lincoln, typically Texan for a well-off doctor, and typically luxurious with leather upholstery that Neva couldn't help but run her hands over. While they drove to Jimmy Walker's, Dr. Mueller tried to make small talk, but Neva was trying to figure out who could have been watching her from the window.

"We've got ourselves quite a handful here, don't we, Neva?" Dr. Mueller asked.

"I'm sorry," Neva said, turning her ear as if she had not heard him right.

"The kids at Morning House," he clarified. "The guineas, I believe they call themselves."

Neva agreed, pulling her hand up off the upholstery and back into her lap. "I've noticed something very peculiar about some of the cases, at least with the girls."

"And what would that be?" Dr. Mueller asked, with a short, incredulous laugh.

"Well, there seems to be a common link, a sexual link that creates abnormal behavior in all three, each of course in their own way. It has me worried and a bit confused. I'm afraid that I'm going to need your help on this."

Dr. Mueller's dark eyebrows piqued with interest. "Oh really? In what way?" he asked.

"To begin with, I would like your opinion, to make sure I'm not on the wrong track."

"I am always glad to help, Neva. That's what I'm here for."

Excitedly, Neva moved in closer. "Okay, this is what we have: one girl who was prostituting, one who was molested by her grandfather, and one who is acting out with promiscuous behavior. Each has some problem directly related to sex and sexuality. I feel like we need to deal with that, but I'm having difficulty finding a way to change the behavior without getting to the root of the problem, without attacking the sexuality issue head-on."

"Have you established the behavior you wish to change?"

Neva was prepared, not wanting Dr. Mueller to end the conversation with his claim that she should just let behavior modification do its job. "Well, I guess it's more the attitude than the behavior that I am worried about. These girls seem to be confused, and they're lacking in self-esteem."

"In what way?"

"Emily seeks attention, love if you will, through sexual contact, but she feels bad about it afterward. With Janeen, prostitution seems to be just her way of expressing her depression. Ironically, both girls are using sex as a form of self-punishment. I must admit; Krista is a mystery. She doesn't seem to be bothered in the least by what has happened to her. She could just be the typical, resilient, flirtatious teenager, or she might be repressing her feelings by using every male she meets in a way to get even with her grandfather. If that's the case, she will never have a decent relationship. Unfortunately, I don't think we have enough time to work with them. None of the girls is going to be at Morning House very long."

"There is always psychotherapy, which they can continue even after they leave Morning House."

"There's no guarantee that they'll even be interested once they leave Morning House. We have them now, and I want to focus on the here and now, what they are feeling, and how they relate to others and handle problems. I have this feeling that nothing will get resolved unless they are provoked into letting their emotions emerge. And I mean their *real* emotions, what the surface is hiding. Right now, they're in a unique situation that might be of great benefit to them if some type of crisis group were implemented. These girls can relate to each other because of the similarity of their problems. I really feel that they can help each other get to the root of these problems—and possibly unite to overcome their poor self-images." She paused for a moment and then added, "with the proper guidance, of course."

"You sound as if you have a plan, Neva."

"I would like for you to be my advisor, Dr. Mueller. You know I'm working on my doctorate, and this opportunity would provide a significant amount of research for my dissertation. I want to show the benefits of group therapy in a crisis environment."

"Are we competitors, Neva?"

"Not at all. On the contrary, I need your expertise."

"I am very flattered, but what you propose will hardly be a controlled experiment."

"I realize that, and I won't approach it as one. My conclusions will deal only with comparative values, showing how each client responded to direct and indirect methods. I can learn a great deal from this, Dr. Mueller. So too, I believe, will the girls."

"You drive a hard bargain, Neva. I promise I will give it careful consideration, if you promise me one thing."

"What's that?"

"Stop calling me Dr. Mueller. You make me feel like your father. Please call me Carl."

Neva was excited. She couldn't help but laugh silently at her own efforts to get on a first name basis with the guineas. As Dr. Mueller escorted Neva into the restaurant, she hooked her arm in his and noticed that look again, as if he had just given her a gift he knew she had been wanting for a long time.

Jim's look had been apologetic. Jim couldn't stop telling me how sorry he was for what happened. I tried to laugh it off, to act sophisticated, to cover up my embarrassment. I teased Jim about sleeping in the nude, about waking up in an excited state. He said it had nothing to do with love, that sometimes he confused it with love. He wondered why girls didn't feel the same way, that maybe it was some chemical difference that made boys more sexually aggressive, more uncontrollable.

"How do you know girls don't have the same urges?" I asked. He was stretched out in the bed with the sheet like a shroud across his body, stopping at the rise of his chest.

"You're right, I don't," he said, intertwining his fingers behind his head. "But there is a difference. Girls want to know that you love them first. They're more willing to release those urges if they believe there's something more serious involved. With boys, the physical need comes first and evolves into something emotional later. Girls feel the emotion first, which elevates the physical to something more than just sex."

"Not always," I said. I wanted to be defiant. I wanted to disagree because I didn't like what he was saying. For some reason, at that moment, I didn't want Jim to make sense, so I refused his premise from the beginning.

Ironically, we had all our beginnings together.

After the waiter took their orders, Dr. Mueller snapped his napkin and smoothed it over his lap. "So tell me," he said. "What did you think about Alec's file?"

"It was very interesting," Neva said. "Although, I'm not sure he has any serious problem that can't be dealt with in the usual way."

"Are you saying that you don't want the boys in the group?"

"Well, I definitely think that the girls will not open up if the boys are there. They're just typical males, for the most part, vying for the attention and affection of the females. With them, everything is so physical." She had to look away to hide her amusement at repeating Jim's theory.

"Don't be surprised at what you find beneath all that chest beating," Dr. Mueller said. "Freud believed there was a connection between aggression and sexuality."

"I'm not arguing the point. I just haven't noticed anything more than inappropriate behavior that can be corrected by sublimating the energy. I'm not sure there is anything there that is emotionally unhealthy."

"Didn't you make a note that the school principal saw a connection between Alec's fight at school and his mother's visit?" He didn't wait for an answer. "Also, in your notes, I noticed that Alec almost got into a fight with Randy when there was mention of Alec's father. I don't see a typical boy here just flexing his muscles for the affection of the prom queen. I see a disturbed boy, possibly with unresolved oedipal feelings that manifest themselves in aggressive behavior."

Bullshit, Neva thought. She smiled momentarily to let the urge pass. "There could be other reasons for both of those incidents," she said. "He hasn't done anything so terrible, so I hope we can give him time to adjust to his new environment."

"Alec is a hebephrenic, Neva. He will never react with normal behavior to some situations. This recurring dream of his, disguised as it may be, is very oedipal."

Neva looked puzzled. "But Dr. Edelstein wrote in the file that the dream was a release of Alec's fears about the physical abuse he was subjected to by his father."

"Nonsense," Dr. Mueller said, dismissing the thought with a slight shake of his head. "Just examine the symbols. The lake and the canyon quite obviously represent his mother's vagina. The fact that he is there in a flock of geese, a company of strangers, disguising himself as one of them, is just that— a disguise so he will not be noticed. His fear of being discovered by his father comes true because it is Alec's wish to bring his secret desires out in the open and relieve his guilt. It is also a reversal of Alec's own wish to use the gun on his father, to eliminate his competition. But stronger still is Alec's wish to be punished for his feelings. In the dream, Alec is discovered as he escapes the vagina, and he is shot by his father. The fact that he does not die signifies that his feelings are not dead. This other boy in the dream had me stumped at first, but I have concluded that he is in fact Alec's own superego with his rebukes and reprimands that are entrenched firmly in Alec's subconscious. If the flock of geese is the secret Alec has kept, it makes sense that they would fly off toward the heavens, signifying death—that there is no longer a need for secrecy because the father is gone."

"Alec hasn't had this dream in a long time," Neva said. "Are you saying that he is still disturbed by what it represents?"

"Alec, like Oedipus, is ignorant of his own condition. It is not something you outgrow. Tell me this, is Alec shy or gregarious?"

"Well, he's not very social, but then . . ."

"This shyness is mainly around females, is it not?"

"To be perfectly honest, he does seem a bit intimidated."

"This fear is just an extension of his confusion about his mother. It all fits together with what I said before. He has a problem with aggression, and the fact is, I am beginning to doubt my decision to allow him in this program at all. If I feel his condition is worsening, I'll have to recommend that he return to the hospital. I can't allow him to jeopardize the program at Morning House. The board of directors wants results, and they control the purse strings."

Jim had picked up one of Dad's National Geographic magazines and showed me an article about grizzly bears. "Did you know that the male bear will kill his own young just so he can mate with the female again? He knows she won't mate until the cubs are gone."

"What does that prove?" I asked.

He just continued as if all the facts would reveal his point. "The female will fight him, to the death if she has to, defending her young—with the same ferocity and determination that the male uses to pursue her. Now tell me, where do two opposite instincts like that come from?"

I still didn't see his point. "Needing sex doesn't justify violence," I said.

"Of course not," he agreed. "Not in our civilized society anyway. It's just that this article got me thinking that sex seems to be at the root of all social behavior, whether it's good or bad. Whatever we do is because of sex. We try to make ourselves look good, we achieve financial success, we

strive for immortality. We even fight one another so we will be more attractive—so we can be desirable."

"You don't really believe all that do you?" I asked.

"No matter what we do on the outside, we won't feel right until we find true happiness, and that can only be achieved with a comfortable and exciting companion. Sometimes, Neva, I wonder if I will ever find someone to replace you."

"Of course, you will," I said.

"You know something else," Jim said. "If I do find her, I suspect she will be a lot like you."

Neva suddenly realized how wise Jim was, and he had never read a word of Freud. She was trying to be sexually appealing to get something she wanted from Dr. Mueller, and she was shutting him out when she felt he was threatening one of her own. Her maternal instinct was protecting Alec from the man who was trying to eliminate him.

Dr. Mueller raised his glass in a toast. "To progress," he said, that boyish look re-emerging through the dim light of dusk on the bay.

Neva smiled and repeated his toast. Looking away through the wide window, she saw the Kemah drawbridge in the distance with its arms raised in mechanical salute, almost waving to Neva, as a tall-masted sailboat moved smoothly through the gap.

"I don't want you to think I have given up on Alec," Dr. Mueller said. "I haven't. I'm just going to watch him closely, as you should. We can't let him transfer onto you the feelings he once had for his mother. We must help him to develop healthy relationships."

"That may be hard with this group."

Dr. Mueller laughed loudly, finishing with a deep sigh. "I see what you mean. We have quite a group of square pegs, but we still must help them fit into the round hole." He took a sip of wine, then contemplatively patted his lips with the napkin. "As for the girls, I quite agree with your evaluation, and I am willing to give this group thing a try under two conditions."

"Really?" Neva tried to contain her elation. "I guess I should wait for the conditions."

"First of all, I will continue to see them individually. This will not interfere with your program. And secondly, you must give Dr. Freud a fair shake."

"Agreed," Neva said, feeling the wine already going to her head.

Chapter Seven

Neva was like a newborn colt, full of nervous energy, as she prepared her office for the arrival of the girls after school. She had placed the chairs in a circle—well, as close to a circle as four chairs could be. That's the way her mind's eye saw it. That was what Neva wanted—a circle of friends, no head, no leader. The circle would protect their integrity, their secrets. Their innermost fears would not escape. The circle would provide protection against outside threats. They would need each other to remain safe. Need and trust. A family circle.

Krista sat with her arms folded and her legs crossed tightly against each other. Emily fidgeted with her hair, avoiding Neva's glance, and Janeen was always the same, looking straight down into her lap, her hands tucked away under her legs, avoiding the spotlight, afraid to be a part of anything.

"We are going to make a contract," Neva began. "I am going to teach, and *you* are going to learn." As she continued to explain the rationale of her therapy, defining the personality states of the parent, adult, and child that govern each person's life script, the girls remained rigid, recalcitrant, almost calcified.

"If we meet with Dr. Mueller, why do we have to meet with you too?" Krista asked when Neva was finished.

"What you do with Dr. Mueller is different. Anyway, not all of you meet with him."

"What if we're happy with the way we are?" Krista asked. "What if we don't want to be changed? That's what this is about, isn't it?"

"No one wants to change you, Krista. I need you here for support. None of you is here because you volunteered to be. None of you asked for help, but let's not kid ourselves. You are all here because you have something going on outside of Morning House that could be considered a problem, so why don't we talk about that? We all might be surprised at what evolves."

"It's not my fault I'm here," Krista said.

"Being here is not a punishment, but being here is not exactly your choice either. I want you to be able to make choices that are free from guilt or impulses, choices that are responsible. That is our contract. You will learn why your lives are so destructive, and I will help you learn a new way of interacting with people that allows you to make choices that are right for you."

Janeen slowly lifted her legs one at a time to release her hands, and for a moment, she looked as though she were about to speak. The moment passed as her hands folded together and pushed between her legs.

"Janeen? What is it?" Neva asked, hoping to draw her out again.

"You want us to talk about ourselves, don't you? About secrets and stuff like that, right? That's not exactly easy to do. I don't know if I can."

"You're not alone, Janeen. Believe it or not, you all have something in common. Life has dealt you a blow that hurts, and it's not easy coming back from that. I'm referring to relationships—and sexuality." Without waiting for reactions, she pressed on. "Talking about it will be hard, even painful at first, and that is where you'll need each other for support. You'll be relieved when you share your experiences, and you just might be surprised to find out that you're not alone. This part is very important. What you tell each other must be kept confidential. We must agree not to let any secrets out of this circle."

Krista tossed her hair forward and then back again with a sweeping insouciance, brushing it away from her neck and shoulders with the back of her hands. "Well, there is nothing I have to say to anyone here."

"I think there is," Neva said.

"Let me put it another way," Krista said. "I don't want to share my experiences with a certain party here."

Neva didn't have to turn around to know where Krista's comment was directed. "That will be enough of that," she said.

"It's all right," Emily said, folding her hands in her lap.

"No, I don't think so," Neva said. "I think we should get it all out. You two don't know each other well enough to have this much animosity. I want to know what's going on and why."

"All I know is she doesn't like me," Emily said. "I don't know why."

"Don't act so innocent," Krista snapped. "I saw you that first day when you showed up here, playing up to Alec, lifting your skirt so he could see everything you own. You might as well wear a sign that says, 'Please fuck me!'"

Neva blushed a bit, thinking of her night out with Dr. Mueller. He had walked Neva to the door last night, and her heart pounded like a schoolgirl's, increasing its rhythm with each step to the porch, until she thought she would faint. She managed to escape the dilemma of a goodnight kiss by extending her hand to thank him for dinner, the lovely evening, and most of all, the therapy group. Dr. Mueller had taken her hand firmly and pulled her to him. She turned away, accepting a peck on the cheek. At least this would be explainable.

"Why does that bother you, Krista?" Neva asked. "It is my impression that you are not beyond flirting. In fact, you seem to enjoy it."

"Flirting is one thing. Advertising is another. Emily might as well hang a billboard."

"But why did it make you angry?"

"It made her jealous," Emily said. "Anyone can see she's after Alec for herself."

"So what if I am? He's cute. At least I don't sneak out at night to meet him."

"You wanted to," Janeen said. Then, her eyes widened, and she put a hand over her mouth, trying to hold back the words that already escaped.

"Janeen, how could you?" Krista scolded.

"I'm sorry. I just don't like the way you're always picking on her. She hasn't done anything."

"Well, you two can have each other then, if you're such good friends."

"You don't have to worry about Alec," Emily said. "I *didn't* sneak out to meet him. It might interest you to know that he means nothing to me. If you want him so much, then he's all yours."

"Why did you sneak out then?" Krista asked. "You never said, and this stolen money thing is still hanging over our heads."

"I was going to run away," Emily said.

"That's dumb," Krista said.

"Why?" Janeen asked. "I've thought about it before. Haven't you ever thought about running away?"

"Well, if I did, I wouldn't tell you about it, you little snitch."

"I said I was sorry," Janeen cried.

"What do you feel like running away from, Janeen?" Neva asked, trying to steer the discussion back on course.

"I don't know. This may sound funny, but sometimes I feel like running away from me."

Krista laughed with a scornful hiss.

"It doesn't sound funny at all," Neva said, glancing at Krista. "I think we all have those feelings at some time in our lives. Each of us has a different way of dealing with it. First, we need to find out what makes you feel this way."

"Just look at me." Janeen laughed. "The make-up only lasts for a short time. Then, it's gone, and I realize it was just hiding what I am on the inside. Wouldn't you want to run away from yourself if you were me?"

"I want to point out one very important thing," Neva said. "You are the lucky ones. You may not feel like it, but because you are here, you have survived, and you have been given another chance. What is on the inside may hurt, but if you don't face the hurt, you will never learn to control it. Facing the hurt means deciding that you will conquer it, and you will no longer be a victim. None of you asked for what happened to you. A woman does not ask to be raped or mistreated. A woman does not invite or entice sex unless she knows it is right, with the right man, at the right moment, when she wants to enjoy it for those reasons. If it is anything else, then what might appear to be enjoyment is really pain."

"Why don't you tell us about it, Emily?" Krista said.

Neva let out an exasperated sigh. "Krista, you must try to keep your comments on a more adult level."

Emily began to cry.

Neva held out an open palm toward Emily but addressed Krista. "Now, do you see where that type of parental criticism leads to?"

"I'm sorry," Krista said. "I only wanted to know why."

"She's right, you know," Emily said. "I *am* everything she says. I've done it with a lot of guys, and it's always been my idea, or I didn't stop them when I knew they wanted it. I made it with the grocery clerk the night I sneaked out. I even made it with a teacher at my old school. I tried with Alec. It was an impulse, but he wasn't interested." She was sobbing now. "I don't know why I do it. I know there's something wrong with me. I always hate myself after. I want to get away from me, just like what Janeen said."

Janeen started to cry too, feeling all of Emily's emotion, and the others looked at her.

Krista sighed heavily. "Is this going to lead to one of those group hug things?"

"It wouldn't be such a bad idea," Neva said. "But it doesn't have to be now. It's better if it's spontaneous."

"Thank God," Krista said, in the slump of her chair, swinging impatiently the pendulum of her crossed leg.

"Why do you always have to be so critical?" Janeen reprimanded, taking a deep breath to stop the tears.

Krista sat up straight, pinching her face up angrily at Janeen.

"I know how Emily feels," Janeen continued, undaunted. "I've done the same things before, only different."

Emily pushed back her own tears. "Really?"

"Go ahead, Janeen," Neva said.

"Yeah, go ahead," Krista taunted. "This should be interesting."

Janeen lowered her head and talked into her lap. "I did it with a lot of guys too. That's how I got sick and ended up here."

"You got sick?" Krista asked. "You mean you got an STD? You told me that welfare picked you up because your parents weren't supervising you."

"That was true. It just wasn't the whole truth. I'm sorry. I was too embarrassed. I don't even know why I'm telling you now."

"There's no need to be embarrassed," Neva said. "What we need to do is look at *why* you made those choices and *why* you thought they were the right ones at the time."

"This is too weird," Krista said.

"No, it's not," Neva said. "Emily and Janeen did what they did because they thought it was the right thing. It helped them for the moment, but when the moment was gone, they felt guilty about it. It's like, inside each of us is a parent who admonishes the child in us for being bad. The hard part is to let the adult make the decision instead of the child, because the child wants to make the easiest decision, but the adult will make the better decision."

A door slammed in the kitchen, and Neva looked disappointedly at her watch. Krista noticed this and stood up quickly. "Maybe I should go. It's my turn to cook."

"I don't think anyone will mind if we're a little late," Neva said. "We've opened up some wounds here, and I don't want to leave them unprotected."

"I'll be all right, honest," Emily said.

"Me too," Janeen said, nervously. "Except for one thing."

"What's that?" Neva asked.

Janeen looked at Krista, then down into her lap again. "I don't want Krista to be mad at me," she said softly.

"Well," Krista said thoughtfully. "If you help me fix dinner, then I'll forgive you."

Janeen smiled and leaped like a child picked for a team. She followed Krista out of the room. Emily waited before she rose from her chair and started to leave. Neva sensed that Emily had something to say and asked her to stay a moment. "There is something I want to ask you."

Emily sat back down.

"It's about that night at Gilley's. I read the police report. I believe, no matter what, that it was rape. You were obviously intoxicated or under the influence of some drug when the police found you. You were unable to make a rational decision, not to mention that you are underage, and that, too, makes it rape. But I would like to know one thing because of what you said here today. Do you believe that you encouraged those boys to do what they did?"

It took Emily a while to answer as if each word was a thorn pricked from her throat. When she finally spoke, the words were deliberate and uncompromising. "I went to Gilley's that night because I wanted to meet someone. I admit that, but I didn't ask those boys to do what they did. I don't remember much of it. They gave me some . . . well, I think I passed out anyway. It doesn't matter though, does it? I would still be the bad girl, even if I fought them, and maybe they would've hurt me real bad."

"But it *does* matter," Neva said, surprised that Emily would still feel this way. "I believe that what you really want is not physical at all but emotional. If you think you need sex to feel wanted, then we must find out why."

"I'm tired of feeling like there's something wrong with me. I'm not sure anything matters anymore anyway." Emily stood up and walked to the door, then turned back to Neva. "Feeling wanted in the wrong way is better than not feeling wanted at all."

When Emily left the room, Neva sensed an unnerving vibration, a sudden barometric plunge, a sensitive movement in the hundred-year flood plain from some freak alignment of the planets. It gave her an out-of-sorts dizziness. She sat still waiting for it to pass, this mild temblor, but it only grew worse. Neva tried to get up, but she couldn't move. She looked down at her hands and realized that they were trembling, and her chest heaved with rapid breathing.

• • •

Neva wanted to forget what happened. She refused to face the possibility that something might be physically wrong with her. The next day, she worked in her office until early afternoon, then drove to the garage to check on Alec. She saw cars inside and parked in the lot out front, but the place looked deserted. Neva looked around for Johnny Rodriguez. He was usually on the telephone with a customer, but she saw no one in the office. As she walked around the tires and engine parts, an air hose snaked across the floor, and Neva jumped as if it had come alive. Johnny Rodriguez rolled out from under one of the cars, revealing only his head, and looked up at Neva. "I thought that was you." He laughed.

Neva breathed deeply. "You're a devil, Johnny Rodriquez. You almost gave me a heart attack."

"I could hear that old bug of yours coming a mile away," he said. "Sounds like you need a tune-up."

"You could let Alec do it to get the experience," she said.

"Oh, he's ready for it now."

"Is he that good?"

They heard a motorcycle start up as she said it; Johnny motioned toward the sound with his eyes. "He's here early every day."

Neva stared in the direction of the sound. "I didn't want him to think I was checking up on him behind his back, but maybe I should have."

"He's a hard worker, Neva. I'm glad you brought him to me. Maybe you should wait here and let me go get him."

Neva listened to the motorcycle's engine rev and unwind like a giant spring. Her jaw tightened. "What's going on, Johnny? There's something you're not telling me."

Johnny sighed and led Neva around the car to the back of the garage. "I keep forgetting you're one of those psycho people."

"That's psychologist, and don't change the subject. Tell me what it is."

Behind the garage, one of the other mechanics was sitting on a motorcycle, revving the engine. Alec stood to the side, his hands in his pockets, a toothpick in the corner of his mouth.

"He reminds me a lot of Jim," Johnny said.

"I was afraid you'd say that. I'm afraid I noticed it too."

"He's heard the story, Neva. Gary over there got to talking, and before I knew it . . ."

"About Jim?"

"I'm sorry. I couldn't stop him. You know Jim is still kind of a legend around here. Alec wanted to hear it all. He wanted every detail."

It was like Neva had the wind knocked out of her. She couldn't breathe, much less talk. When Alec noticed her standing with Johnny, he offered a grin that clinched the bobbing toothpick. She could barely manage a modest smile.

"I knew you were going to be there," Alec said, as they walked down to the lakeshore beyond the field behind the garage. "After Gary told me about your brother, I just had this feeling. It was more than coincidence."

In the distance, several sailboarders in angular suspension skimmed the surface of the lake. A lone jet ski churned up the surf near the shore. For a moment, Neva watched in silence, preferring the distant serenity of the sailboards. "I came to tell you about a court hearing scheduled for tomorrow, to make sure Johnny knew about it in case you were late for work. It had nothing to do with Jim. I didn't have any idea . . .. Oh dear."

She sat down on an overturned rowboat embedded in the sand, where a fringe of tall grass had taken root.

"I told you, I'm not crazy," Alec said. "I'm not hallucinating. From the first day I came to Morning House, I felt something. It was almost like I had known you before."

Neva was quiet, contemplating her response., She knew that she would have to reveal things, personal things, to gain Alec's trust. "Jim and I used to talk like this," she said. "We talked about what bothered us and what made us happy. We had a secret place in Seabrook where we went. It was on a sandbar near an old boatyard. We crawled up under this abandoned skiff near the dunes, and it was like we were in another world, a world of our own."

"I like it here. They're good to me at the garage. I feel like I finally fit in, like I can make something of myself—forget what happened in my past."

"We're all looking for a sense of attachment, a sense of identification. It gives us a reason for living. I hope this works out for you," Neva said, changing the subject. She was having second thoughts about confiding in Alec—letting a part of her past slip out.

"This is all so strange, though," Alec said. "I feel as if I have been here before. Do you know what it means?"

"I'm not sure," Neva said, fearing that he would sense it, that he would want to hear her tell the story, fearing that he already knew her innermost fears—that everything was happening all over again.

• • •

Jim turned off the engine of his motorcycle and waited until I got off. In the distance, the bridge looked like a mountain rising into the morning twilight. He just wanted to look at it. He seemed to stare in awe of it, like he was offering his respect before he conquered it. For a moment, the world was still and so quiet, I could hear my heart beating and my breathing quicken. A truck with bundles of newspapers in the back drove by, the drone of its engine fading away as it reached the bridge, lighting it up with flickering headlights before it disappeared over the other side. Soon, the sun was simmering on the horizon, threatening what was left of the night.

"This couldn't be more perfect," Jim said.

"I don't like it," I told him. "I don't want you to do this."

"Don't ruin it, Neva."

"I'm scared."

"What for? You're not the one jumping the bridge."

"I know, but . . ." All the plausible reasons vanished like thistledown. I could see them floating away, but I couldn't grasp them. I was faced with the stark realization that Jim was going to perform this needless stunt.

"You know you can't talk me out of it," he said. "Everything is too perfect. I've been watching the bridge. I have it timed. I know when to hit it before it gets too high. This is going to be an unforgettable morning."

Jim drove me up to a spot just below the bridge, where I could see the front slope up to a control booth and then the drawbridge. He left me there and headed back around the curve toward Seabrook. When I couldn't see him anymore, I looked back at the bridge, and everything seemed brighter; the sky was beginning to glow. Orange streaks of fire burned up into feathered clouds that lay over the horizon, and I knew Jim was right. It would be an unforgettable morning, and I knew it wouldn't be long now.

I didn't see the man come out of the booth. I just saw the ship sitting in the channel like it had come out of the fire, and it wasn't real. It was just there, waiting. The man moved across the bridge, looking around like he was checking something. When I saw him, I wanted to call out to him and make him raise the bridge. My heart was racing, and I was angry with myself for coming at all. I just wanted it all to be over. The man went back to the side where the booth was and waved a car over. Then, he stepped inside the booth. The car was an old clunker with a clattering engine and fishing poles sticking out of the trunk. The dark faces of a Mexican family stared at me from within. I imagined they were on their way to the Clear Lake levee to catch breakfast. They probably thought I was just standing there waiting for a ride.

The ship was bigger now, and darker, silhouetted against the glowing horizon, looming closer in a strangely twisted shape. It was clawing the air like a mechanical demon, and I only stopped thinking about it when I heard a bell clang. I turned as the guard barrier was lowering. I watched it pass in front of the booth, first blocking, then releasing a reflected ray of sunlight, a spark that glinted off a window and momentarily blinded me. When I heard Jim's motorcycle, I wanted to run into the middle of the road and stop him. I wanted to warn him about the glare, to tell him not to look into the light. I couldn't see him at first. I just heard him getting closer. I shielded my eyes and saw him crouched low on the motorcycle. He was driving fast now on the left side of the road so he could pass the guard barrier.

The bridge suddenly jolted and shook, then groaned as the gears screeched together, and the middle opened like a great, dispassionate yawn. Jim went by in a blur, still leaning forward but sitting higher on the motorcycle now. On his face, I thought I could see a look of conquering will, an overpowering sense of knowing that he had defeated fear.

I didn't see the man come out of the booth until it was too late. I didn't see him at all until Jim was going down. The man was waving his arms and yelling, but I couldn't hear him because of the noise from the bridge and Jim's motorcycle. Time stopped, and yet, in that instant, an entire dream passed, and I awoke realizing that it was all very real when Jim's motorcycle hit the side of the bridge and then disappeared over the opened mouth. At first, I thought Jim had managed to jump free of the wreckage, because he flew through the air so perfectly, actually sailed so delicately, that I thought he had planned out what to do in the event he took a spill. I waited, thinking he was going to come up behind me, thinking he was going to jump out and surprise me.

The police couldn't get me to stop shaking until Jim's body was pulled from the channel later that day. They said that when I saw him, I just stopped, without warning. He looked so peaceful, but they couldn't see the darkness that had fallen like a shroud over that perfect day.

They didn't see that inside, I died.

Unforgettable.

Part Two: Chaste And The Chaser

Chapter Eight

From Clear Lake to Houston, the drive was tedious and barren of vistas. A column of skeletal towers towed thick cables, escorting the cars along the flat, unbending highway. Distant communities were guarded by tall water towers that stood like giant toadstools in an otherwise vast, empty plain. Alec watched a military jet sweep out of the emptiness. It banked twice, then strafed the highway before dissolving back into the low, gray clouds. No more than a minute passed before it dipped again into view. Alec watched through the rear window until the plane disappeared. This time, it did not return. They seemed to be traveling along the border of a strange, foreign land.

"They come from Ellington Field," Neva said.

Alec settled into the seat, and again, silence pervaded the car.

In the stillness, Neva thought about her previous night's dream. *Alec was bound hand and foot to a cross buried in a large rock at the base of a hill. The parched earth was a desert of rocks and cactus. Attending Alec was Emily, Krista, and Janeen. Overhead, in and out of a glaring sun, a large vulture spiraled downward, getting closer with each pass as the girls frantically worked to loosen Alec's bindings. Just as the vulture made what appeared to be its final descent, the girls were able to free him. Alec jumped down from the rock and rode away on a motorcycle that had been lying in the dust like bones of a decayed carcass. He drove toward a canyon, where I was waiting for him on the other side. As Alec got closer, he drove faster and faster, rising into the void, flying over the emptiness, and I could see him coming toward me, but before he landed, I woke up.*

That was the way Neva would tell her dream to Dr. Mueller. She wanted his opinion, the psychoanalytical interpretation. She also wanted to compare her own interpretation. She knew neither of them would be totally correct. For that, she would have to tell the whole dream.

A fine mist settled on the car, stirring a rhythmic monotony in the wiper blades as they screeched and groaned across the windshield. In the rearview mirror, Neva could see Alec reading a book and intermittently staring at the passing shopping malls and car dealerships. He had not said a word all morning. Sitting next to Neva in the front seat, Emily listened as Neva explained what they could expect to happen in court. Occasionally, Emily glanced over at Neva and nodded, but only because this afforded her a better look over her shoulder at Alec. Neva saw poignant apprehension in her eyes, and she knew that Krista had put it there. Before she left for school, Krista caught Emily at the bottom of the stairs and told her to remember what she had said in the group.

"Have you ever dreamed something you didn't understand?" Neva asked, not addressing either one.

Alec remained silent.

Emily glanced back at him and frowned, bewildered. "I usually have nightmares," Emily said. "Just scary faces—or someone chasing me."

"Freud believed that dreams are expressions of our desires for fulfillment of wishes," Neva said, and as she said it, she thought about it in her own dream. She had avoided thinking about it before, consciously analyzing it, because she feared the obvious. Of course, Alec finding out about the accident was enough to cause the dream, but why would she wish her greatest fear? And why was Alec on the motorcycle, and not Jim? And why was she waiting for him, almost coaxing him? That bothered her most about the dream, what she had been avoiding, what she would have to leave out when she told Dr. Mueller. She had been waiting for Alec, lying on the opposite bank, watching him through the V of her arms and legs, then waking before he got too close. Freud would jump all over that one. Any interpretation would be incomplete because there was one detail she would never be able to tell Dr. Mueller.

"Even nightmares can be interpreted to hold a wish fulfillment," Neva said.

"What if your dream is only a woman standing alone in a field?" Alec asked. "What kind of wish is that?"

"Do you know who she is?" Neva asked, pleased that she had drawn him out of his silence.

"No. I've never seen her before. Last night, I moved closer than I have ever been before, but I never get close enough to see her face. The dream just stops."

"I'm not that knowledgeable about dream interpretation," Neva said. "We each have such personal experiences, desires, and fears. Every dream must have more than one interpretation. We could ask Dr. Mueller for his opinion. Dreams are supposed to reflect our subconscious mind at work when the conscious mind has no control over it. Understanding what lays beneath our consciousness helps us understand ourselves better, whether you believe dreams are the fulfillment of wishes or just the release of our desires and fears."

She hated it when she sounded like a textbook.

The rain fell steadily, easing the strained rhythm of the wiper blades as Neva pulled off the Gulf Freeway and headed toward downtown. Distant buildings rose like stalagmites to meet the low clouds. Before long, they navigated the dark spaces in a stone and steel forest, illuminated through the rain with glaring reflections of reds, yellows, and greens. The top floors of buildings disappeared into a shroud of mist above the windless rain that fell like a whisper. Policemen in yellow raincoats stood on busy street corners, watching the traffic. Neva avoided their glances. When the light changed, she was too close to stop without skidding on the rain-slick street. She coasted through the intersection, exchanging a smile with the policeman at the corner who admonished her with a naughty wave of his index finger. Alec and Emily shared a chuckle at Neva's narrow escape. Several blocks later, Neva pulled up in front of the Family Law Center.

"I only have one umbrella," she said. "You two better get out here and wait for me while I park the car. I'll just be a minute."

Emily got out of the car and looked around for Alec, but he had already dashed up the stairs and was holding the heavy glass door. "Hurry up," he called out. "I'm getting wet."

Emily hurried up the stairs. "You don't have to scream at me," she said. "I didn't ask you to stand in the rain."

"I'll remember that the next time," Alec said.

Inside, several groups of people huddled near the elevators. Others read the daily court calendars displayed in glass cases in the center of the lobby. Some looked up at Alec and Emily as they entered. Alec avoided their stares, preferring to find a secluded corner where he could read his book. Emily wandered beyond the elevators, where a flight of stairs descended to a coffee shop. She stood at the top for a moment, listening to friendly chatter drift up through the stairwell with aromas of sweet bread and coffee. Emily walked back to where Alec stood against a wall.

"I'm sorry about snapping at you a while ago," she said. "I really did appreciate you holding the door for me."

"It's okay," Alec said, not looking up.

"Are you ever going to finish that book?"

"I'm in the depths of Mordor now," he said, half-smiling. "Sort of symbolic, huh?"

Emily looked at him askew, not understanding. "Why are you here anyway?" she asked.

"Didn't you hear what Neva said?"

"I know about that. I was wondering if you knew what it was about. I mean, is it because . . ." Emily struggled for the right words.

"What?"

"Is it true you really killed your father?"

"Where did you hear that?"

"Randy was talking the other night. He said he knew you years ago."

"Well, Randy doesn't know everything."

"He scares me. There's something about him I don't like."

There was another gap of silence, then Alec returned to his book.

"I'm sorry," Emily said. "I shouldn't have pried. I was being nosey, and I hate that when other people do it."

Neva entered the lobby shaking the rain from her umbrella and laughed at herself when she saw them watching. "Whew. I feel like a drowned rat. Are we ready?"

From across the lobby, a raggedy man approached, smelling of sweat and rain, and covered with soot from head to toe. His long hair and dark beard sprang from his head like a bed of moss on an old tree. His eyes shone like a startled owl. He mumbled to himself as he walked, and every few steps, he jerked and looked around as if someone had pulled him back suddenly. As he passed, he turned and looked straight at them, not seeing them, and shouted to some invisible force. "The smell of death! But they shall see the light!" He turned back with a sweeping motion of his arms. "No more the light of day, but the true light!" He walked on, muttering to himself. "This day have I paid my vows. I have been gone on a long journey, for forty days, and I will return on the full moon."

As they entered the elevator, Emily giggled. "How does someone get like that?"

"He's a politician, I think." Neva chuckled.

Alec looked up at the numbers above the closing doors. "He definitely sees something the rest of us don't."

They got off at the third floor and entered a crowded courtroom. Emily stuck close to Alec, waiting for Neva to lead the way. Neva glanced around the room, then spotted Anna Gogarty sitting in the back row, only a few feet away. In the bowl of her lap were colored beads, which she was threading onto a string. April sat next to her on the bench, reading a book in whispers to Anna. Neva noticed that April's manner of dress was still casual but respectably discreet. Neva addressed them, and Anna's eyes almost immediately filled with tears when she saw Alec.

"My baby," she gasped.

Emily giggled.

"Why are you here, Mother?" Alec asked. His voice was cold and distant.

"Please don't be cruel to me, Alec. I came because I miss you."

Alec remained silent as they filed into the row. When he sat down, April reached across Anna's lap and took Alec's hand. She introduced herself as a friend. "You should try to be understanding, Alec. Your mother's actions may appear confusing, but she is filled with emotion because of her deep love for you." She looked at Anna. "And you shouldn't talk about Alec as if he were a child. He is obviously a young man now, and quite handsome, I might add." April released Alec's hand and took Anna's, giving it a quick squeeze. "You should be very proud of him."

"I'm glad you could make it," Neva said.

"A social worker came by the house to tell me about the hearing," Anna said. She reached into her purse on the floor and pulled out a business card. "Julia Simpson. Do you know her? She said she was Alec's caseworker."

Emily had been watching April, Anna, and the string of beads in Anna's lap. She leaned toward Alec and whispered, "Julia Simpson is your caseworker too?"

"I don't know," Alec said. "I've never met her."

"She must be here somewhere," Neva said.

"Julia Simpson is the one who brought me to Morning House," Emily continued. "She doesn't talk much. I figured she was just new."

"She hasn't talked to me at all," Alec said.

"She seemed like a nice person," Anna said. "Like Ms. Bell here. She's trying to help us. Not like these other people." Anna pointed toward the judge's bench. "They wouldn't have told me what was happening. They don't care. But they'll get theirs. That's what these are for." She held up the beads she had been stringing. "This one is for the judge. I have one here for the district attorney too." Anna searched through a canvas bag beside her feet.

"Is it still raining out?" April asked, changing the subject quickly.

"It was when we came in," Neva said.

"Oh, I was hoping it would stop," Anna said, losing interest in her search for the beads. "I hate riding the bus in the rain. I don't know what we'll do if it's still raining when we're ready to leave. I have such trouble with the rain. I can't even sleep at night if it's raining. I used to have Alec to ease my nerves." Anna patted Alec on the leg. "My protector."

Alec shifted on the bench, sliding closer to Emily. Their shoulders and legs touched, and Alec could feel her warmth.

Emily didn't move.

"Where is your baby this morning?" Neva asked.

"Oh, a neighbor agreed to watch him," Anna said. "I needed April here for support, especially with this rain and all."

Neva smiled, then spotted Julia Simpson in the crowd of attorneys standing at the front of the courtroom. Julia waved, hurried down the aisle, and slipped into the row next to Neva. She clutched a portfolio to her breast and delivered a smile like an evangelist selling bibles. Glancing down the row without readjusting her smile, she greeted everyone. "Oh, what a lovely necklace, Ms. Gogarty. You must be very handy. We'll probably get going here soon, right after the judge takes the bench. It looks like you've got them all prepared, Neva. Oh, Emily, your mother should be here too. I'm expecting her, anyway."

"What?" Emily asked. "Why?"

"We'll have to talk about it later," Julia said. "I want you to understand everything. I also have a little surprise for you."

The bailiff's voice rose above the low chatter in the courtroom and called everyone to order as the judge entered from a door behind the bench. An uneasy silence fell over the crowded room.

Julia leaned toward Neva and whispered, "I'm going out to find Marion English. She should have been here by now."

Neva smiled and nodded.

A clerk stepped up next to the judge, opened a file, and read softly into his ear.

"He's the judge who took Alec away from me," Anna said. "Blind as a bat. They say justice is blind or should be. I think he was struck down as a reminder of it. I can't help but think that some witch got to him before me."

"I'm sure he thought he was doing the right thing for Alec under the circumstances," Neva said.

"Circumstances? What do you mean? Alec got a little out of control, that's all. He had some emotional problems but nothing serious. Nothing I couldn't handle. It was all like a bad dream."

Anna Gogarty was a different person today. She was prepared, angry, and armed with her beads and spells.

The judge called the first adoption case, and a well-dressed young couple carrying an infant approached the bench. The judge's face seemed to be directed toward something on the ceiling more than toward the couple, but it didn't matter because the couple gazed adoringly on their small bundle, as it squirmed and cooed. They only occasionally looked up at the judge as he talked to them about the responsibilities of being a parent.

"What does he know," Anna said defiantly. She leaned close to Alec and whispered, "I had a very mysterious dream about you last night. I think it was telling me that you'll be coming home soon."

Neva overheard this and was suddenly overwhelmed with curiosity about the coincidence of their dreams. "It will be a little while. Why don't we go out into the hall?" Neva asked, wanting an excuse to get Anna Gogarty out of the courtroom before she created a disturbance.

They walked to the end of the hall, where a large window offered a hazy view of Allen's Landing, the antique shops and nouveau restaurants that revitalized the market square once composed of sleazy discos and nightclubs. They watched the silent rain as it fell like snow to the street below. On the sidewalk, they could see the raggedy man in smoke-stained clothing, his arms spread in exaltation, his bearded face turned in raptured prayer to the sky.

"There but for the grace of God," Anna said.

Neva looked down at the man, who spun around, joyfully splashing his boots in the rain puddles. A blue and white police car made its way slowly around the corner.

"Yes," Neva said, "sometimes our own misfortunes become trivial when compared to the misfortunes of others. It makes us appreciate the world we live in."

"I don't like the rain," Anna said. "The rain gives me nightmares. You were in my dream too."

"I was?"

"I dreamed that the rain woke me up, and I was walking through the house looking for Alec. When I opened the front door, the rain had stopped, and all I could see was this brilliant rainbow. It was crossing over the street—only the street was flooded and had become a river, and Alec was on the other side. He started to cross the rainbow to get to me. He was walking on the rainbow, and when he reached the highest point, he fell. When I looked down, you were standing in the river."

"That's interesting."

"I don't know why you were there."

"That is a mysterious dream," Neva said, watching the policeman who had gotten out of his car and was walking toward the raggedy man. She was numbed by the certain similarities between Anna's dream and her own. "Do you know what it means?"

"I believe Alec is trying to get back to me, Ms. Bell." Anna's eyes narrowed. "You're either there to help him—or to stop him. I don't know which. I want to believe you're there to help."

"Of course, I am," Neva said.

The policeman and the raggedy man were talking, but when the raggedy man turned away, the policeman grabbed his arm. The raggedy man jerked his arm away, and they scuffled. Neva and Anna watched silently as the policeman and the raggedy man fell to the sidewalk, struggling. Suddenly, the raggedy man stood up and waved a gun in the air. He turned and fired one shot at the policeman, who ducked between the cars parked at the curb.

"My God. I don't believe what's happening down there." Neva gasped. "We should get help."

As she spoke, the policeman tried to run toward his own car. The raggedy man fired again, and the policeman fell in the street. Two patrol cars almost simultaneously skidded onto the street at opposite corners as the raggedy man walked slowly up to the fallen policeman.

The raggedy man noticed the patrol car driving toward him and fired at the car instead. The door to the police car swung open, and another policeman reached through the open space and fired back. The raggedy man took off running across the street, waving his weapon at passing cars and spectators, who backed away from his wild ranting and returned inside buildings when they saw the gun. The raggedy man turned around and, without warning, pointed the gun at the two policemen chasing him. They fired back, almost endlessly, and the raggedy man fell to the sidewalk.

Neva and Anna had not moved. They stared silently at the scene from high above, unable to speak, unable to comprehend what had taken place. Neva remembered the man's prophetic words as he passed her in the lobby, and now as she stared at the two still bodies, the lives ruined, she wondered how such a person could evolve, slip through the spectrum of sanity, and fall, with all his apparent mystical insights, like an errant meteor from the sky, delivering death.

Emily stepped into the hall and called after them, waving, signaling for them to hurry.

"We mustn't tell them about what happened," Neva said. "I think it would be too upsetting."

Anna turned back toward the window and whispered, "Sort of makes you feel like God, doesn't it, standing up here, watching it all happen?"

"That's the problem I have with God," Neva said.

Emily was on her toes, shaking her hands. "Hurry," she said. "The judge is hearing Alec's case."

Julia Simpson waited in the front of the courtroom. She motioned to Anna, then toward an empty chair next to where Alec sat at the attorney's table. Anna cautiously approached the front, clutching her precious cargo of spells and divinations, which she had carefully stowed away in her large handbag of bright tapestry. Neva waited near the back with Emily.

"What are they going to do?" Emily asked. "Is Alec going home with his mother?"

"I don't think so," Neva said, trying to shake away the memory of the bodies lying in the street. "I hope he will be with us a while longer."

"And what about me? Will I be able to stay at Morning House?"

"There's nothing wrong with you telling the judge what you want."

The district attorney explained what she referred to as the 'facts' in Alec's case, and she paused for a moment as the distant crescendo of a siren wailed closer before it expired like a great, troubled breath. A young woman, not much older than Emily, entered the courtroom and scanned the audience. Emily looked up, drawn to the young woman's presence. "Loretta!" she shrieked.

The young woman turned toward Emily, then excitedly moved into the row next to her. They embraced, holding tight. They held each other's hands. They gazed into each other's eyes through curtains of tears.

"I was afraid I would miss you," the young woman said.

"How did you know I was here? I don't believe this." Emily was so excited, she forgot where she was. She noticed several people turning to stare. She sank slightly on the bench and whispered, "I thought I would never see you again."

Neva leaned in and extended her hand. "I'm Neva Bell."

"She runs Morning House," Emily interjected, "where I'm staying."

"I'm Loretta," the young woman whispered. "Emily's sister. I've come to see about getting custody of her."

"Does Julia Simpson know about this?" Neva asked.

"Yes, she knows I want Emily to come live with me."

Neva realized that this was Julia's surprise. She patted Emily on the leg. "You two go into the hall and talk about this," Neva said. "I'll come get you as soon as Alec's case is settled."

Neva sat back, wondering why Julia didn't tell her about this. Her mind whirled, thinking about her group and the progress they had made already. Neva hoped the judge would at least order an evaluation of Loretta's home before placing Emily there. She had to talk to Julia and get this worked out, but Neva shook her head and focused on the judge, speaking to Anna about Alec.

"Alec is almost an adult, Ms. Gogarty," the judge said. "He is of an age where he should be accepting responsibilities, but he is not *yet* an adult. He has been confined to an institution for the past four years and therefore deprived of what might be considered a normal maturing process. He is not ready to accept or be burdened with the responsibilities placed on the head of a household. That is *your* job. The court, as custodian of Alec, must also be convinced that he is no longer affected adversely by the death of his father—or by other factors that caused him to be placed in the institution in the first place."

"*You* did that," Anna said.

"What did you say? Speak up, Ms. Gogarty," the judge said.

"You're going to leave Alec in that home, aren't you, judge? You're never going to give my baby back to me, are you? *You* are the one who is depriving Alec of a normal life, not me."

"Be careful, Ms. Gogarty. I am not responsible for what happened to Alec, but I *am* the one who determines what is right for him now. I will make a decision after your present living situation is evaluated. You see, I am not thoroughly convinced that you are capable of providing for Alec's special needs."

"I am his mother. I know what he needs."

"As part of the evaluation, I am ordering that you submit to a psychological test as well."

"A test? Someone is going to know all about me after giving me a test? They had four years to get to know Alec, and they couldn't do it. How can you sit up there and tell me I have no right to my own child when you have never talked to me for even one minute outside of this courtroom?"

With a slight trembling of her hand, Anna reached into her purse, but before she could withdraw her hand, the bailiff rushed across the room and grabbed her arm. He yanked the purse away to display her twisted hand, from which dangled a string of colored beads.

"I'm sorry, your honor," the bailiff said. "She reached into her purse so quickly—I thought she was going for a weapon."

"Thank you, bailiff," the judge said as he turned slightly toward the bailiff's voice. "Is everything okay now?"

"Yes, your honor," the bailiff said. "She just has some beads."

"Ms. Gogarty," the judge said, looking slightly confused, "please sit quietly while I hear from Alec."

Neva heard muffled voices behind her in the hallway. Someone arguing. One shouted in anger, "You're only doing this to be evil."

The other was more restrained but tense, "What I am doing is *my* right. I only have her best interests at heart."

The judge raised his head toward the sound as everyone else turned to see what was causing the commotion. The bailiff headed down the aisle, and as he opened the door, the voices exploded into the courtroom.

Neva immediately recognized Emily's voice and followed the bailiff into the hall. Loretta was batting her arms as if swatting madly at a fly. Marion English defiantly faced her with arms crossed over her large chest.

"Our sister is going to die because of what you're doing," Loretta screamed, now swinging her arms as if the fly were right in front of Marion English's face.

"I am still Emily's mother," Marion said, grabbing Emily's arm.

"No!" Emily cried out, trying to free her arm.

Loretta then pulled Emily back and reached across the two of them to push Marion. The bailiff stepped between them and seized Loretta's arm.

"Ladies, please!" the bailiff pleaded. "Court is in session. You'll have to keep it down out here, and if you can't, I will have to arrest all of you."

Still holding fast to Emily, Loretta's voice quivered. "Yes, yes, of course. I didn't mean to . . ."

The bailiff relinquished her arm and looked toward Marion English for a similar response. She remained smug and unyielding. "I was not the one creating a disturbance," she said.

"Excuse me, officer," Neva said, stepping boldly into their midst and placing her hand on Emily's shoulder. "This young lady is my responsibility, and I'll see to it that there are no more disturbances."

"Thank you," the bailiff said, turning with an admonishing glance toward Marion English before returning to the courtroom.

Neva introduced herself to Marion English and asked her to wait inside the courtroom. When Marion English was gone, Neva sat Emily on a bench in the hall and walked with Loretta to the window overlooking the street. The ends of the block were taped off with bright yellow tape and guarded by several policemen. The sidewalks were empty now, except for a few spectators who watched a group of men measuring distances along the sidewalk and street. One man photographed the area from different angles while another snapped shots of small placards scattered about on the street and sidewalks. They all could have been mistaken for surveyors if Neva had not known what had transpired only minutes before.

"Emily told me that her sister was sick, but you're not Emily's only sister?" Neva asked.

"Why, no," Loretta said, stretching out each single syllable into two as she gazed up at the silver mist drifting between the buildings. "Our other sister is sick. Emy tells me that you're nice, that you really seem to care about her. I like that. And she trusts you. I think that's important." Loretta turned quickly back toward Neva. "If Emy can trust you, then I guess I can too. I'm going to tell you something I've never told a soul before."

Neva waited patiently, watching Loretta now instead of the men in the street.

"Katie, she's the oldest of us three girls, you see. She's in prison, and she's had this drug problem ever since what happened when we was all living at home." Loretta paused again, as if having second thoughts. Then, she blurted it out. "We was raped by our stepbrother, me and Katie that is. For five years, he raped us. We began to worry that he was going to do the same to Emy. We got Emy out of there 'cause our father wouldn't believe us, and he wouldn't do nothin' 'bout it. So anyway, Katie just couldn't handle it afterward, and now she's dying 'cause that woman in there won't let Emy have this operation that could save her."

Neva looked puzzled. "Emily's records say that your parents abandoned you."

"That's mostly true. Mama left us when we was all real young. Emy don't even remember her. The rest of it's a lie, but we only lied to protect Emy 'cause we wanted her to get adopted if she had a chance."

"Do you know where your parents are now?"

"Our father still lives in Houston with his wife, I suspect. I don't know where our mother is or even if she's still alive."

"Has Emily talked to anyone about this?"

"No. I don't think so."

"I think it's time, don't you?" Neva asked.

"Maybe," Loretta said. "But I got to think about Katie too. She's the one who's dying."

"Of course," Neva said. "Of course."

They entered the courtroom with Emily, feeling the unified strength of confidence and promise, when the air suddenly erupted with the heavy clap of a legal tome upon the attorney's table.

Anna Gogarty was standing in front of the judge, pointing up at him with an accusing finger he could not see. "You'll regret this," she admonished. "Mark my words. Your injustice here will swell like a tidal wave and roll back upon you with a vengeance."

Anna turned and held off the bailiff with a stare, then swept down the aisle, stopping only to address Neva in the same portentous tone, her eyes narrowing to shield against impending evils in Neva's aura. "Beware, Ms. Bell, there is something evil approaching. I felt it that first day when I took your hand. This is just the beginning. If you are a part of this—if you are using my son, only you know why, but beware it does not destroy you. God may not be able to change things, but my companion is a different force. Remember that, and beware. Before this is over, vengeance will declare his victims."

And then, she was gone.

Chapter Nine

"Yesterday we were talking about dreams, and you said you had nightmares about someone chasing you. Do you remember? Would you tell us about that dream now?"

They were sitting cross-legged on the floor. Neva had removed the chairs and brought in pillows.

"I don't remember very many details," Emily said.

"Try your best," Neva said.

Emily paused a moment, then drew in a deep breath. "It always starts the same. I'm in bed when I hear someone in the hall. The door opens, and I see a man in the doorway. He's very dark—like a silhouette. He walks over to the bed and just stands there, looking down at me. I can't see his face. I'm afraid, but I can't move. He reaches for me, and suddenly, I'm running down the hall to another room. No one is there, so I hide, but he finds me. This happens over and over. I run to different rooms, and he always finds me. The last room, I'm hiding in a closet, and when he opens the door, I can see he has a knife in his hand. There is no place I can go. I can't move. It's like my muscles are frozen. And I think there is someone behind him, because I can hear laughter, and it sounds like a woman's voice. That's when I wake up."

"That's spooky," Janeen said.

"Sounds like you've been watching too many Hitchcock movies," Krista said.

"Don't make fun, Krista," Janeen said. "It sounds like a dream I've had."

"Oh God," Krista sighed sardonically with a roll of her eyes. "I don't believe this."

Emily ignored Krista and spoke to the floor. "Neva said that dreams are really our wishes coming true. I guess that means I want some pervert to attack me."

"I didn't say that about wish fulfillment in dreams. Freud did," Neva said.

Krista's eyes narrowed, then widened. "Then, the knife would be a phallic symbol . . . and you want it because when it hurts, it feels soooo good."

"Oh God," Janeen screeched. "Shut up!"

"You shut up," Krista snapped back.

"Actually, Krista might be onto something," Neva said. This time, she ignored Krista and Janeen sticking their tongues out at each other. "If dreams come from what we want to hide, it would be very logical that they would be symbolic in order to conceal their true meanings. Freud probably would interpret your dream as a sexual fantasy because of the closed doors that the man has to open to get to you. Symbolically, he must cut away your hymen to get to your virginity."

Emily and Janeen giggled, then looked at each other, and shouted in unison, "It's a little late!"

"Do you really believe all that Freud mumbo-jumbo?" Krista asked.

"No," Neva said. "And I don't want to quote Freud too much because I think he was on the wrong track when it came to women and sexual fantasies. In Emily's dream, however, there very well may be some truth to the juxtaposition of danger and wish fulfillment. I call it the dichotomy of womanhood. As a girl becomes a woman, she can both desire and fear the loss of her virginity because it can mean the loss of youthful innocence as she is suddenly thrust into an adult world. That can be kind of scary. But there could be another way of looking at it. Another psychologist by the name of Carl Jung was right on track when he said that we are all afraid of becoming conscious of ourselves. He called it our secret fear of the unknown perils of the soul."

"I don't understand," Emily said.

"No one likes to feel guilty," Neva continued. "To get rid of bad feelings, you need to cut out that which makes you feel guilty."

"Sometimes I wish I didn't feel at all," Emily said.

"You would be dead, then," Krista sneered.

"Or reborn," suggested Janeen.

"Well, you obviously can't go back in time," Neva said, "but you *can* change your lives, if you want to stop making the same old mistakes that continue to hurt you."

"But it doesn't hurt, so how do we know when we've made a mistake?" For a moment, Janeen tilted her head and thought about what she had just said; then, thinking it was funny, she laughed.

Emily, too, began laughing and leaned into Janeen's shoulder to give her a nudge. Krista just blew air through her pursed lips as she rolled her eyes.

"Okay, girls," Neva said. "I can tell this is not going to be easy. Nothing in life is, I suppose, but we can learn to take control of our lives."

"That would be impossible for these two," Krista said.

Neva talked about negative forces and feelings that do nothing to improve the quality of life. She talked about smoking and drinking, and hatred and jealousy, guilt and depression, and other physical and emotional consequences until she realized that they were no longer listening, and she was about to lose them permanently, so she called on Emily again.

"Why do you always have to pick on me?" Emily asked.

"We started talking about your feelings, and I wanted to follow up on that. It all relates to your dream and this man who's chasing you. Why do you think you're afraid of him but not afraid of men when you're awake?"

"Well, most men aren't trying to kill me," Emily said. This drew a laugh from Janeen and a fleeting smile from Krista.

"Okay, girls. Let me explain. When you allow yourself to have sex with someone you don't care about, does this help you or hurt you in the long run?"

Emily squinted as if flipping a coin in her head for a response. "I guess it hurts me," she said.

"For God's sake, then why do you do it?" Krista asked.

"That's an unnecessary criticism, Krista," Neva said. "Please keep your comments on an adult level."

Krista smirked and arched her eyebrows in defiance.

Neva sensed that Emily was squirming with a thought and asked her to keep going.

"This may sound dumb," Emily said, "but it makes me feel good for a while. I mean, they wouldn't want me if they didn't like me, right?"

"But once they get what they want, do they stick around?" Neva asked. "And when you sneak out at night and hitchhike alone, you place yourself in a position where your chances of getting hurt are very good."

"You mean I *want* to get hurt? Why would I want that?"

"Let's not get confused about why you would do this. You're not making conscious choices to do something that will make you feel bad, but you might be making these choices totally unaware that somehow you want to punish yourself because you think you deserve it, perhaps for having the sexual urges in the first place. When men or boys show you attention or desire you, that feels good, so you might seek out that attention, but you know that ultimately, they will hurt you because this is what you have learned, and your dream is a way of undoing that."

"That can't be true," Janeen jumped in sharply like a knife. Then, she tried to back out slowly, apologetically, hoping to close the wound. "I'm sorry," she said.

"That's all right," Neva said. "Go ahead."

"Well, like I said, I have kind of the same dream, but I know the man in my dream. I know he wants to hurt me. I know why, and I'm afraid of him all of the time." Janeen stopped and stared into her lap.

"You can't just stop there," Krista said. "That's like getting a call from someone who has some juicy gossip, and then, the phone goes dead."

"You don't have to say," Emily said.

"Of course, she does," Krista snapped. "Right, Ms. Bell?"

"If you're ready."

"It's the man I used to work for," Janeen said.

"Why does he want to hurt you?" Krista asked frantically.

"He used to tell me that if I ever turned him in to the cops, he would get me, and now, they want me to testify against him at his trial."

"Who is this guy?" Krista asked. "He sounds like some Mafia creep. And what did you see him do?"

"It's a long story," Janeen said.

"But that's what we're here for, isn't it?" Krista said. "Come on, Janeen, I didn't know you were such a mysterious person."

"Everything you say here is confidential," Neva reminded them.

Janeen sighed heavily. Something in her eyes disappeared, leaving someone else to tell the story. "My friend told me that her boyfriend knew this guy who could get us some drugs. It was nothing heavy. Just some grass. We didn't have enough money to pay him, though, so we did some things with him to pay for the grass."

"Oh God," Krista exclaimed. "You mean you had sex with him."

"Sort of," Janeen continued. "It didn't seem like such a big deal, but I guess one thing led to another. Once, when we were really ripped, some friends of his came to his trailer, and they all did it with us. I was so stoned, I didn't know what was happening until it was too late. I was a little afraid, but they didn't hurt us. He told us we could make some money doing it, so we did it to pay for drugs at first. But then, he started to threaten us if we talked about quitting."

"You were working as a prostitute?" Krista asked. "This guy was your pimp." She stared at Janeen in disbelief.

"It's not like I wanted to do it," Janeen said, and tears ran down her cheek.

"That's awful," Emily said. "I mean you must be glad that you're out of there."

"What did your parents say when they found out?" Krista asked.

"Nothing. I didn't really get to talk with them about it. The caseworker said that they should have looked after me better, and that's how I ended up here."

"I thought you said you dropped out of school," Krista said.

"Well, that wasn't a lie; it just wasn't the whole truth."

"Aren't you afraid that this guy will get to you?" Emily asked.

"Of course. I think that's why I have the nightmares about him," Janeen said.

"So how do you think your nightmare is similar to Emily's?" Neva asked.

"We're both being chased," Janeen said.

"You couldn't get a . . ." Krista began, then stopped as Neva gave her an admonishing glance.

"You and Emily both put yourselves in potentially dangerous situations in order to fulfill a very fleeting need," Neva said.

Janeen thought about this a moment. "I guess you're right," she said.

"I think your dreams are trying to tell you something," Neva said. "One, you have to conquer your feelings of guilt, and two, you have to stop placing yourself in positions that allow men to hurt you. To put it another way, the child inside of you wants attention, but the parent inside of you keeps saying no, and punishing you, and you're playing out both of these roles when you put yourself in a dangerous situation. You must learn to use the adult inside of you to control what the child wants so the parent stops judging you so harshly."

"That sounds easier said than done," Emily said.

"Exactly, but identifying the problem is the first step. You have to find a more acceptable way of achieving those good feelings. You need to rely on yourself, not others, to do something that makes you feel good about yourself. That's how you build your self-esteem, and that's what protects you against those who want to harm you."

"It's not really that hard," Krista said. "It's all just a big game anyway. Guys only want what's under your skirt, so make them work for it, but always make sure you have the advantage. There's no rule that says you have to give them what they want."

● ● ●

Sunday morning was shamelessly cool—a day toward the middle of June, which no native Texan would mistake for a lingering spring. Folks were quick to take advantage of the unpredicted pleasantness, of the resurrecting breezes that swept down from tall clouds and stirred the music of the earth, as dry aching leaves twitched in the dark branches, and hummingbirds darted among daylilies and honeysuckle, and the surface of the lake played in equal measures against the shore.

In the stairwell, Neva overheard Krista and Janeen planning a walk to the mall in Clear Lake, and she quickly reined them in with the task of painting the front porch. A choral groan erupted around the breakfast table as the others realized that this was a community project, and although Neva had to admonish Warren into joining, she eventually compromised with the promise of an afternoon of freedom in exchange for a morning of devoted labor.

Still, they dragged themselves through a clattering cacophony of breakfast dishes as they cleared the table and washed the pots and pans, delaying the inevitable, until Neva pushed them like a demanding Kapellmeister. She tuned up the brushes with satin eggshell and orchestrated the theme and variations of the task at hand. She then dropped in her tape of Mozart's K. 525 sonata and settled into a melodious drift over the window trim, timing her bristled baton along the hungry wood, quieting the violins or bringing up the cellos with her free hand.

Through the first movement, everyone worked diligently, hoping that time would pass quickly, or if not time, then work. The second movement brought muffled complaints, which Neva did not hear, that the work was beginning to seem endless.

By the third movement, both spirits and progress were lost in a decrescendo of despair. Neva was so enraptured by the music that everyone else seemed to disappear.

Krista noted her first, and with rolling eyes, she signaled Janeen, who got Emily's and Randy's attention on the opposite side of the walkway. A tremolo of laughter exploded as Warren and Spinner noticed Neva's preoccupation. When Alec, who was working on the ladder's third interval, leaned to his left to see what they were laughing at, a measure of paint dripped onto Spinner's sleeve, and a howl leapt through the air with such grand fortissimo that Neva's feet pirouetted off the deck.

Warren slipped up the stairs while Neva was trying to quell the ensuing paint fight. He furtively replaced Mozart with the Rolling Stones, and a sudden ragtime rock and roll thundered out into the warming summer air. Spinner moved away from the ladder and resumed his painting next to Janeen, who swung her hips to the Stones' infamous thumping beat. She smiled shyly at Spinner, and together, they danced down the rail, painting with a Jagger swagger as Krista joined in. Before long, the three of them were singing into their brushes. Neva sighed helplessly as she watched them dance onto the lawn. Even Randy joined them with a clumsy rendition of Keith Richard slamming out a riff on his paintbrush.

No one noticed Emily walk to the base of the ladder and tug at Alec's pant leg. "Hey wallflower, you want to dance?" she asked.

"I'm no good at this," Alec said.

Emily looked at Randy stomping on the grass and leaping as if he were trying to bring rain. "I don't think you have to be." She giggled. She pulled Alec with both hands away from the ladder and guided him out near the others, coaching him to sway with the music, never taking her eyes off his efforts, then taking his hands again when the music ended so he could not escape back up the ladder. "You're really very good," Emily said. "You shouldn't be embarrassed."

"I'm just not used to this," Alec said.

"You mean you haven't ever done anything just for the fun of it?" Emily asked, tugging again at his hands as the music started with a long, electric screech. "I won't push you, if you don't want to." The music tumbled into a brisk dance rhythm, but before they got started, Emily stumbled from a bump against her side that sent her sprawling onto the grass. Krista moved into her place.

"If you two aren't going to dance, then maybe Alec will dance with me," Krista coaxed.

"Why did you do that?" Alec asked. "You could have hurt her."

Emily stood up, rubbing her hip. "It's all right. I can sit this out." She started for the porch.

"No, wait," Alec pleaded.

"I was just playing," Krista groaned. "I didn't mean to knock her down. Come on, Alec. Let's dance. Please."

The others had stopped dancing and were watching them now. Warren came down the steps, sensing turmoil.

"Maybe some other time," Alec said.

"Shit," Krista screamed. "Why does that little slut always have to spoil everything?"

"That's not fair, Krista," Warren said. "There's no need for that kind of attitude."

"I'm just telling it like it is," Krista insisted. "Just ask her. She admitted it. She's done it with everyone."

Neva stood on the porch, stunned.

"You just lost all privileges for one week, Krista," Warren said.

"You can't do that!" she squealed.

"I just did."

Krista turned a pleading glance to Neva, who remained silent. Krista turned back to Alec, who turned away. "I don't believe this," she cried out. "I didn't do anything!" Krista narrowed her eyes at Warren. "I hate you, and I *will* make you pay for this." Before Warren could respond, she ran into the house.

The magic of the morning had passed, and the sky commiserated with dark clouds that brought a steady rain. The house fell still as if in anticipation of something stirring in its shadows.

Chapter Ten

"Prometheus," Dr. Mueller said. "That's the first image I got. Are you familiar with Aeschylus?"

"I'm more familiar with Shelley, but it's been a long time."

"The myth is the same, I agree. Prometheus brings fire to the world and is punished for it. Fire is knowledge. But is the opposite true? Some believe that knowledge is a dangerous thing, and in certain cases, it *can* be. With these kids, for instance, sexual awareness might just be the fire which can burn them."

"I see what you mean," Neva said.

"I don't think it is Alec, however, that is being punished, but what he represents, some missing knowledge. What I find amazing is the similarity between your dream and Anna Gogarty's." Dr. Mueller stretched out his long frame in the chair and settled into a posture of comfort and contemplation.

"Frighteningly so," agreed Neva. "That's why I felt the need to talk to you about it."

"There is one striking difference, though. Where your dream is arid, almost void of life, Anna Gogarty's is satiated with water—life-giving water according to another myth. The Fisher King, I believe."

"Do you mean that my cup is half-empty while hers is half-full?"

"Possibly. However, I find it ironic that in your dream, life comes from death, whereas, in Anna Gogarty's dream, just the opposite is true."

"Are you saying that the two dreams really are different? That any similarities are just a coincidence because of our connection through Alec?"

"Again, possibly. But they could also be parts of a continuum, different chapters or seasons in the cycle of life. If we look at the Fisher King, he is cursed with impotency, and his land is sterile. A knight of purity must find the Holy Grail before he can heal the king and bring fertility to the land. Just as the earth rejuvenates itself from winter to spring, we seek knowledge to fill our loss of spirituality, to give life from death."

Neva got up and filled her cup from the coffeepot on the table against the wall. With her back to Dr. Mueller, she felt uneasy. She was glad she had worn jeans and her favorite blue work shirt. Neva kicked off her shoes and settled back on the sofa, bringing her feet up under her legs. She sipped her coffee before speaking again. "I want you to know that I'm bringing all this up out of curiosity. I'm not going to obscure my objectivity because of one restless night."

"Still fighting Freud?" Dr. Mueller observed. He smiled broadly, and Neva felt a chill run up her back, the same puzzling shudder she noticed in their last meeting.

"I'm just leaving an open mind for all the possibilities."

"An active subconscious is a healthy thing. Dreams flow from the blood of recognition. Freud made the analogy to Ulysses' journey to the underworld, where the shades of his past awoke to new life when they tasted blood."

"I'm trying to keep this in perspective, and I have no trouble accepting that Alec has stimulated some deeper feelings in both me and his mother. What bothers me is the role Anna Gogarty sees me in—and the possibility of her black magic turning into something very real and very harmful."

"There is no doubt that she views you as someone who can either help or hinder her efforts to get Alec back. She still sees him as the child who was taken away from her four years ago, and now she has a chance to have him again. She is still afraid, nevertheless. This is evident in the rainbow he is crossing to get to her. Rainbows can be interpreted as death, like a tall bridge where the person either leaps or falls. I don't think Anna Gogarty has any wish for her son's actual death, so it might mean some other kind of death, perhaps the death of his dependence on her. Or you," Dr. Mueller said after a pause.

"I don't know what she has to fear from me."

"She would be the one to ask that question."

"Alec makes it across the bridge in my dream. Couldn't it be interpreted the same way?"

"Does he? You said that you woke up before he landed. As far as interpretation, your dream is more involved, more allegorical. I don't think it's going to be so simple. In fact, as I think about it, I wonder if you lost something in your past, something you miss very strongly. In your dream, Alec could represent that which is missing, which you desire to have back. Tell me Neva, are you very religious?"

"No. I guess you could say I was once. My family was anyway. I don't believe anymore, though."

"There is a lot of religious symbolism in your dream. For instance, the rock as the foundation of the church and the desert as the place where Jesus spent forty days of redemption. The crucifixion is fairly obvious. The girls could be angels, or disciples, or even some earthly representation of the Trinity. I find the motorcycle a curious feature, but the fact that Alec pulls it from the dust could represent the Resurrection. It would then follow that Alec's jump across the canyon would be the Ascension. Waiting for him on the other side could be your own desire to have your religion back again. Of course . . ." Dr. Mueller paused, but this time he did not continue.

"What is it?" Neva asked.

"Well, there is the sexual issue, if Alec plays the knight of purity to your Fisher King. After all, you *are* still a young woman. Alec could represent your own desire for sexual fulfillment, and the religious symbolism just keeps it all in perspective. The superego controlling the id."

"And what about the vulture?" Neva asked.

"Certainly a vivid image of death. Perhaps the punishment for an uncontrolled id. The ire of Zeus for playing with fire."

"Sometimes I think Freud was a pervert." Neva laughed.

"These are just my observations. If you are looking for an easy answer, I don't know if I can provide it. We would have to talk more. Analysis wouldn't hurt. Do you think you need it?"

"No."

"Is everything going all right with the group?"

"It could be better. Perhaps if the girls didn't interact so closely on a daily basis, they wouldn't violate the rules of the group so easily. We're still dealing with surface problems instead of getting to real issues. I feel like I'm lecturing at them, and they don't really understand. It would be better if the girls opened up more. In fact, I can't even get Krista to talk at all. She's very reticent about her own problems and only seems to react to what the other girls say. Even then, she's critical with her remarks."

"A defense mechanism probably, when she perceives a threat to her ego. Don't overlook the obvious, which might actually be a sign or a symptom of something more serious. You'll have to think of a way to use the little things to get at the big ones. Is there anything else?"

"No. Yes, Doctor . . . I'm sorry . . . Carl."

"Thank you. I didn't think you would ever call me by my first name. I feel as if we've made a breakthrough."

Neva smiled briefly. "There is one other thing."

"Something about the group?"

"Something you said about my dream." Neva wanted to say that she didn't mention it before because she knew what Freud would say. It was the part where she was waiting for Alec, lying on her back, and watching him approach through the V of her open arms and legs. She knew that the image couldn't get more sexual than that. "I don't have any secret sexual desire for Alec," Neva said.

"The image might relate only to your frustration over the absence of certain religious feelings. Alec is just a symbol. You are a very caring woman, Neva—and a very sensual woman. It only follows that you would relate to something important in that fashion."

Neva wondered why he would say that, about her being sensual. He didn't know her. "I just wanted you to know," she said.

"You mustn't take these things too seriously. You need a break, time to take your mind off your work. I have tickets to the ballet, Neva. Would you like to join me?"

The vulture was turning.

"The ballet?"

"The Royal Ballet is appearing at Jones Hall. It's called Raymonda . . ."

He swept down from the sky, gathering speed.

"Really?"

"... with Rudolf Nureyev and Cynthia Gregory."

"Oh my God ..."

In the dream, it was not a vulture at all, but a very vivid image of Dr. Mueller, with arms spread, talons exposed, and a wide, threatening grin, which Neva could not forget.

"... yes."

● ● ●

Neva's meeting with Dr. Mueller should have been therapeutic. It should have relieved her mind about many things, especially the convergence of these mysterious dreams. Troubled still by Anna Gogarty's warning and Dr. Mueller's haunting countenance circling above her, Neva went out to the backyard garden, where she was always able to expend a certain amount of stressful energy by kneading dirt and yanking weeds from her favorite rose garden.

Emily had gone into the office to talk with Dr. Mueller while the others were preparing dinner. Alec had not yet returned from his job. It gave Neva time to be alone. She was turning the rain-softened soil with a spade to get at the roots of the weeds when she thought about the religious symbolism Dr. Mueller had mentioned, how neatly it had fallen into place, everything except the motorcycle, and his assumption that it was her belief in religion, or the loss of it, that was longing to be resurrected, somehow sexually. Neva knew that she desired a renewed relationship with her mother, but her mother was nowhere in the dream. What kept coming back to her was the motorcycle. She knew what the motorcycle meant, and she hadn't told Dr. Mueller about that either. Neva knew she was beginning to feel Jim's presence.

Jim was being resurrected in Neva's life, but she feared that she was replacing him with Alec, bringing him back alive in Alec. And yet Neva wondered if she was responsible for this at all or if it was something on the outside, something more than just her mind playing with fire. Neva knew she did not bring Alec to Morning House, and it was not her imagination that Dr. Mueller seemed to be against his being there.

The vulture could have been death, as Dr. Mueller had speculated, but then, he wasn't aware that he was the true image, circling over Alec. The vivid image came back to Neva as she pulled at deep, pertinacious weeds, losing herself in the vision, the image fading as he circled away, then returning as clear as before. This time, though, the vulture was not Dr. Mueller but her Uncle Spencer, who was standing on a pulpit high above his congregation, his arms spread inside a flowing robe, his fingers extended like grasping claws. And that same disturbing smile, transferred from one vulture to the other, was pressed across her uncle's face.

● ● ●

Sitting low on the motorcycle, Alec drove out of the parking lot in front of Rodriguez Auto Repair and onto the highway toward Kemah. His grip on the accelerator was tight, and the power vibrated in his hands as he shifted through the gears. Alec felt the front-end rise up with each acceleration, felt the freedom of flight and of control. The wind brushed against his face and furiously through his hair. It was the best feeling he had experienced in a long time.

Alec rode several miles before he realized he was approaching the drawbridge in Kemah. He stopped as the guardrail lowered across the road, watching the bridge split at the middle and open to let two tall-masted sailboats pass underneath. He could only see the flags on the mastheads as they bobbed slowly through the channel. The bridge jolted, and sunlight glinted off the windows in the control booth near the top as the two arms of the bridge began to lower.

Alec gazed at the sun sitting low in the sky and frowned as if watching a distant enemy. He revved the motorcycle's engine several times, listening impatiently to the tone and pitch. When the guardrail lifted back away from the road, he moved cautiously forward, feeling the incline of the road and the textured surface in the movement of the front tire. As Alec crossed the bridge, the tires hummed over the metal grating like a fly in his ear. When he reached the other side, he saw an opening in the approaching traffic and circled quickly to drive back over the bridge.

Alec looked down at where the different sections came together and were supported by larger pieces of steel. The middle sections looked as if they had been welded together with a flat strip of steel slightly wider than the tires on his motorcycle. He coasted back down the side as the tires sang over the smooth, black asphalt. When he reached the bottom, Alec punched the accelerator again and headed back toward Morning House.

He hadn't driven far when he noticed a police car filling the space in his rearview mirror. Alec thought about the turn he made at the top of the bridge, a mistake he now regretted, and one that was compounded by the fact that he didn't yet have his license. His heart thumped madly in his chest as he slowed down, hoping the police car would pass. It came closer but made no move to pass. Another police car appeared from the opposite direction. The driver looked at Alec as he drove by, then made a sharp turn in the road, squealing tires and churning up dust as it took a position behind the first car. Then, red and blue lights filled the mirror, and a sharp wailing cry came at Alec like a fist.

Alec pulled the motorcycle off the road and into a parking lot by a boatyard. He got off slowly, thinking how short-lived his freedom had been. Alec turned around, expecting to see the officers approaching him, but instead, he saw them crouched behind their open doors and pointing guns at him. One of the police officers spoke to him through a microphone that made his voice sound metallic and full of static. He told Alec to keep his hands away from his body and not to make any sudden moves. Something wasn't right. Alec knew this was about something more than his U-turn on the bridge. The officer told him to turn around.

"What's going on?" Alec asked.

"Turn around!" the voice screamed, barely discernible through the speaker on top of the car. When Alec turned around, the voice continued as before. "Now, step away from the motorcycle and lie facedown. Do it slowly and do it now."

Alec was lying with his face against the rough surface of the parking lot for a few seconds, wondering what the voice would tell him to do next, when he felt a sudden heaviness in the middle of his back that nearly took the wind out of him. Alec tried to look back, but his head was pushed down against the gravel. Pieces of gravel and dirt went into his mouth and one of his eyes. They wrenched his arms behind his back, pulled at his clothes, and brushed their hands roughly over his body. Alec was pulled to his feet. He couldn't see because of the dirt in his left eye, and he could taste it in his mouth. Pieces of gravel were embedded in his forehead and left cheek. His arms hurt at his shoulders, and something was digging into his wrists.

"He's clean," the one behind him said. "Not even a wallet."

The one facing him looked down at the motorcycle. "There's nothing here either," he said. "He fits the description anyway, so we better take him in and get some photos."

Alec retched up several white clods of dirt and gravel. He kept retching even when there was nothing left, and he couldn't even spit. When his stomach was calm again, Alec stood up straight and tried to open his eyes. The gravel had cleared out of his eyes, but some of it still clung to his eyelashes. He tried to wipe it away with his shoulder, but he couldn't.

"What's your name, kid?"

"Alec Gogarty."

"Why aren't you carrying any identification?"

"I don't have any."

"That's convenient. Why did you turn around then on that bridge when you saw me?"

"I didn't see you. I turned around because I had to get back . . ." Alec wanted to say home, but it wouldn't come out. "I'm late for dinner."

"And you're gonna be a whole lot later, kid."

● ● ●

"Neva?"

The voice called to her from outside the well of afternoon light that pierced through the trees. It drew her up in a lightness of air, buoyed on a warm, invisible current. In that narrow tunnel of light, a blur of stones rose up to meet her and swept by so close, she feared she would crash into them. Neva reached out to stop her momentum, but the stones transfigured into faces. She saw Jim, but his image passed too quickly, and in her dizziness, she saw her mother, her Uncle Spencer, and finally Dr. Mueller. The images repeated in a kinematic array of shades, drawn from the depths, calling to her as she neared the top. Something grabbed her arm and pulled her out of the light. Neva screamed, or thought she did, and whatever it was released her arm.

She was on her knees, and when she turned around, Warren was standing next to her.

"You scared me," Neva said.

"I'm sorry," Warren said. "You lost your balance and nearly hit your head on that rock. I called, but you seemed to be lost in thought. Are you going to plant something there?"

Neva looked down at the flowerbed where she had been pulling weeds near a large rock. In front of her, she saw a hole deep enough for a new plant, but much too close to the base of the existing roses. "That's odd," Neva said. "I was turning the soil. I didn't mean to . . . Is it getting late?"

"Yes. Dinner is almost ready." Warren looked puzzled. "Anything you want to talk about?"

"No. I'll be all right."

"Dr. Mueller left. Janeen and Randy just got back, so everyone is here but Alec."

"Did he call?"

"No. I called the garage, but they said he left some time ago."

"I guess we can all lose track of time," Neva said. "I'll be along in a minute, as soon as I fix this."

Warren went back inside while Neva replaced the dirt in the hole, then put the tools away in the shed. She was returning to the house to wash up when she heard a car stop in the driveway. Neva walked up the drive along the side of the house and saw a pale blue sedan—plain, like a company car or a rental.

There was a conversation at the front door. She heard Warren's voice, which was friendly but firm. Neva looked up through the boxwood hedge and the freshly painted porch rail. The stranger was dressed neatly with the polished look of a company man. Warren wasn't buying whatever he was selling.

Neva walked around to the front and up the steps. The man glanced at her with a hint of suspicion, then smiled with a recognition of her relationship to the others. "You must be Ms. Bell," he stated simply. His voice was deep and soothing, capable of putting someone at ease and, Neva suspected, off guard.

Neva could see the others behind Warren, whispering nervously. They weren't leaving, which meant that the man wasn't selling bibles or encyclopedias. The man kept his attention on Neva, studying her response, her demeanor, the lines and color of her face.

"I'm sorry," Neva said, "we were just about to sit down to dinner."

"Oh, no, thank you," he said. "I can't stay. Perhaps another time." His smile again drew her in as he waited for her recognition of his joke at her polite effort to dismiss him. He introduced himself. "I'm Detective Kelly with Harris County Sheriff's Office."

Neva repeated his name as if she had not heard him correctly. "Kelly? Detective Kelly?"

"With the Sheriff's Office," he said. "I won't keep you. I just came by to ask a few questions about a robbery that took place about an hour ago just down the road."

"A robbery?" Neva asked, still as if it were not registering correctly in her mind.

"Yes. Actually, there have been several robberies in the area recently. This one was at the gas station across from the Space Center."

"Why would you think that we would know anything about these robberies?"

"We're checking every home and business in the area, to find out if anyone might have seen something. Sometimes an event like a man speeding away on a motorcycle may draw your attention, but you don't associate that with a robbery unless someone is chasing and yelling, 'Stop, Thief!'" Detective Kelly looked around, trying to get a better look at everyone standing behind Warren.

"Is that what happened?" Neva asked.

"Not exactly," Detective Kelly said. "But something like that. A motorcycle may have been involved. Well, I won't keep you. If anyone remembers something, though, would you give me a call?" He handed Neva a business card, and as he was heading down the steps, he turned. "No one here has a motorcycle, do they?"

"Actually, we all do," Neva said. "In fact, we fly our colors when we ride, crossed bones under a teddy bear, pale blue, like your car."

"Sounds pretty dangerous to me." Detective Kelly chuckled.

"We could surprise you."

Warren stepped out of the doorway and gently took Neva's arm to draw her attention. "We'll keep an eye out for anything unusual," he said.

Detective Kelly got into his car and was driving away before Warren let go of Neva's arm. "He was smooth," Warren said. "I thought he was going to ask you for a date."

"He would have been disappointed," Neva said. "There was something about him that I didn't trust. I think it was the casualness of his authority."

Warren made sure the others were gone before he addressed Neva again. "Do you think we should have told him about Campbell's Market?"

"Why? It could be totally unrelated."

"We could also be interfering. I know what I saw that night, and money *was* stolen."

"We don't know anything for a fact, and I think it would be unwise to create more grief in the lives of these kids when we owe them protection. Anyway, Duffy Campbell believes his clerk stole the money, so why shouldn't we?"

While they were still standing on the porch, the pale blue car drove back up the drive and stopped in front of the house. Detective Kelly walked around the car and stopped at the bottom of the steps before saying a word. This time, his face was serious. "I have to ask you to come with me, Ms. Bell."

"What is this about?" Neva asked warily.

"One of your wards was picked up in connection with the robbery. His name is Alec Gogarty. He was asking for you."

• • •

Alec sat in a small, gray room on a metal bench bolted to the floor. He stared at a gray metal toilet in the corner of the room. He had been in this type of room before. It was a room for crazy people and criminals—people who somehow had broken the rules. It was a room where you went crazy.

Alec remembered staring at the ceiling for hours, counting tiny holes. He counted his fingers and his toes, moving each one as he counted just to keep in touch with reality, to prove that he was still alive, that he wasn't crazy. Lying on his back in the hospital, in a bed in the middle of the room, he couldn't see his hands or his feet, and if he tried to move them, the straps would cut into his wrists and his ankles. Alec could tap his fingers against the side of the bed. And he could gather several deep breaths and scream at the top of his lungs. It was a voice that wasn't his voice, a voice that was deep and raspy. "Witch, witch, cast your spell! Must be quiet, mustn't tell!" Alec cried and muttered to himself while he counted the holes in the ceiling tiles. "Ten, nine, dead is fine. Eight, seven, get to heaven. Six, five, once alive. Four, three, why choose me. Two, one, pick up the gun." And he tapped his fingers to keep from slipping over the line.

Alec had never been so afraid before. On the bench, he leaned over and placed his arms on his legs so he could see his hands and feet. He sat that way for a long time, without moving, without thinking. When the door opened, Alec sat up and put his back against the wall. The man stood in the doorway, smiling and waiting, like he expected Alec to say something first. Alec had decided that he was not going to say anything until someone explained why he had been arrested.

"Alec, I'm Detective Kelly. You seem to have gotten yourself into quite a mess here."

"I don't understand. Why am I here?"

"Well, I'd like to talk with you about that so we can get this straightened out."

"Fine."

"Would you come with me?"

Alec walked silently beside Detective Kelly down a white, tiled hallway. They entered a room where Neva sat at a table. Several empty chairs surrounded the table, which was empty except for an ashtray. Alec glanced at the bare walls and noted a "No Smoking" sign. Neva stood as they entered. The look on her face was more worried than angry.

When she approached him, Neva's eyes switched from worried to angry. "Oh my God! What did they do to you?" she asked as she reached out to touch the red marks on his face.

"Nothing." Alec backed away from her touch.

"It's one of the hazards of officer safety," Detective Kelly said. "You didn't resist the officers, did you?"

"I didn't resist anyone," Alec said.

"Surely this wasn't called for," Neva said, glaring at Detective Kelly as she pointed to Alec's cheek.

"Shall we sit down and talk about it?" Detective Kelly motioned toward the chairs.

Alec's chair was comfortable, with a thick, cushioned seat that relaxed the muscles in his legs. But his stomach churned with hunger, and his cheek stung, and he didn't trust this cop. Alec leaned back in the chair and crossed his arms over his chest.

"I want to go over your rights, Alec, because I want to make sure you understand them before we talk about what happened."

"That won't be necessary," Neva said.

"It is if we're going to talk," Detective Kelly said.

"But that's just it," Neva said. "We're not talking about this."

"That's up to Alec," Detective Kelly said with a smug smile.

"I want to know why I was arrested," Alec said. "I don't know why I'm here."

"If they're going to arrest you, they have to tell you why, but you don't have to tell them anything," Neva said.

"They'll think I'm guilty if I don't," Alec said, and he noticed a childlike pleading in his voice.

"No, they won't," Neva said, looking at Detective Kelly. "They better not."

"But I don't have anything to hide."

"Look, Alec," Neva said. "They know I haven't talked to you about this. I'm not protecting you because you're guilty. I'm protecting you because you're innocent. If they can prove you're guilty, then they know where they can find you."

"I'm not going to hide anything either," Detective Kelly said. "We called your employer, and he confirmed your story about the motorcycle."

"What?" Neva asked.

"I'll explain later," Alec said.

"But Johnny Rodriguez left the garage before you did. In fact, he left the garage at 4:30, which leaves you without an alibi during the time the gas station was robbed, and you had plenty of time to do it."

"All that seems pretty circumstantial, doesn't it?" Neva asked.

Detective Kelly sighed with an audible rush of air through his nostrils. "Are you sure you're not a lawyer, Ms. Bell?"

Neva raised her eyebrows. "Are we free to go now, Detective Kelly?"

"Your motorcycle is parked in the lot where you were stopped," Detective Kelly said to Alec. "But if you're going to drive, I suggest you get a license."

• • •

"What did you go and do, man?"

The silver reach of the moon parted the darkness and lay across their faces. They were undisturbed, gazing at the ceiling in their bedroom.

"Nothing," Alec said. "I bought a motorcycle, that's all."

"That's enough. Don't you know cops don't like bikers?"

"Neva didn't go for it much either."

"How's that?" Spinner turned his head in the cradle of his hands locked behind his head and looked at Alec.

"She didn't say much, but I could tell she was upset."

"Looks like the cops did a number on you."

"They thought I was someone else. I was just in the wrong place at the wrong time."

"They must be lookin' for that guy who hit Campbell's Market. That's why they lookin' here. They think it has to be one of us."

"Ever notice how bad things just seem to follow some people? Well, I'm proof of that." Alec pushed a soft groan from his throat. Even with his cheek still throbbing, he didn't want sympathy.

"Don't expect any handouts, cowboy. One thing I learned a long time ago is you have to make your own way."

"Easy for you. You can fight. Someone like me won't even get a chance. There's always going to be something in the way or someone to push me back down."

"I don't know. You handled yourself pretty good against that dude at school."

"I just got lucky. And you were there to back me up. If I had to do it all myself, I wouldn't know the first thing."

"You did what you had to do. That's what it takes. Sometimes you gotta be the first one there with the first blow to take home the prize. Ain't no time to strategize in the real world. I can't figure why you're in such a big hurry anyway, want'n to fight all the time. Only means that someday you'll get hurt. No matter how good you are, someday there will always be somebody better."

"I used to get beat up pretty regular. I guess I just got tired of it."

"Your old man?"

"Yeah. Randy, too, back when I knew him before."

"Is that why you did it? I mean, what they say you did to your old man. But hey, if you don't want to talk about it, I understand."

"It's all right. One day he just went crazy. I guess I couldn't take it anymore, him always beating up on me and my mother. I thought he was going to kill us. I mean, I didn't even think about it. It just happened."

"Oh man, that's harsh, but hey, I don't blame you. You do what you got to do to survive. I learned that early 'cause I never even knew my parents. Never saw my father, and my mother's been in prison most of my life. I lived with my grandma, but she's too old to take me in now. Not sure where I'll go. Boxing is my only hope."

"There's got to be something better than this," Alec said as he turned back toward the window. "I was thinking I might enjoy flying jets. Saw one fly over the car on the way to court. It looked real cool, but that's a long way off. I need something right now. I feel like I could change everything if I could just do one great thing, something no one else has ever done before. That would be my ticket, my way out of here. I could change my luck and get everyone off my back—mothers, fathers, psychiatrists, cops, social workers—the whole world."

"I hear you, cowboy. You're thinking like me now. And what you're talking about is freedom, real freedom."

"You're lucky 'cause you have boxing. That's your ticket out of here. All I have is a dream."

"You can come by the gym anytime. I'll introduce you to my coach."

"No. I have to do something else. Or at least I've got to try."

"I hate to ask what's going on in that crazy head of yours, cowboy."

"You can't tell."

"Why would I?"

"I got that bike 'cause I'm going to jump the Kemah drawbridge."

"You're crazy, cowboy. There's no doubt. But let me ask you something. What if you do jump that bridge? What's that going to get you? Have you thought about that?"

"Yeah, I've thought about it. I know it sounds crazy, and it may not get me anything except some broken bones, but if I make it, I'll be the only one to do it, and everyone will know that. I'll always be the one who jumped that bridge, and no one can take that away from me."

Chapter Eleven

Neva sat down on her pillow, her audible sigh accented with an exaggerated shrug of her shoulders. "I was thinking about asking your parents to come join the group for a session." She waited for a response.

Janeen looked startled. "Why?"

"Why not?" Neva asked. "They're still the primary people in your lives. They're the ones you will ultimately have to deal with when you leave here."

"But what if we don't want to leave? What if we don't want to go back there, to the way things were?"

"Morning House is only a crisis placement, Janeen. You can't stay here forever. It's only good for a few months, at most."

"You're just going to toss us out?" She looked betrayed. "You just send us back, even if we would rather die?"

Neva was stunned by Janeen's frailty, her rag-doll existence with seams unraveling and frayed edges too weak to withstand new stitching. Neva wondered how she could be expected to erase all the years of emotional destruction in just a few months or weeks. And yet, that was all the time she had to deal with the shades that lay beneath these frail shells.

"Good luck even finding my parents," Emily said.

"In your case, I was actually thinking about Loretta."

"Really?"

133

"Yes, really. I got a call from your caseworker, and she feels like Loretta's home would be a good placement. Since the judge didn't appreciate Ms. English's fickleness about her responsibility for you, he might be willing to give Loretta a chance."

Emily fidgeted joyously. "That's great. In fact, that's better than great. When can I go?"

"It's not that simple. Marion is contesting, so it may mean more court hearings."

The joy in Emily's face trembled for a moment, like a flower in a summer breeze before it shook loose and was gone. "What does that mean?"

"She still wants you back, and maybe you should give her a chance. That day in court, I didn't see her and Loretta arguing over you. I saw them arguing over whether or not you should have this operation. Personally, I think that should be *your* decision. Ms. English is frustrated because she has lost control of you, but that doesn't mean she doesn't want you. These are things you need to talk over with her."

Krista cleared her throat. "Mind letting us in on what you're talking about?"

Emily explained about her sisters and the operation, which could save Katie's life, and the argument in court between her adoptive mother and Loretta.

"They just want to use you," Janeen said. "They're just like every other adult." She realized what she said, and bit her lip. Janeen glanced at Neva. "Sorry. I guess I don't think of you as . . ."

"That's all right," Neva said. "But I think you should explain why you feel that way."

Janeen lowered her head. "Because it's true."

"We're talking about parents here, Janeen. Are you talking about your parents?"

Her voice faltered. "I don't want my parents to come here. I'll leave. I'll run away if you try to make me go back there. Please don't bring them here," Janeen pleaded.

"I'm not going to force you to do anything you're not ready for," Neva said.

"You can forget about my parents too," Krista said. "I don't want to talk to them, and I don't ever want to go back home."

Neva was watching Janeen and the trauma that lay beneath the chalky grip of her entwined fingers. Neva knew she had opened a wound, and she didn't want to leave it exposed, but this was the first time Krista had opened up in the group. Ignoring her now might mean losing her for good. She chose to pursue Krista. "Was your life at home really that bad?" Neva asked.

"What do you think?"

"What I think is not what's important. Do you want to tell Janeen and Emily what happened?"

"For starters, they moved my grandfather in and moved me out as if suddenly I was just a stranger in the house. They gave him my room, my phone, my space, my privacy. I hate them for what they did."

"And what about what happened later with your grandfather? Did your parents blame you for that?"

"He's still living there, isn't he? He's still in my bedroom, isn't he?"

"Are you having trouble facing him about it?"

"Exactly."

"What exactly did he do?" Emily asked.

"None of your business," Krista said.

"Sounds like you're protecting him," Emily said.

"No, why would I do that?"

"But if he's the one who . . ."

"I just want to forget about it."

"Do you think that's a good idea?" Neva interjected.

"I don't . . ." Krista screamed, then pulled it all back inside and looked away. "I just don't want to talk about it," she said.

"He raped you, didn't he?" Janeen asked.

Krista turned sharply toward Janeen, but Janeen just shrugged. "Well, it must have been something like that," Janeen said. "Neva said we're all here because of something to do with sex."

"Janeen and I have talked about our problems," Emily said. "I think it's only fair."

"You just want some dirt on me," Krista said.

"We're not the ones who snitched to everyone," Emily said. "We all agreed that anything said in here is a secret, just for us, and I plan to honor that."

135

"You broke your promise to stay away from Alec," Krista said. "I was just getting even. If I said I was sorry, would you just drop it?"

"We're not the enemy, Krista," Janeen said.

"Okay!" Krista screamed. "He molested me! Is that what you want to hear? Do you want all the dirty little details too? Do you get off on that?" She got up and walked to the window, where she began to sob. At first, Krista tried to hide it, and then, she turned and asked, "Why is everyone always against me?"

Janeen went cautiously to the window and gently took Krista's arm. Krista didn't move. "We won't tell. I promise. You've got to trust us. We're not against you. If anything, we're just jealous because you always seem so strong, like you don't need anyone. I envy you, Krista, and I need you as a friend."

Krista turned slowly to face Janeen. They both began to cry. They held each other until the comfort melted away, and they laughed awkwardly and wiped away the tears. They continued to hold hands until they sat back down in the group, and Neva handed each of them a tissue. "Affection and support can feel good when it's wanted," Neva said. "Are you ready to trust us?"

"This is not an easy thing to talk about," Krista said.

"I think you've already gotten past the hard part. Just getting it out can help you deal with it better." Neva was feeling so excited she wanted to jump up and scream. She felt her heart beating wildly against her chest when Krista began.

"The trouble all began when he moved in just after my grandmother died. My parents gave him my room, and I moved in with my sister. I guess he felt bad about this because he was always apologizing and kissing me. He started treating me like a little girl, making me sit in his lap while he told me stories. I didn't really pay any attention to it when he put his hand on my leg or patted me on the bottom. I thought he was just being affectionate. He came into my bedroom one night and said he wanted to tuck me in. He pulled the sheet up and leaned over to kiss me on the forehead, only he didn't stop kissing me. He actually kissed me on the mouth and squeezed my breasts through the sheet as he pretended to tuck me in. I was so shocked, I couldn't move. He pulled the sheet down, and pushed up my nightie, and started kissing my breasts. My sister started to wake up in her bed, and that's when he stopped. At first, I was repulsed and angry, but I also thought that maybe he was just lonely with my grandmother dying and all. It didn't go any further, so I didn't say anything.

"But this just seemed to encourage him. He started touching me again when no one was looking. Then, one day at a dinner party my parents were giving for some friends, he grabbed my ass, and I screamed at him to stop. It was embarrassing, and it upset my parents. We had a big blowout right there, and they accused me of making too much out of it like it was all just some innocent affection. I couldn't take it anymore, so they sent me here." Krista stopped suddenly and stared at Neva. She seemed to be waiting for a response that never came.

Neva's eyes were fixed on a place somewhere beyond Krista. Her face was ashen, and beads of sweat emerged on her forehead. She dabbed at them with the back of her wrist. "I'm sorry," Neva said. "Suddenly, I'm not feeling well. I don't know what has come over me. Please forgive me Krista, but can we pick this up next time? Of course, it's important, and I'm so proud of the breakthrough you made. It's just that I'm feeling faint, and I think I need some fresh air."

• • •

Neva took several deep breaths. She had regained her physical composure, but she was still confused about what took place, and she was angry that she had allowed herself to become transparent in front of the girls. She had gotten no argument from them about ending the session. Their minds seemed to race between events with little thought of the consequences, as if a change of scenery or a new day was like a bath for the soul. Neva clinched her fists and slammed them down against her sides. *They are more than clients*, she thought. *Being with them every day has made them that*. She was angry that her feelings were too subjective, that she had gotten too close.

Her mind raced with what she had sensed before, when she went to Campbell's Market to pay Duffy for the stolen money.

The oak trees stood around Neva like old men with mossy beards. In the cloak of leaves, she heard a rustle like faint Japanese chimes. Several bone-bare branches reached out through the cloak, pointing. Neva was drawn toward them. She looked toward the channel where a small boat was tethered and made her way down to the broken dock. Someone had been fishing and had fallen asleep in the boat, his arms folded across his chest. The image wasn't clear. She blinked to bring it into focus, but it just seemed to dissolve and play tricks with her mind.

The trees closed in, creating a sanctuary, where Neva made her way down the aisle with other mourners toward a casket where a body lay with its arms folded across the chest. She couldn't see who it was and thought she was in the wrong place. When Neva got close enough, she saw the face. She recognized it, and she saw how peaceful and serene it looked, and she wanted to slap it. Uncle Spencer had no right to be at peace, not after what he did. It was settled for him now, forgotten. Neva could see it in his face, in his haunting smile, and she became very frightened.

A side door opened, and Jim emerged in the doorway. Neva heard his slow, reassuring voice reach out to her. "You're just hurting yourself by holding it all in." Jim tilted his head toward Uncle Spencer. "He can't hurt you now. He's dead." Dead. "You've got to put it all behind you so you can find happiness. Find someone who can make you happy. You deserve happiness. Stop repressing everything."

Neva was angry that Jim associated happiness with finding a man. "You're not Freud!" she screamed. "Freud wasn't even right!"

"Freud was repressed too," Jim said and laughed. "Come on, Neva, lighten up."

Neva closed her eyes, and when she opened them again, Uncle Spencer was gone. A fallen tree limb was lying in the boat next to the boathouse, where Alec was now standing in the doorway. He looked stunned, and Neva was embarrassed.

"It was you," Alec said. "You've always been the woman in white."

• • •

Through the windshield, Neva saw the dirty house from a distance. She knew it must be the right place because of the way it looked, but she slowed the car and searched for the numbers on the front of the house anyway. When Neva and Warren drove up, Earl Combs was standing in the driveway, staring at the flat tire on an old primer gray Chevy pickup. They didn't see him at first, but he saw them. Earl didn't like strangers, especially the fancy-dressed, high-minded ones who acted like they were only there to help you. His eyes narrowed to thin slits as the young woman stepped from the car and shook loose an abundance of brown, wavy hair.

Neva's eyes moved over the bags of trash, the broken chairs, and the rusting refrigerator in the front yard. Warren came around the car and nodded toward Earl, and then Neva saw him. Earl inhaled a deep, sputtering breath and wiped the back of his hand across his nose. He then wiped both hands down the front of his shirt and trousers. He made no effort to cover the exposed swell of his belly.

"You folks ain't sellin' religion, are you?" Earl asked without moving away from the car.

"No," Neva said. "Are you Mr. Combs?"

"Yep."

"We're from Morning House, where Janeen is staying. We'd like to talk with you and Janeen's mother. Is she here?"

"Inside," Earl said, drawing out the word long and low, more like an order than a fact.

Warren nudged Neva toward the front door, where a musty, dirt floor-basement smell lingered. When Mary Combs opened the door, the smell got stronger. It was a part of the house, within the walls and in its breath. Mary Combs was a small, plain woman with hair cropped short and a skittish look in her eyes. Neva and Warren introduced themselves, and Mary invited them in, stepping to one side. When Neva crossed the threshold, she let out an audible gasp.

Except for the space that allowed the door to open freely, the entire floor was buried beneath several inches of newspapers, discarded clothing, and trash. A television buzzed in the corner of the room, its harsh, flickering light creating agitated shadows on the walls.

Neva and Warren only noticed the boy because he moved. He looked about ten, and he was lying in a small, cleared space on the sofa, his curled-up legs resting against a mound of clothing. He twisted to a fresh position and continued to watch the out-of-focus television.

"We've been cleaning out the place," Mary said. "Sometimes Earl just don't feel up to it."

"I didn't know you had another child," Neva said.

"Oh, he's a neighbor child," Mary said, staring at the boy. "He just comes over to watch television."

Neva smiled nervously.

"Should we go back outside and talk?" Warren asked.

"No," Neva said. "I think we need to see the rest of the house."

Mary Combs sighed helplessly.

"You don't mind, do you, Mrs. Combs?" Warren asked apologetically. When Mary turned away, Warren grabbed Neva's arm and whispered in her ear. "Look at the walls."

Neva squinted again at the large, quivering shadows, but in the darkness behind the television's glare, she saw nothing.

Mary Combs led them to the kitchen, stepping over more trash and scattering tiny roaches from the crevices. There was a gaping hole in the ceiling above the stove, where streaks of light entered the room. The stove was cluttered with cooking pots. Roaches boldly foraged on the dried food and caked grease.

"How can you live like this, Mrs. Combs?" Neva asked. She was almost pleading. "This is not healthy."

"My husband's been ill," Mary tried to explain. "He can't work."

Warren watched a rat dart out from under the stove and scurry across the floor behind Neva and into the cupboard. Neva didn't notice. "He doesn't have a job?" Warren asked.

"No."

"How long has he been out of work?" Neva asked.

"'Bout a year, I think."

"How do you pay for food and rent?" Warren asked.

Mrs. Combs forced a sad smile. "Earl gets a disability check. We do the best we can."

Neva's voice sank to a deeper, determined tone. "Mrs. Combs, Janeen was giving you her money, wasn't she? She was working for that man and turning over her money to you to pay the bills. Isn't that true?"

"You don't have to answer that, Mary," Earl said. He stood in the doorway behind Neva, and she turned around quickly, startled by the sharpness of his voice. He stepped in closer to Neva. "Why did you come here anyway?" he asked her, staring into her eyes. "Did you come here just to cause trouble where there ain't none? You already got Janeen. Ain't that enough?"

Neva stood her ground. "Janeen is afraid of you, Mr. Combs. She thinks you're going to hurt her because of what has happened. She blames herself, and this is causing her a great deal of pain. I was hoping you would help us with Janeen. Dealing with this as a family can be helpful for all of you."

"Janeen has done what she wanted to do for a long time now," Earl Combs said. "She got herself into this, so she can get herself out. I don't think it's a family problem."

"She at least deserves a clean, safe environment at home," Warren said. "A lot of people are having hard times, but they don't live like this."

"How we live ain't none a your business," Earl snapped.

"You could have stopped her, Mr. Combs," Neva said. "But you didn't. Instead, you let her continue what she was doing in that man's trailer just so you could have the money she made."

"Is that what she told you?" Earl smiled, causing his eyes to narrow at a sharp angle. "You have to know Janeen. She can lie pretty good."

"I believe her," Neva said, holding fast to what she had started, hurling accusations like feathers. "I also believe that that boy in the next room is your son, not a neighbor, and you're lying about him so child welfare won't come here and take him away from you too."

"I think maybe it's time for you to leave," Earl said.

Neva turned to Mary Combs, who had been standing quietly behind her with her head lowered. "I am sorry about your situation, Mrs. Combs. I really don't want to cause you any more problems than you already have, but I am concerned about Janeen, and I would like to help her. It's time to start thinking about your children and what this is doing to them. You need to change the way you are living."

Earl left the room quickly, his heavy footsteps pushing through the debris in the hallway that led to the bedrooms.

"Earl is all I've got," Mary said meekly. "Yes, I knew what was going on, but I couldn't stop it. He woulda left me. You'll never understand because you don't know what it's like."

"He's not all you've got, Mrs. Combs," Neva said. "You have your children. There are shelters where you can live."

They could hear drawers opening and closing and boxes toppling over in the back of the house.

"You better leave before he comes back," Mary said.

Neva handed Mary a business card. "Here's my number. Please call me. I can help you."

Warren grabbed Neva's arm and escorted her out of the house before she had time to work up the courage to face off again with Earl Combs.

"I don't believe this," Neva said as Warren helped her into the car.

"Believe it," Warren said. "That man is dangerous."

As they drove away, Warren looked back at the house in the mirror. Earl Combs stood in the front yard holding a rifle or a shotgun. Warren couldn't tell. He didn't want to find out, and he didn't want Neva to know.

"They live like rats," Neva said, still disgusted and angry.

"They certainly live with them," Warren said.

"What?"

"Nothing. Did you see the walls?"

"All I could make out were shadows."

"Those shadows had legs. The biggest roaches I've ever seen."

Neva shuddered, thinking of what Mary Combs had said about knowing but not being able to do anything about it. Neva's thoughts took her to another place.

• • •

I thought I was being punished for what I had done. It was a sin, and all that was happening was God's retribution—first our father's death, then Jim's. I was so overwhelmed. Our father's death was the warning—one I failed to heed. I felt guilty, knowing I had been a part of it, though not directly. I didn't want to face what I had done. In some way, I enjoyed it, even encouraged it by not telling Jim to stop.

My loneliness for Jim became a physical ache, like a phantom pain in the amputated part of my life, and I mistook my longing for desire, that same desire I had hidden away and refused to acknowledge. I was angry that Jim had to die as a lesson to me, angry at myself for not making things right while he was alive. I wanted to punish myself, so I refrained from eating or bathing. I went so deep within myself, I didn't even notice my mother's depression until my uncle came one Sunday after services to see why we had not been attending.

"This place is like a dungeon," he said, opening the curtains in the living room.

My mother's voice called from the back of the house. "Spence? Is that you?" A weakened spirit from the other side.

"Yes, Margaret. Now get out of bed. I order you to get in here and talk to me this instant. It is time you re-entered the world of the living."

Mother made her way to the front of the house, clutching her robe over her breasts. She shielded her eyes from the harsh light chasing motes of dust around the furniture.

"My lord," Uncle Spencer exclaimed with a mournful gasp. "You both look like hell."

"There is no call for talk like that," Mother said. "You of all people should know better."

"Sometimes it is a pastor's calling to advise God about his wayward children, and there is no better way to express the seriousness of a matter than with language he understands."

I watched my mother's bent and tortured frame, the sallow texture of her skin, the matted strands of hair that fell in front of her vacant eyes as she groped her way past Uncle Spencer for a chair to support herself. The horror on my uncle's face fell away, replaced by sorrow and pity. From the way he studied us, I realized that my mother was just a mirrored image of myself.

"It's been three weeks since the funeral, Margaret. You can't continue to live like this. Have you even eaten?"

"Did you come here just to ridicule me, Spence? Is that God's answer to my problems? It's not enough that he has taken my husband and my son from me."

"Please, Margaret. I'm concerned about you. And Neva too. You have retreated from life, both of you, and I don't think what you are doing is right. If I have to force myself on you, I will."

"We can take care of ourselves."

"We all need God's help sometimes, Margaret. Let's talk. Make some of your good coffee, and we'll talk."

Mother went to the kitchen, and Uncle Spencer turned to me and held out both of his arms. "Come here, child," he said. I readily accepted his embrace and his offer, in a word, his comfort, to place me in his complete care and protection. "You know I love you, Neva. You know I want to help you get past your loneliness and grief." My head was against his chest, where I could smell a sweet perfume, and he was stroking the back of my hair. I felt myself starting to cry.

"I need help, Uncle Spencer," I said.

"That's why I'm here," he said. "Not to replace Jim or your father, but to help you hold on to their memory. To use that memory to make you stronger." My chest shook with the sobs. "Perhaps the best place to start is with a good cry," he said. I let loose while Uncle Spencer held me, and when I was through, he took my chin in his hand and held my face up to his. "That's a good beginning, Neva. I'm proud of you." His voice was soothing. "I want you to come to my office at the church after school, and we'll talk in private."

Through my sniffling, I told him that I would be okay. Uncle Spencer put his arm around my waist, and we walked into the kitchen, where mother was trying to remember how to make coffee. Before we crossed the threshold into the world of my mother's depression, he gave me an extra hug, and very quickly, his hand slipped up my side and pressed against my breast. I was confused and shocked, thinking that he had only gotten close to me to 'cop a feel,' as Jim used to say.

Uncle Spencer devoted the rest of the afternoon to my mother, and his attention to her was both sincere and respectful. I told myself that the whole incident was just an accidental slip of his hand. He must have chosen to ignore it rather than acknowledge it with an embarrassing apology.

Chapter Twelve

Dr. Mueller closed the curtains and locked the door. "There," he said. "Now you won't have to worry about someone watching or walking in unannounced."

Krista shifted nervously in her chair.

Dr. Mueller placed his black bag on the edge of the desk and smiled at Krista over the top of his glasses. "It's just a standard physical exam," he said. "You can leave on your underwear, but remove everything else."

Krista removed her shirt and shorts and left them on the chair. She sat on the desk where Dr. Mueller had placed a towel, crossed her legs, and folded her arms across her chest.

"Just relax," Dr. Mueller said as he began the exam, peering into her ears, eyes, nose, and mouth through small, lighted instruments. He then felt the sides of her neck and under her arms. Krista jumped when Dr. Mueller placed the stethoscope on her back. He apologized and warmed it in his hands. At his instruction, Krista breathed deeply while he moved the stethoscope around her back and chest. "Do you know how to check for lumps?" he asked.

"What?" Krista was confused.

"Lumps," Dr. Mueller repeated. "In your breasts. Here, I'll show you how." He grabbed Krista's right elbow and raised it over her head, placing her right hand at the back of her neck. "Pay close attention so you will be able to do this yourself." Dr. Mueller moved his fingers around on Krista's right breast, outlining small, spiral galaxies. He took her left hand and placed her fingers on her breast, guiding her back over the same motions. "It's a very easy examination, but it's important to do this about once a month. If you find a lump, it's important to get it checked out." Dr. Mueller guided Krista's right arm into her lap and her left elbow over her head to examine her left breast in the same manner. "It's important to catch these things before they become serious." He guided her left hand to her lap, where Krista clasped it tightly with her right.

Dr. Mueller placed his hand on Krista's legs and tapped her knees with a small rubber hammer. Her legs jerked under his touch. "Are you getting a regular period?" he asked.

It took Krista a moment to find her voice. She cleared her throat and muttered softly, "Yes."

Dr. Mueller completed his examination and sat down in a chair facing Krista. "I understand that yesterday you had quite a cathartic experience in your group session with Neva," he said.

Krista crossed her arms over her breasts. "I guess. They got me to talk about my grandfather, if that's what you mean." She looked puzzled. "Excuse me," she said. "Are you through? Can I put my clothes back on?"

"I still have a few more questions," Dr. Mueller said. "Does it make you nervous?"

Krista attempted to conceal herself. "A little, I mean, I know you're a doctor and everything, but . . ."

"You shouldn't be embarrassed," Dr. Mueller said. "You should feel comfortable with your body. You should never be ashamed of it. Let me ask you this. If someone you cared for a great deal, a boyfriend, touched you the way your grandfather touched you, would you have reacted the same way?"

"Of course not—not if I wanted him to touch me."

"What I am getting at is that this problem with your grandfather is an emotional one, not a physical one. Your body has not changed since this experience. Only your attitude has changed. Just a moment ago, as I touched you, it didn't bother you because of the circumstances. I am a doctor, and I was examining you. With other circumstances, your reaction would probably be different because your psyche has been wounded, as your trust in your grandfather was violated. The typical response would be to project this new defensive attitude onto all men, but this would be very damaging and would not allow you to develop a normal relationship with any man, even one you felt you were in love with. Understanding this is the first step in feeling at ease in a relationship."

"I don't think I have any problems with boys," Krista said.

"Do you remember the test I gave you when you first came to Morning House?"

"Yes."

"It was a personality test. It rated different parts of your personality, and one of those ratings said you like to be in control no matter what you are doing. Is this how you see yourself?"

"I don't know." Krista shrugged. She paused and then seemed to find herself in that moment of silence. "I don't really see anything wrong with it though."

"We all want to feel in control of our lives," Dr. Mueller said, "but it could be a problem if we feel we have to be in control of others, especially ones we have close relationships with."

"I don't know. I guess so, but I've always looked out for myself. It's the only way to make sure I get what I want. Isn't that what it's all about?"

"Sometimes it doesn't hurt to share."

"Can I get dressed now?"

"Yes, of course."

Krista slipped from the desk and began to put on her clothes as Dr. Mueller watched her patiently. "That didn't hurt now, did it," he asked, "being without your clothes?"

"No," Krista said, turning away to adjust her breasts in her bra.

"You seem to be very healthy, Krista," Dr. Mueller said. "Both physically and emotionally. You have positive self-esteem, which is good, but don't use it as a shield against future relationships. We all have chinks in our armor. Now and again, we have to make some necessary repairs. I would like to talk to you more about this next time."

Krista turned to leave, and Dr. Mueller asked her to tell Emily he was ready to see her. Krista was not in the mood to be a messenger for Emily's benefit. "I don't know if I can find her," she said. "If Alec is back, she'll probably be with him."

"Oh? Have they been seeing each other?"

Krista noticed his interest. "Yes. I thought you knew."

"Have they been alone? I mean, do you think they are getting serious about each other?"

"I don't know. Maybe," Krista said, twisting the word like a knife. She walked back to where Dr. Mueller was sitting. She stood in front of him, her bare leg close to his knee. "I could keep an eye on them for you if you want."

Dr. Mueller's knee trembled. "Thank you, Krista," he said. "I would appreciate that very much."

• • •

Warren saw the light flash across the kitchen window, a glare from the evening sun that always caught the windshield as Neva drove into her space at the rear of the house. Warren leaned toward the window enough to see without being noticed.

It wasn't Neva after all. A truck he didn't recognize had pulled up next to the toolshed. Randy got out of the passenger side and held the door open as Janeen got out. The driver exited the vehicle and walked around to the front of the truck. His yellow hair glowed with a flash of light as if his head were on fire. He grinned as he dug deep into his pocket and pulled out something, which he gave to Randy. They shook hands, not the way strangers or old men shake hands, but with thumbs hooked like close friends who share a secret. The boy pointed at Janeen, and Warren thought he heard him call her Angel. The boy seemed to be in a hurry as he got back into his truck and drove away.

Warren went back to helping Krista prepare dinner, but his mind replayed the exchange. If Neva were there, she would ask them about it immediately. He wondered why he hesitated to do the same.

Warren was chopping vegetables, and he didn't look up when they came through the door. "Who's your friend, Randy? You should have invited him in."

Randy frowned and glanced back toward the shed where he had been. He smiled. "He's not a friend. We know each other from work. He's just a guy who gave us a ride home."

Janeen stared at the floor, giving Warren the suspicion that she knew differently. "My mistake," Warren said. "When he gave you something and then you shook hands, it looked like you knew each other pretty well."

Randy turned his pockets inside out to show they were empty. "He didn't give me anything. He's just a guy. He gave us a ride because it was on his way. There's nothing wrong with him bringing us home, is there? We missed the bus, and he offered a ride, so we thought it was easier than calling you."

Warren looked at his watch. "No. There's nothing wrong. You could try to make it a little earlier, though."

"We had to work late. Like I said, we missed the bus."

Warren didn't know how to pursue the issue without outright calling Randy a liar, so he shrugged, as it wasn't a blatant violation of the rules. "How is your job?" he asked. "Are you two getting settled in?"

"Work is work," Randy said.

●　●　●

Emily and Janeen faced each other in the middle of the room. With nervous anticipation, their eyes met. They couldn't help but laugh. They turned away and tried again. They attempted to talk, but again, laughter erupted. Forming the simplest word was impossible. Emily bit her lip and looked toward the window, away from where Neva and Krista were sitting. Janeen looked down, covering her mouth with her hand.

"You can do this," Neva said. "Just remember that you're someone else. You have to become that other person."

Emily turned back, lowering her eyes. She tucked her hands between her legs as if she were going to curl up inside herself.

Emily was roleplaying Janeen.

Janeen played her own mother.

"Mom, I miss you," Emily said, still looking down at her lap.

Janeen looked up quickly. "I wouldn't say that."

"Emily can say whatever she wants," Neva said. "Just react to it; don't comment on it. Say what you think your *mother* would say if you *did* tell her that. Krista and I will give you our observations when you're through with the exercise."

Janeen signed, "Okay."

"Go ahead," Neva said. "That was a good start."

Emily took a deep breath and said, "I don't like working for that man. I want to stop, but I need your help."

"You know I can't do that," Janeen said.

"Why?"

"Your father won't allow it."

"But that man said he's going to do something to me if I tell. He said he would hurt me if I went to the cops. He scares me. I need your help," Emily said, a pleading tone in her voice.

"What do you want me to do?"

"Don't let me go."

"It's not that easy. I can't go against your father. You know I can't handle these things. Why can't you just leave me out of it?" Janeen mimicked a frustrated voice.

"You're my mother, that's why! Why can't it be just you and me again? I want a mother, someone to do things with, someone to talk to when I have problems, someone to hold me when I need to . . ."

"Because," Janeen interrupted. "You ruined that."

Emily frowned. "Is that why you left me there? I was being punished? All I wanted was for you to come back and get me."

Janeen shaded her eyes for a moment with her hands. She placed them back into her lap. She looked at the ceiling in agony. "I'm sorry. We needed the money. Your father can't work. He said it was helping out the family, you being there and all."

"It's not my fault. I didn't ask for any of it."

"You could have stopped anytime on your own."

"No, I couldn't. He would have come after me. I needed help. Why didn't you just help me?"

"Your father would have gone to jail, that's why. That's why he told you to keep it a secret."

Krista and Neva looked at each other, puzzled, as if searching for the right place in the script to interrupt.

"I need you, Mother," Emily said. "I need to know that you love me. I'm just a kid. I need someone to take care of me. I need to feel loved."

"Well, that's what you got."

"I didn't want it that way. I wanted *you* to hold me. I wanted to be like all the other kids. I wanted to feel normal."

"You're making too much of this. You're always upsetting the applecart."

"But I was afraid. I didn't want to do it. I needed help."

"You know your father. He wouldn't listen to me. You know how he can be. I suspected what he was doing, going into your room all the time. He said he was going to check on you, but I knew different. I knew, but I couldn't stop him. I knew that, so I guess I just didn't try. It was easier to look away than have it mess up all our lives."

Emily blinked as if coming out of a trance. She, too, now looked puzzled.

"Don't act so innocent," Janeen said. Her eyes narrowed as if staring through Emily. "I know you really didn't mind. It's not like he was the only one. At least I knew he wasn't going outside the family."

"What?" Emily asked, with real hurt in her voice.

"And if I had told, it would have ruined everything. He would have left. We would have been alone. I can't work. We would have all been out on the street. Did you want that for your little brother? It was easier to just let it happen."

"Janeen?" Emily said.

"No!" Janeen screamed. Her eyes were now full of tears, and she screamed at the ceiling. "Don't let him near me again. He told me when I was locked up that if I told anyone about what he did, he would hurt me. He's an evil man, and I hate him for what he did, and I hate you, too, because you just let him do it to me. I hate you both."

"Janeen?" Neva asked, getting up and taking Janeen by the shoulders.

Janeen was tense and frozen, with tears streaming down her face, staring without any sense of what was around her. She took several deep breaths until her muscles relaxed and her breathing returned to normal, and her eyes cleared with the recognition that Emily and Neva were standing over her. "You were right," Janeen said. "I have so much inside, and I'm afraid to let it out, but I know I need to."

Neva pushed back a strand of Janeen's hair that had fallen into her eyes. "You're safe here, Janeen. Take your time."

"I need to say it," Janeen said. "I need to tell you that my father made me do awful things to him. Awful things. Oh God, please don't tell. I'm so ashamed." She sat still for a moment, while the others stood around her, and she cried into her hands, unearthing the sorrow and despair and anger like heavy rocks and thick roots that had kept her buried alive.

• • •

Broadway was an ancient street in Galveston with a long row of three-story mansions that loomed out of the sidewalk like gargoyles, crusty and dark, with iron fences and verandas as wide as the road. Alec guided his motorcycle cautiously as he marveled at these relics. He followed the boulevard until it met the seawall at Stewart Beach, where girls in string bikinis walked undaunted down the street, past drive-in restaurants and surf shops and bicycle rentals. Alec saw the pier, where couples dressed in white strolled the boardwalk out to the Flagship Hotel and its view of the Gulf of Mexico, heavy with foam and a thick smell of salt. Beyond the pier, curio shops held colorful souvenirs, hanging like ripe fruit from the windows and awnings. Alec pulled his motorcycle to the curb, drawn like a child to the sparkle and wonder of a rainbow.

This summer was going to be a hot one. Neva felt it. Spending the day at the beach would be good for everyone. After all, the past week had been difficult, and they deserved a break. She wanted to take some of the pressure off. At dinner the night before, no one spoke, not until Neva suggested it. Going to the beach was Neva's first successful effort at bringing everyone together without a single complaint.

They were waiting on Alec. There would be no lunch, no volleyball, and no rides up the strand until he arrived. Neva reluctantly allowed Alec to ride his motorcycle to Galveston, but she emphatically refused to allow anyone to ride with him on the highway. Alec said he had to run by the garage first to finish up something. Neva didn't like the idea, but she had to show she trusted him. Especially now. Detective Kelly had called last night to tell Neva about another robbery in the area. She knew that Alec was getting his motorcycle driver's license at the time the robbery was supposed to have occurred. She was relieved until Detective Kelly told her that the time wasn't exact. The clerk hadn't reported the robbery right away. He claimed he had been tied up, but Detective Kelly thought the clerk's story was suspicious, so he wasn't sure of the exact time that the store was robbed. It could have been just before Alex was getting his license or just after.

"His alibi isn't any good," Detective Kelly told Neva.

"You still can't talk to him," Neva said, "so you better come up with some evidence."

Neva told Alec that they would be on West Beach near the jetties. Warren had set up the grill and was lighting the charcoal. Neva had spread out several old blankets and anchored them at the corners with all their discarded shoes. She placed the cooler with the drinks at the convergence of the blankets so no one would have to walk far when the sand got hot.

Spinner, Janeen, and Randy were setting up the volleyball net in the soft sand, and Krista was lying on a towel near the surf, propped on her elbows, reading a Vogue magazine, her back to the sun, one foot swaying capriciously from the bend of her knee. Emily was walking in the surf, occasionally stopping to dig for small, colorful shells that lay hidden beneath the surface of the wet sand.

The beach was getting crowded as families set up picnic spots, and groups of teenagers walked up and down the strand. Alec was late, and this was bothering Neva as she stopped at the barbecue grill to check the fire.

"I think I know who Bubba is," Warren said.

"What?" Neva asked, startled out of her thoughts.

"Alec's dream. The Bubba from Alec's dream. I think it's Randy."

Neva gave Warren an incredulous look. "Why would you think that?"

"A few nights ago, Randy and Janeen were dropped off at the house by this boy. I heard him call Randy Bubba, and he called Janeen Angel. It was like they had known each other a long time."

"That must be a coincidence."

"Why? We know Alec and Randy knew each other before they came to Morning House. It's not as far-fetched as you think."

"Who was this boy . . . the one you saw with Randy and Janeen?"

"I don't know. I asked Randy, and all he'd say is that they work together. Randy was being evasive, which made me suspicious. I just don't trust him."

"Maybe he doesn't trust us either. We still need to try to reach him somehow. Maybe we just need to ask Alec." Neva guarded her eyes from the sun and stared down the beach, where she heard a faint hum. Alec rode toward them across the hard sand. The air around him glistened. Neva narrowed her eyes and smiled.

Alec was almost upon them when he accelerated, and the front wheel came up off the sand. He roared by, causing Krista, who had not seen him, to shriek and hide her face in her Vogue magazine. When the front wheel came down, Alec skidded to a stop, spinning around to where he was facing them again, the back wheel fanning out a fine spray of wet sand.

"He just got to be a cowboy," Spinner said.

Alec got off the motorcycle, which was now still and silent. His smile was innocent and boyish. Neva couldn't bring herself to spoil the moment by getting mad at him for being reckless. Krista was capable enough, chastising Alec with a slap on his arm. "That's for scaring me," she said.

"You gonna let her get away with that?" Randy asked.

"I'll let her think that for now," Alec teased.

"That was quite a stunt," Warren said. "When did you learn to ride like that?"

"Just now, right here." Alec laughed. "It was an accident. I didn't mean to punch it so hard."

"In that case," Neva said, "you're lucky no one got hurt."

"Cowboy looked like he knew what he was doing," Spinner said. "That's what counts."

"It doesn't matter that he could have killed me?" Krista complained.

"No," Spinner taunted. "Well, I guess it would've made a mess on the beach. We'd have to move to another spot."

Krista slapped Spinner on the arm.

"Why don't you show us how good you really are, hot shot," Randy said. "Try jumping those dunes over there. I've got a sawbuck that says you'll chicken out."

"Where you gettin' money to place bets like that?" Spinner asked.

"Tips have been real good at the hardware store," Randy said. "Anyway, this is a sure thing."

"I think you can do it," Krista cooed. "I'll take back what I said if you jump it for me, Alec."

"Save your money," Neva said. "It's a safer bet if you put it in the bank."

"Let me at least check it out," Alec said. "I promise I won't do anything stupid. The dunes look too soft to jump anyway."

Neva's look said she disapproved, but Alec somehow knew she didn't really mean it. He took the saddlebag off the motorcycle and handed it to Spinner. The motorcycle started up quickly, and Alec rode back along the edge of the dunes toward an opening where the road entered the beach. He swerved the motorcycle up and down the dunes several times, each time testing the sand farther up than the time before.

"I don't like this," Neva said to Warren.

"Don't worry," Warren said. "If the sand is too soft, that'll be his way out of the bet."

Alec drove slowly over the top of the dunes and down the other side. He was almost to the opening of the road when he turned and headed back down the other side. He tested the sand again, nearly reaching the top before he returned to the road and headed back toward the opening.

Krista looked disappointed. "He's coming back."

"I knew it," Randy said smugly.

Neva smiled at Warren, who shrugged complacently. "Okay, how about we choose sides for volleyball," Warren said. "Take out your aggressions on the court."

"I hate choosing sides," Neva said. "It reeks of favoritism."

"That's the argument of everyone who is picked last." Warren laughed.

Alec reached the opening in the dunes, then slowly turned around and raced down the road along the dunes.

"He's gonna jump," Spinner said.

"Alec, no!" Neva screamed.

It was too late. Alec had already swerved off the road, and before Neva could bring her hand up to cover her eyes, he was upon the dunes, then in the air. The front wheel twisted to an angle that would have flipped the motorcycle in the sand, but Alec was able to straighten it just before he landed. The motorcycle wriggled through the sand like a rodeo bull trying to throw its rider. The tires dug in and lurched forward, clearing the dunes.

"You better cough up that sawbuck," Spinner said to Randy.

"Hell no," Randy said. "He didn't bet. He said he was just going to check out the sand."

Spinner started forward until Warren checked him with a look. "Okay, let's forget it," Warren said.

Alec pulled up grinning. Spinner came up and held out his hand. Alec slapped it, and Spinner slapped Alec's. "I got to hand it to you, cowboy," Spinner said, "that was pretty slick."

Randy stepped in front of the motorcycle and kicked the tire. "Well, I guess you're not the wimp you used to be. You should've bet."

Alec let it go. "Coming from you," he said, "that's better than taking your money."

Neva watched from a distance, hearing Randy's words and remembering something else from Alec's dream. She was almost sure that Warren was right.

"I knew you could do it," Krista said, "and this is to make up for slapping you." She put her arms around his neck and kissed him on the cheek. Her lips were warm and wet, and her skin smelled sweet. Alec could feel her ample breasts press against his arm. They were soft and full, and when she backed away, he could still feel the sensation. Alec couldn't look at her; he couldn't move. He thought he heard Spinner say something that got Krista mad again, but it was all like a small echo in his head.

Warren grabbed the volleyball and tossed it up in the air. "All right," he said excitedly, "it's time to get down to some serious volleyball. How about the boys against the girls? Losers do all the chores tomorrow. We'll even spot you five points."

"Not that I'm afraid of the challenge," Neva said, "but why don't we just play for fun?"

"Okay, how about this," Warren said. "Me, Randy, Emily, and Janeen against you, Alec, Spinner, and Krista."

"Oh my god," Neva said. "Where is Emily?"

Alec looked around, but just then, Krista grabbed his arm and pulled him toward the volleyball net. "Would you give me a ride later?" she coaxed. "I've never been on a motorcycle before."

"She never gives up," Warren whispered to Neva.

"That's where we women get our strength," Neva said as she pushed Warren from behind. Then, she teased loudly, "Enemy spy in our territory! Get over there on your own side." Warren planted a foot in the thick sand, which stopped his momentum and caused Neva's hands to slip around his waist until she was up against his back. She had to hug him to keep from falling.

"You two get a room," Spinner said. "You're setting a bad example for the children."

"She can't help herself," Warren said.

"Get out of here," Neva said, kicking sand at Warren's legs. "You're in for a good thrashing now. Come on, team, let's plan our strategy."

Janeen came back with Emily, who glanced shyly at Alec through the veil of the net. He smiled and waved, and she smiled back. Then, Emily darted to her shoes on the sand and placed a small bundle under one of the tongues. Warren could still feel the warmth of Neva's hands wrapped around his waist, which engendered a moment of fantasy.

They played one game while the barbecue fire was getting hot and one more while the hamburgers were cooking. A fierce competition quickly developed between Spinner and Randy, who always came up to the net at the same time. When Janeen set up a spike for Randy, Spinner was right there to block it, and when Neva set up a spike for Spinner, Randy's hand was almost always on the ball before Spinner's. Some of the drives got through on both sides, and by the time lunch was ready, each team had won one game. They had all decided to have a big playoff game after lunch, but by the time they finished eating, everyone was too full to play, so they sat on the beach while Krista studied the young boys who walked by and gazed at her. She concealed her eyes with sunglasses and didn't smile no matter how much they smiled at her. Janeen giggled and pointed out the ones she thought were cute.

Randy made suggestive remarks to girls walking by, such as "What a pair!" when two girls walked together, or "Paint two hands on that butt, so you can wave goodbye next time," and to one who wore a string bikini, he called out loudly, "Shake that thing, baby!"

Spinner told him to can it, and everyone agreed.

"I'm just having fun," Randy insisted.

"You're cramping my style," Spinner said.

"You don't have a style for me to cramp," Randy said.

Alec turned to Emily, who sat next to him on the sand, and asked if she wanted to ride down to the jetties with him. Overhearing that, Krista gave Alec a reproachful look, then turned back to a group of approaching boys.

"Oh my," she cooed, nudging Janeen, "how would you like to have that hard body on top of you," and Janeen giggled, more at being included by Krista than by the implication of her remark.

"Yes, I'd like to go with you," Emily whispered, glancing over at Krista. "But let me get something first." Emily retrieved the bundle in her shoe, slid onto the motorcycle behind Alec, and put her arms around his waist. It only took a minute to reach the jetty, but she wanted it to last forever, feeling the warmth of his body against her cheek, the tenseness in the muscles of his stomach under his shirt. Emily let the wind sting her eyes and sweep through her hair as she pressed her cheek against his neck.

When they stopped, Alec pulled a bag out of the pouch on his motorcycle, and they climbed up the rocks and walked down the jetty, where fishermen crouched beside their poles, waiting for the lines to twitch with activity in the strong surf.

Emily spoke first. "You know, what you did back there, jumping over those sand dunes, that was very brave."

"It was just dumb luck. I really wasn't showing off."

"I was afraid you were going to fall."

"Yeah, me too. I was scared a little, but I had to do it. If I didn't, everyone would think I'm a coward."

"That's silly; you shouldn't care what others think."

They turned toward each other and said in unison, "I've got something for you."

They both laughed, and Alec handed her the bag he had been holding. "Oh, wait a minute," Emily said. She took a folded napkin out of the larger bundled napkin and placed it into Alec's hand.

"It's so light," Alec said.

"It's not very fancy," she said.

"I didn't mean anything by it. It doesn't matter."

Emily opened the bag and gasped when she saw the pale pink shell. She held it up in the palm of her hand, holding it up like an offering. "It's very pretty. I've never seen one like it before."

"You can hear the sea if you put it to your ear."

She held it to her ear and frowned as if she was having trouble hearing the person on the other end of a telephone.

"I guess you have to wait until you're not sitting right next to the ocean before it works right," Alec said.

"But I love it," Emily said, smiling broadly. "I will always be able to remember this moment now when I hear the sea in the shell." She held it to her ear again and covered her other ear. "I can hear," she said excitedly. "It sounds so far away, and yet it sounds like another world right here inside this shell."

Alec opened the folded napkin and held up the delicate white disc that lay on the napkin like a jewel on a velvet pillow.

"It's a sand dollar," Emily said. "I found it while I was looking for shells."

"Can you buy anything with it?" Alec asked.

"You're silly. What if I said that maybe you could?"

"It's wonderful," Alec said. "Whatever it could buy must be very special." He held it closer. "These markings, see how they come together? It looks like a flower or a star. How do you suppose it got there?"

"I don't know. It might have been there in the sand a long time, just waiting for me to find it."

"I suppose that would make it lucky. Why would you want to give it away?"

"It has already been lucky for me. I want it to be lucky for you now."

Alec smiled. "Maybe it will be lucky for both of us." He took a deep breath of warm salty air and stared out at the gulf water, dark under the glistening surface, splashing nervously against the rocks.

"A penny for your thoughts," Emily said.

"I was thinking how good it would feel to get on that motorcycle and just ride off and keep on riding. Have you ever felt like doing something like that? You know, just take off and look for something better."

"It sounds scary, but I would do it with you," Emily said shyly.

"You would?" Alec sounded surprised.

Emily smiled, then looked down at the other bundle that she still held. "I also found these," she said, opening the napkin. Tiny, colorful shells sparkled like a broken rainbow in her hand. "They were all under the sand, where people walk and don't even notice they're there. Isn't it funny how something so small and insignificant can be so pretty?"

"They look so alive," Alec said. "Maybe they're lucky too."

"You have to make a wish on these," Emily said and tossed the shells into the water. They disappeared quickly in the surf. "Did you make a wish?" she asked.

"I can't tell you. If I do, it won't come true."

"I won't tell you my wish either, then, but I bet they're the same."

Alec laughed and took Emily's hand as they returned to the motorcycle. They put the shell and the sand dollar in the pouch and rode back down the beach to where the others were waiting.

Emily got off, and Alec asked if anyone else wanted a ride. Krista didn't turn around. Spinner wanted to give Janeen a ride, and Alec said it would be okay. Neva didn't like the motorcycle business, but Warren calmed her down by assuring them that they'd stay on the sand. He told them not to take a long ride because the playoff game was about to start. Spinner and Janeen rode off toward the jetty and returned a short time later.

Janeen clung to Spinner's back and wouldn't open her eyes until he turned off the motorcycle. Even then, he had to pry her hands loose to free himself from her grip. "Crazy white girl." Spinner laughed. "The way you was screaming, you'd think I was riding through fire." He helped her off the motorcycle, and for a moment, she fell limply into his arms, laughing at herself and pleading with him to forgive her.

The volleyball game started up again with Warren expressing the most excitement. He said he would serve because they had lost the last game, so Randy took a position at the net, and Spinner quickly set up across from him. The score was even to the last remaining points, when Spinner and Randy came up to the net again. Neva returned Warren's serve to the back, where Emily hit a weak volley toward the net. It was too low, so when Janeen tried to set it up for Randy, she hit the ball too hard, and it went too high. By the time it came down, Spinner was at the net to block the ball, and it fell at Randy's feet.

Randy turned angrily to Janeen. "You'd think by now you'd know how to hit the damn ball right."

"I'm sorry," Janeen said. "I tried . . ."

"You're just too stupid," Randy said.

"Lay off her," Spinner said.

"You'll stay out of this if you know what's good for you," Randy said, pointing at Spinner through the net.

"That's enough!" Neva said, coming up to the net. "This is just a game. Try to remember that, Randy."

They went back to play. Krista served down the line to Emily, who could not get to the ball, which put Neva's team one point away from winning. Krista served again, and this time, Warren returned the ball to Alec, who volleyed it to the net, and Neva set it up for Spinner. The ball was high above the net when Spinner went up, aiming for the open sand behind Janeen. He didn't see Randy come across with a sweeping arm that brought down the net, and he caught Spinner on the ear, sending him backward into the sand, but not before the ball had sailed over and rolled up to Janeen's feet.

Spinner came back up with a fistful of sand, which he tossed into Randy's eyes. He had pulled back a fist, ready to unleash it on Randy's jaw when Warren called out for him to stop. Spinner's rage was suddenly trapped inside his clinched fists and his taut muscles. When he brought his hand forward, he just pointed at Randy.

"You just went too far," he said. "You think you can bully everyone around, but now it's time you learn a little humility."

Randy wiped the sand from his eyes. "I'll be happy to settle this however you want," he said.

"Anyplace, anytime," Spinner said.

Warren stepped between them. "The only way we are going to settle this is by sitting down and talking it out," he said.

Spinner continued to stare at Randy. "Sometimes that just ain't good enough, Mr. Mac."

Neva slipped under the net and stared up at Randy. "I want to talk with you right now, before any of this goes any further," she said.

The others walked off toward the beach.

"Does anyone want to go for a swim?" Alec asked.

"I think the party's over," Krista said. "What I really want is a cigarette."

"Oh, come on," Alec said. "We *did* win the game. We need to celebrate." He nodded at Spinner, who came up on the other side of Krista.

Krista looked at them and realized what they were up to. She squealed, "Oh, no you don't," and started to run. "Get away from me!"

Alec caught up to her and grabbed her around the waist, and Spinner lifted her legs. She wiggled and kicked and shrieked as they carried her into the surf, counted to three, and tossed her into the water. Krista came up screaming, madder than an angry cat.

Chapter Thirteen

Neva felt aristocratic and decadent, strolling in the warm evening air, in the surreal city lights, with a delicate grasp on her sequined purse, her hair pinned in a French braid to expose the slender length of her neck. Her sensible smile acknowledged the other women who passed beneath the lofty colonnade, women with bare shoulders and low necklines adorned with simple strands of pearls or diamonds. Neva felt beautiful, more beautiful than she had felt in a long time, as she lifted her skirt to climb the maroon-carpeted steps. Her heart leaped as the joyous, discordant sounds of the gathering crowd drifted out over Jones Hall lobby.

Carl Mueller waved to someone on the balcony as he took a program from an usher, then escorted Neva to the landing. "I want to show you off," he said. "You don't mind, do you?"

"Would you prefer I cling to you like an ornament or just walk several paces behind?"

"Please, Neva. I support the ERA. I'm just a bit overwhelmed, you see. You look so lovely tonight, and I confess, I'm feeling proud."

"Well, I guess you're off the hook for now, but I must warn you that I have a difficult time responding to conditional flattery." Neva noticed the bewilderment in his contemplation. "If I accept your compliment," she explained, "then I am forced to forgive your innuendo. That's part of the feminine mystique."

Carl Mueller let out a hearty laugh. "I knew I hired you because you were smart, but I didn't know it would backfire on me."

When Carl Mueller introduced her to Harry Harwood, Neva recognized the name, a well-known Houston defense attorney who mesmerized judges and juries into letting murderers go free, a man who accepted millions in retainer fees from willing clients. She was amazed that Harry Harwood was a man not half as big as his reputation. Even with his pock-marked, but charming, grin, Harry Harwood had managed to attract a beautiful, blue-eyed, blond wife nearly half his age, perhaps only slightly older than Neva, which made her wonder where the original Mrs. Harwood was—if there was one. The new Mrs. Harwood carried herself with the dignity befitting Harry's reputation— and the accoutrements befitting his income. From the Stuart Weitzman pumps to the Pat Sandler beaded gown, she wore more than a month of Neva's annual salary.

When Jeanette Harwood placed her hand on her husband's shoulder, laughing at one of his crude jokes, the light reflected through the ostentatious diamond she displayed on her arched finger. Neva felt herself slip into an abyss of weakness, turning on Carl Mueller's profile with the scrutinizing possibility of it being a permanent fixture in her future. Where was this night leading?

"I really admire what you're doing with those kids at Morning House," Jeanette Harwood said to Neva. "It's so foreign to me. You know, I've often thought of adopting a child, one of those precious babies from Peru you see in the commercials, but I don't think I could deal with all the problems on top of the simple adjustments that must come with that type of thing. You must have to face that every day."

"I don't think you would ever encounter that, unless you plan on moving to Peru," Neva said. Realizing this might be taken as an insult, she laughed and added, "Do you have children of your own?"

"Well, yes, but that's quite something altogether different, isn't it? I was speaking more of those less fortunate who have nowhere to turn and only end up disrupting the system. What you see must be very depressing."

"Not really," Neva said. "I enjoy the work—and the kids. They both can be very rewarding. It is true that less fortunate kids have different ways of dealing with problems, but emotional trauma is just as demanding whether a child can afford one of Carl's private sessions or has to work things out living at Morning House."

Jeanette Harwood smiled sympathetically but said nothing.

"Knowing that I'll never get rich doing what I'm doing is a little depressing, though," Neva quipped.

It seemed that old Harry Harwood was paying attention after all. His roar of laughter drowned out Carl Mueller's polite chuckle. "You come see me, Neva, dear," Harry said. "I think you have a good case of equal pay for equal work on your hands."

"You have a conflict of interest, remember, Harry," Carl Mueller said. "As a board member, you would be suing yourself."

Harry Harwood let out another storm of laughter, which seemed to cause the house lights to flicker portentously. Neva's nervous reaction was to run for cover. Jeanette Harwood unceremoniously handed Harry her champagne glass, which he set on the railing next to his own.

Neva felt herself become a part of the parade again, as Carl Mueller took her arm and escorted her through the doors. She was filled with awe at the grandeur but remained silent, thinking that any comment would reveal her as an intruder in this world where she didn't belong.

The concertmaster entered, and the applause broke her thoughts, which fluttered away on the rise and fall of the A note of the tuning orchestra. The lights dimmed, and the spotlight guided the conductor to his place in the pit, where he bowed to acknowledge the applause. During a moment of breathless silence, Neva remembered why she accepted Carl Mueller's invitation in the first place, as the elegance and charm and fantasy suddenly unfolded on the stage before her.

Driving back to Morning House, after praising the ballet and reminiscing about how magnificent the performances of Cynthia Gregory and Rudolf Nureyev had been, Neva mused, "Do you think art interprets life or just romanticizes it?"

Carl Mueller thought for a minute and said, "Probably both. Art is certainly more demonstrative."

"How's that?"

"I doubt that people really say and do all the things that playwrights and novelists and librettists have them say and do."

"I suppose not, but we certainly think like them, or at least we would like our thoughts and deeds to be like those in novels and plays. I believe that sometimes we act out our thoughts, but somehow, the result is always different, not as romantic. Art is more tolerable."

"Fantasy is usually a good thing, as long as it doesn't get out of control. It can help us soften some of the hardships of life."

"Then, there are people like Jeanette Harwood, who can purchase life and keep it at a safe distance, like Peru. She lives what some only fantasize—and fantasizes what others are forced to live."

"You're not being fair."

"You're just defending your friends. I'm being realistic."

Carl Mueller stopped the car in front of Morning House in the fading yellow glow of the porch light. Neva had started to open the car door when he took her hand. "You know, it could be that *your* fantasy is right in front of you," he said.

Neva thought to ask what that was. In the dim light his eyes appeared searching and forlorn.

"But you just won't allow yourself to experience it," he added.

Neva laughed softly as she gently slipped her hand out from under Carl Mueller's, then pushed back the hair at the side of her face, even though it didn't need it. "Fantasy and romance are only in the imagination. The age of computers has seen to that. People are too much in love with money to be in love with each other. Rhett Butler and Scarlett O'Hara are gone with the wind."

Carl Mueller groaned.

"Okay," Neva said, "bad example. How about Catherine and Heathcliff?"

"You can't mean what you're saying . . . about love, I mean."

"Oh, but I do."

"Even a stuffed shirt like myself can fall in love."

"I'll wager you that most men can't tell the difference between physical love and romantic love."

"I would win that bet, Neva, because I have fallen in love with you."

She was quiet for a long moment. "This is getting complicated. Our relationship was easier to understand when it was based solely on our work."

"I think it can survive totally separate from work."

"Maybe it could if our work was different, if we were teachers or actors or farmers, but not a psychiatrist and a psychologist. We will always be analyzing each other, picking at each other's subconscious."

"Not if we practice what we preach." Carl Mueller leaned across the plush leather of his Lincoln Continental and kissed Neva on the mouth, pressing her against the seat so that when she grabbed him, he thought it was her passion, and when she moaned, he thought it was her pleasure. Finally, she was able to turn away and gasp for air.

"Stop!" Neva screamed.

Carl Mueller was stunned. "I'm sorry. I don't know what came over me. Here I am acting like a child who can't even control his own libido. Please forgive me."

"Something's wrong here. I think we should stop seeing each other, except at work, of course."

"Let me explain, please. I want you desperately, Neva. I have for a long time, and with the romance of the night, well I guess I got the wrong message."

"There was no message."

"Why did you go out with me if you weren't the least bit interested?"

"Why is it that men feel a woman must put out to pay them back for a nice evening out?"

"I didn't mean that you had to put out. There were no obligations. Just now, I strictly acted on impulse—on my feelings, and I regret that now. I apologize. I just thought that if you knew my feelings, then maybe you would feel the same."

"You are just like every man, Dr. Mueller, unable to control your own libido and your fantasies about women."

Neva got out of the car and slammed the door. She had started up the steps when Carl Mueller called after her. She turned around, ready to fend him off, but he was standing next to the open driver's door.

"I'm only human, Neva."

"That excuse is overrated and overused to justify bad behavior. The problem is that someone always gets hurt. We have a whole house full of kids who are victims of someone's bad behavior, and no one has been held responsible." Neva then hurried inside before Carl Mueller had a chance to respond, shutting the door behind her.

A light was on in the stairwell. It was just a little thing, but Neva was already in a bad mood. This type of carelessness was inexcusable. She stopped in the hallway when she heard voices. Neva checked her watch. It was midnight. *When the cat's away.* Warren had been reliable up to now. But she had never been away this long before—and never at night. Two shadows stretched over the floor and out into the hall. Neva stepped around the corner, pinning the shadows and the two figures they cast in surprised immobility. Alec and Krista stood silent on the stairs.

"What are you two doing up?" Neva whispered angrily.

"Krista's hallucinating," Alec said, managing a smile.

"I thought I heard someone," Krista explained.

"It was probably just me," Neva said. "Now, get back upstairs. You know this is against the rules."

A muffled sound came from the office, and Neva turned as a clear groan came in answer. Krista looked toward the office, then back to Neva. "See? I told you I heard something. I tried to get Warren," she said, "but he didn't answer his door. That's when I got Alec."

Neva turned back to the door to the office and leaned in closer. There was silence, then a small, female voice. "I'm sorry," it said. "I didn't know . . ."

Neva opened the door quickly and flicked on the light.

Warren was on the sofa, trying to sit up. Something held him in a suspended state between sitting and lying down. His movements were sluggish and weak. He was swimming in a viscous cloud, unable to hold his head right enough to focus on them. He attempted to shield his eyes from the sudden, harsh light.

Emily was trapped in the final moment of backing away from the sofa where Warren was struggling with his equilibrium. When she stopped, she stared at the floor as if waiting to disappear.

Neva saw the scene in a counterclockwise motion, beginning with Warren's apoplectic struggle, ticking through the scattered beer cans on the floor, to Emily's bare feet and legs, and ending with the teddy Emily was wearing. Inside, Neva's patience ended with the explosive abruptness of an alarm clock at three in the morning.

"I don't believe this," Neva said. "I really don't believe what I am seeing."

As if in another time zone, Warren followed the same clockwise motion from Emily to the beer cans to Neva, squinting in confusion. "What the . . . are you . . . time," he muttered incoherently.

"I want everyone out," Neva said. She turned, but Alec was already gone. Neva told Krista and Emily to go to their separate bedrooms. She would talk with them in the morning. Krista smirked at Emily, then walked away.

Emily started to cry. Slowly, she walked past Neva, her head down, as if walking past a strange dog that might lunge with bared teeth at any moment, sensing more than watching.

"You can save those tears for tomorrow," Neva said. "That should give you enough time to come up with a good story." When Emily was gone, Neva walked over to Warren, who was now sitting upright on the sofa, his head in his hands. "You're drunk, aren't you?" she asked in a way that was more a statement of fact than a question she needed to confirm.

"Very," Warren said.

"That alone is enough to get you fired, but how could you be so stupid as to be down here with Emily?"

"What?" Warren squinted up at Neva.

"Getting fired will be the least of your problems. If I can prove that you touched Emily to get off on your cheap little thrills, I'll have you arrested."

Warren suddenly looked very sober. "What are you talking about?"

"You know damn well what I'm talking about. Now get out of here." Warren stood up and started to address Neva, but she cut him off. "Get out!" she screamed.

Warren stopped in the doorway. "This is not what you think it is," he said.

Neva remained silent, looking away, holding back the alarm that was about to go off again. With his head throbbing, Warren made his way up the stairs and across the landing to his bedroom. Neva, downstairs, exploded with angry tears, thinking about what she had long tried to put out of her mind.

His office walls were dark and smooth, cold and wooden, grained with dark rivers flowing through the panels from floor to ceiling. Against one wall was a hat tree where he hung his robes, and next to that was a leather sofa. Above the sofa, the wall was bare except for a simple, beautiful cross. Another whole wall was nothing but books, large, leather-bound tomes of ecclesiastical thought where I was sure he researched his sermons or pondered the moral justification for the tragedies brought to him daily by members of his congregation. I imagined Uncle Spencer a brooding intellectual.

"God took Jim away from me." I told him just like that, and it took him by surprise, I could tell, but I knew that was the only way I was going to be able to get it out. Gradually, I could see his eyes come to some recognition of the significance of what I had said.

"We mustn't blame God for Jim's death," he said. "That's not the way God works. He may have called Jim for a higher purpose, but he didn't take Jim to hurt you."

I started to cry, not uncontrollably, just very slowly, the tears sliding down my cheeks and into my mouth, not out of my sadness, but more because the tears inside of me just didn't have any more room, and they had gone somewhere. "I am trying to understand, I really am, because the bible teaches us that God is good, but it also teaches us to fear God, and you said yourself that God might have taken Jim for a higher cause. Well, if he can take Jim for a good reason, then he can also take Jim to punish him—or me."

"God is very mysterious, I agree, but maybe we shouldn't try too hard to understand his reasons. Sometimes things just happen, and we have to learn and grow and be stronger."

"But Jim and I did things. We thought it was harmless at the time, but now I think maybe that's why Jim died. I'm being punished, you see, for what we did."

Uncle Spencer wanted me to tell him everything. Drawing his body up from the slump in his chair, he said I should never blame myself, that the guilt stemmed not from Jim's death, but from an uneasiness about my sexual enlightenment. Uncle Spencer wanted every detail about what Jim and I had done. Getting it out in the open was important, he said, cathartic and healthy.

And I believed Uncle Spencer, even when he moved from his chair and sat down next to me on his studded, leather-bound sofa, where all I could see was the framed photograph of his wife and children on his desk. Even when he gave me avuncular hugs of assurance—hugs that became caresses, then kisses on the top of my head, then on my cheek as he told *me he loved me. Even when Uncle Spencer put his hand on my knee and told me he would tell my mother what I had done with Jim if I didn't let him show me how much he loved me.*

• • •

Planned for three rounds, which would have been enough to settle any score, the bout only went two. Not even one and a half really, and that was only because Spinner let Randy use up the best part of his energy in the first round.

Randy charged like a bull out of the chute, his head lowered deep between his shrugging shoulders. At ringside, audible breaths puffed from his nostrils. Clumsily, he copied Gerrie Coetzee's form, how he had seen it on closed-circuit television, attempting to make it a boxing match instead of a brawl.

Warren had asked for that—it had to be a fair fight. "We want to prove that we can get our differences behind us," Warren said. "Expend all this unwanted hostility because no one needs negative energy. I want each of you to come out of this with some dignity."

Randy danced around first, much the same way he danced that day on the lawn when everyone had taken a break from painting the house. He rolled to his left with a bucking hop as if his legs and arms were receiving different signals from his brain. When Spinner stopped and laughed at him, Randy charged in with his arms flailing, swinging with abandon, right, left, right. Spinner bobbed and weaved, successfully avoiding all of Randy's efforts, then ducked under a roundhouse and came out behind Randy, gliding across the pad in a fluid motion. He waved a 'come on' for Randy to try again, taunting with the same psychological tactic made famous by Muhammad Ali. This only got Randy more irritated, which was Spinner's goal.

Warren watched from ringside with an amused interest. Alec had given him the idea the previous afternoon, but it didn't flower until just before two in the morning. Alec had been sitting in the dayroom with a book of poems by Dylan Thomas. "That's pretty heady stuff," Warren said. "What happened to *The Lord of the Rings*?"

This is schoolwork," Alec said, "and I don't understand any of it."

"Are you aware that there is no school tomorrow? Teacher training day, I think. And if we don't think of something to do, Neva will have us all painting the house again."

That was when Alec said that he and Spinner were going to the gym to work out on the heavy bags, and he was going to watch Spinner spar a few rounds. It was like a tiny seed blew into Warren's ear and lay dormant until the sobering hours of the morning. He was staring at the ceiling in his bedroom and trying to think of a way to end the animosity that had led to his being set up. Stupidly, he had gotten drunk, but the rest of it was just too convenient to be merely a case of poor timing. When Neva was late getting up, Warren quickly gathered everyone into his van and headed for the gym. He knew something drastic had to be done. What did he, or anyone else for that matter, have to lose? He was at odds with Neva, Spinner was at odds with Randy, Alec was at odds with Emily, and Krista was at odds with everyone, collectively and individually.

Warren wanted to get out before Neva chose to amuse herself with his public flogging. He left her a note, one he had taken all of a sleepless night to compose. Before breakfast, he stole the kids away on a field trip he hoped would be educational. Perhaps a change of venue, Warren thought, would save his skin and his job.

"What is this all about anyway?" Alec asked.

"I'm going to give everyone a chance to settle their differences," Warren explained. "I've concluded that sometimes we must fight to protect ourselves. I'm going to channel all your aggressions. It will build character. Might for right. We need to learn how to overcome all the evil little tricks life plays on us, whether for real or just in our minds." He didn't tell them the real outcome he hoped to gain. "Spinner is going to provide us with a demonstration."

"I am?" Spinner asked, rolling his eyes at everyone as if Warren had lost his mind.

Krista was being cautious. "After last night," she said, "I don't think we have to do *anything* you want us to do."

"What happened last night was someone's version of twisting reality," Warren said. "And when *that* happens, people get hurt." Emily exchanged a glance with Warren that seemed to say she understood and was thankful for what he was trying to do.

When Spinner invited Randy to spar a few rounds, Krista giggled to Janeen how wonderful it was to have someone fight for your honor.

"I don't think that's what this is about," Janeen said.

"Sure it is," Krista insisted. "Ever since Helen of Troy, women have been at the center of history. Men are only motivated by their desires to prove themselves for women, and today, Janeen, you are Helen of Troy."

"Helen of Troy was a myth," Emily said.

Krista glanced scornfully at Emily. "I didn't expect you to understand."

That's when Randy charged, and when Spinner ducked out of the way, Randy caught him in a headlock and held him in his large, fleshy arms. The gym manager, acting as referee, tried to break them up, but Randy wasn't going to give in until he was ready, and when he did, he threw Spinner across the ring—actually flung him. Randy charged again, thinking he had caught Spinner off balance, but Spinner danced backwards, weaving from side to side, leaving only air to catch Randy's punches. The bell rang as Randy stumbled into the ropes, sweat spraying from his forehead out over the front row seats where the girls were sitting, causing them to scream squeamishly. Spinner strolled casually back to his corner.

By this time, several other boxers in the gym had gathered around, including Kid Gomez, Spider Johnson, and Terry "The Termite" Clark, who had been working out on the speed bags and heavy bags. Then, Moon Marshall joined the crowd. He was South Bay Gym's only contender, who had dropped his first name and shaved his head after seeing Marvin Hagler fight. Now, he was going for the middleweight title and stopped his workout only to view the entertainment in the gym's big ring.

"Are you going to fight this time?" Randy taunted as they came out for the second round.

"What makes you think I wasn't?" Spinner asked.

"Cause all you been doing is running away."

"Be careful what you ask for." Spinner laughed as he stirred his arm in the air and feinted with his body, which caused Randy to jerk backwards.

They circled slowly, sizing each other up. From the ruddy glow on Randy's cheeks, Spinner deduced that he was not in very good shape but suspected that Randy's punch could do some damage or at least sting. Spinner calculated how to get inside and waited for the opportunity.

"Maybe you just don't have any punches to throw," Randy said.

"Maybe you should show me how," Spinner said.

No sooner did Spinner get out the words when Randy obliged with a left jab that whizzed past Spinner's ear. Spinner countered with a right cross that snapped Randy's head back. Randy shook it off and came straight back at Spinner as if he were going to do the same thing, but instead, he ducked to the left and brought his fist down blindly out of the sky. Though Randy didn't aim it and Spinner didn't expect it, the punch landed squarely on the side of Spinner's face, causing him to stagger backward into the ropes as Randy lumbered toward him. Using the ropes as leverage, Spinner managed to duck a left hook before pushing Randy back. They exchanged a sporadic flurry of harmless blows before Spinner moved around to the outside.

When Randy turned, Spinner caught him with a left hook that dazed him and a right uppercut that drove him back into the ropes where Spinner had been. Spinner moved in with several quick body punches, then another uppercut, which caused Randy's arms to slump at his sides. Seeing what was about to happen, the referee moved in quickly to stop Spinner from landing the final blows to Randy's unprotected head.

"I knew I shouldn't have allowed you to do this," the referee said as he pushed Spinner back into a neutral corner. "This fight is over," he announced.

With an equal force, Neva burst through the front door, causing everyone, including Kid Gomez, Spider Johnson, The Termite, and Moon, to look up as if it were a police raid. Neva marched over to ringside, and looking at Randy who had not moved from where the ropes held him upright, she demanded, "What the hell is going on here?" Seeing Warren through the ropes, she pointed at him with the challenge of a contender. "I hope you have an explanation."

Krista, the only one without a startled expression, smiled cagily.

"Why don't you have a seat and watch," Warren said. "We still have a couple of fights left."

"Oh, I think you're through," Neva said.

"Oh no," Warren said, smiling coolly. "You see, Krista and Emily haven't gotten their chance in the ring yet, and after them, maybe you and I will go at it a couple rounds. Or we could just shadowbox. That would be like fighting all the demons in our heads, which we all seem to be very adept at."

Neva stopped. Suddenly, she realized that she had missed something—she had walked in on a play in progress and needed to let it play out a little further.

"We're settling our differences here," Warren said.

"This doesn't settle anything," Spinner said, climbing down from ringside. "I don't feel any better."

Warren smiled. "At least I got through to someone."

"Do you think this was the wisest way to handle this?" Neva asked. "Look at Randy. He's hurt."

"I'm not hurt," Randy insisted, testing the puffiness below his right eye with the tip of his glove.

"The hell you aren't," Alec said. "If it wasn't for the referee, you'd be lying flat on the canvas."

"This is Spinner's turf," Randy argued, wiping his brow with the back of his glove and then pointing at Alec. "Why don't you come up here and see if you can knock me out?"

"He's not going to," Neva interjected, "because Spinner was right. It doesn't prove anything."

"It's just a game," Warren said. "And yet, it's more real than any therapy or mumbo-jumbo psychology."

"What?" Neva waited to hear Warren's explanation as if it were his final speech just before his execution.

"It's all just a game with different names. Psychotherapy, reality therapy, gestalt, behaviorism, transactional analysis, emotive therapy. Take your pick. There's plenty more in the hat. So many theories, so many ways of saying the same thing. I'm beginning to think that psychologists are more concerned with publishing than with curing patients, because no one has the guts to just come out and ask someone what's bugging him."

Neva had enough. "Warren, this is neither the time nor the place."

"Oh, yes, it is," Warren said. "There is never a better time than right now. Putting off what we should deal with right now is what always gets us into trouble." Kid Gomez, Spider Johnson, The Termite, and Moon moved in closer. "No one asked me last night why I was drunk. No one asked me what I was doing in the study. No one asked Emily why she was in the study—and why it looked like we were doing something, which we weren't. I think we can get the answer to all of those questions if we just ask Krista."

"Oh no," Krista said, standing up and starting toward the door. "Leave me out of this."

"You can't keep playing this game, Krista," Warren called after her. "You tried to destroy me and Emily with a very cunning and intricate lie. Who else have you destroyed? Who else will you destroy before you learn that it doesn't make your life any better?" Warren waved a sweeping arm over the ring where Randy stood in silence. "That's what this is all about. We can't keep fighting each other. It doesn't do any good. One day, you have to answer the question. What's bugging you?"

Krista began to cry. She fell into Neva's arms. "Make him stop," she cried. "I didn't do anything."

Warren walked past them, stopping only for a moment to tell Neva he would be back to pick up his things. Then, he was out the door.

Chapter Fourteen

Warren was gone. He had packed up and left even before Neva brought the others back from the gym. This disappearing act was hard to understand. It stung the group into a silent sadness because no one wanted to point the finger, even though they were all thinking it—the real reason he didn't want to stick around, that is. It was all a hoax, an act to throw them off the track. Warren must have been guilty.

This is what Neva was thinking, but for some reason, when Dr. Mueller called to say he would not visit until the Monday after July 4th, Neva neglected to tell him about Warren. She told herself that it wasn't worth dragging everyone through more trauma. Dr. Mueller wanted her to take Emily to her sister's house tomorrow. Neva concurred that a visit with Loretta would be good for Emily. She couldn't remember if she actually told Dr. Mueller that.

Neva could have told Dr. Mueller that Warren had just up and quit. She could have said it and left it at that, but curiosity and the puzzling questions that Warren posed in the gym compelled her to leave off any final decision about Warren's employment until she got answers.

"Did you hear what I said?" Dr. Mueller's voice came over the phone with some insistence.

Neva came back to the moment. "Yes, of course." She thought quickly, realizing that she had not heard.

"I had nothing to do with this," Dr. Mueller said. "I want you to understand that. It was a court decision."

"I understand." Nothing registered.

"I want you to express to Emily's sister how important it is that she get some continued therapy for Emily—to monitor her progress through this change. Emily might be depressed or angry, and she might say something negative about Morning House to vent her anger."

Emily is leaving? That's what he said, what I missed. "Wait a minute. I'm taking Emily to *live* with her sister? Custody has been granted to Loretta, and Marion English agreed to all of this?"

"Yes, Neva. Where have you been? I don't know all the details. Emily's caseworker was in court when the judge handed down his decision. He apparently feels that Emily will be better off with her natural family. I'm sorry, but this means the end of your group."

"But what if Emily's sister could bring her to the group on an outpatient contract?" Neva heard her voice plead, something she had never done before. She didn't like what was happening.

"If that happens, then Loretta can just bring her to me."

To me. Bring your problems. Nothing is so big we can't overcome. We'll talk in my office. My office with the paneled walls and the photograph of my family and the cross above the sofa to remind us of God's love. My love. Don't be afraid.

"But I still have the other two girls. And there will be more soon. We were starting to make some progress."

"No," Dr. Mueller cut her off. "It's over. I am convinced that in the long run, it was going to do more harm than good."

• • •

Emily was all packed in the morning and ready to go before breakfast. She was the first guinea to linger at the door, hanging on words she wanted to say to the others, to say goodbye in a way that didn't really mean goodbye, that meant I'll write or we'll see each other again soon, that this really isn't goodbye. Spinner was the only one who came up to her while the others were on their way to the bus stop—Alec never looking back and Krista dragging Janeen with her voice, warning her as if she were going to turn into a pillar of salt.

In the end, Spinner was optimistic. "Don't you worry, girl. This isn't over between you two. He's just mixed up right now. I'll bring him around. You write him, okay, and I assure you, he *will* write back. I'll make him see what he really wants, instead of fighting it."

Emily smiled shyly as Spinner gave her a one-armed hug, and then he was down the front walk as Janeen ran back, nearly in tears, and wrapped her arms around Emily. "I'm so happy for you. You're so lucky to have someone. Please write to me."

Emily cried too. "Of course, I will. You know I feel that you're my best friend, even though we've only known each other a short time."

"I feel the same way," Janeen said. They looked at each other, wondering what to do next. Their smiles were awkward. Janeen said, "I gotta go," and Emily nodded, waiting as Janeen went down the steps and turned in the walkway to wave goodbye.

Emily wiped away the tears. "I think I'm ready now," she said to Neva.

● ● ●

Loretta's husband worked at the Pasadena Oil and Gas Refinery, and when he answered the door, Neva's first thought was that he had taken the day off to welcome Emily to their house. He looked at them as if he was looking right through them, and he didn't say a word. His body blocked the doorway, and his eyes dropped for a second to the suitcase beside Emily. Turning his head sideways, but still looking at them as if they would run by him if he looked away, he called out toward the back of the house for Loretta. "It's your sister."

They could hear Loretta's voice come from another room. "Oh my God, I completely forgot." She came to the door with a baby slung on one hip. She was combing her hair and buttoning her blouse with her free hand. Her eyes were red and watery.

Loretta tried to hand the baby to her husband, but he held his hands up like he was under arrest and moved away. "No way," he said, "I'm busy." He glanced back at Neva and Emily in the doorway and leaned down to whisper to Loretta—only it wasn't a whisper. "Make it fast," he said firmly.

"Gary, please," Loretta said, frowning at him. She turned and smiled at Neva and Emily. "Come in; come in. I'm so sorry. Things are kind of hectic around here." She didn't invite them to sit. She just stood in the small space that was a part of the front room. "I feel terrible," Loretta said, jumping the baby higher on her hip. "I should have called, but I just found out myself only last night." She reached out to Emily and stroked the side of her face. "Are you all right, Emy?"

"I'm confused," Neva said. "I thought you knew we were coming."

"Oh, I did," Loretta said. A puzzled expression registered on her face. "Oh, I thought the caseworker was going to tell you." She took Emily by the arm and guided her to the sofa. She placed the baby beside her, and it jerked its arms and legs as if struggling with this new environment. "I don't know what to say, Emy. It has all been such a shock. Katie was transferred to St. Joseph's Hospital last week when she got sick. That's where she was going to have the operation." Loretta looked down at her lap. The baby started making gurgling noises, but she ignored it.

Emily didn't move.

"I don't know how to say this," Loretta said, starting to cry. Then, abruptly, she said, "Katie died last night." Loretta pressed her fingers to her mouth as if to apologize for saying it, trying to stifle any burst of grief.

Emily sat silently for a long moment, just staring into her lap. "She must have hated me," she said softly. "She needed me, and I . . . I could have saved her, but I didn't. And now, it's too late."

"There is no way you could have known," Neva said. "You mustn't blame yourself."

"No!" Loretta's husband shouted from the back of the house. "You'll have to go ask your mother!"

Loretta jumped, and the baby started to cry. As she struggled with the infant, another child, no more than four years old, dirty faced and ragged, came from the doorway. Neva thought at first that this child with pasty skin and long stringy hair was a girl, but she wasn't sure. The child saw them and stopped, then started forward quickly as Loretta motioned for the child.

"What is it, Tommy? What have you done now?"

The child made himself invisible with his hands over his eyes, then climbed onto the sofa and burrowed his face into Loretta's available breast.

"Is Tommy your son?" Neva asked.

Loretta grinned innocently. "Yes. They're both mine. It's not easy, but we get by."

"You must have had Tommy when you were very young."

"Sixteen," Loretta said.

Neva looked at Emily, who was watching something in her idle hands. She tried to imagine Emily in Loretta's place, at sixteen, a newborn at her breast, a future heavy with emptiness, a willingness to accept anyone who would take them in, even a foul-smelling, ill-mannered man child with no future of his own. Neva tried to imagine herself in that same place, backtracking through the seven years of hard work to get where she was today. She had made the right decision back then, she thought.

"So you see why I can't take you now," Loretta said.

"What?" Neva asked.

"It would be impossible. You've seen my husband and this brood. He was only allowing it because of Katie. It's no use now. I'm so sorry, Emy. You must think I'm rotten, but there's nothing I can do."

"Can I go back to Morning House?" Emily asked Neva.

"Of course, you can."

"I think I'd like to go now."

"I'm sorry," Loretta said. "Please forgive me, Emy. You know how it is, don't you?"

"It's all right," Emily said. "You have trouble enough. You don't need me here to make things worse. I'll be fine."

Emily got up and walked to the door without another word. Neva waited at the door, waited for Emily to get out of earshot before she turned back to Loretta, who had followed, one child still at her breast, the other clinging to her leg. Neva looked down at Tommy and managed a smile, which caused him to hide his face in the folds of his mother's skirt. "You were living at home when you got pregnant, weren't you?" Neva asked.

Loretta looked out toward Emily, then nodded.

"What happened was not his fault, you know." Neva nodded at the child grasping her knee. "I hope you remember that. Now that he's here, he deserves as much love as your other one."

"I know that," Loretta said. "It doesn't make it any easier, though, when I look at him and see my father. Please don't tell Emy," Loretta said.

"No. She was right. You have trouble enough."

● ● ●

Neva knew that one day her fears about Alec would come true. All the telltale signs—the sense of impending change was growing stronger, like the smell of rain before the sky lets it fall.

She had invited Alec into her office to ask him about Randy when he sprang it on her. "I'm going to jump the Kemah drawbridge," he said.

Neva didn't respond. She couldn't. All of her mental efforts focused on pushing his words back out.

"This is something I've thought about a lot," Alec said finally, "something I have to do, and you won't be able to talk me out of it."

Neva didn't try. She simply asked why.

"Because if I don't, then my life won't be worth anything," Alec said. "Not a plug nickel. I've figured it out, you see. Part of it anyway. We're all here on this Earth chasing dreams because that's what seems to give some meaning to all of it. Funny thing is, sometimes we don't even know what they are. We just keep on running, chasing, and running. Well, I've found out why I'm running, and now I've got to do something about it. If I can jump that bridge, I will have beat death. I'll be remembered for something, and so will your brother because he's tied to this whole thing, somehow."

Neva couldn't bear it anymore. She wasn't going to stop him. She knew she couldn't stop him any more than she could have stopped Jim. All Neva wanted was to find out more before it was too late. "What does Randy have to do with this?" she asked.

"Randy?" He looked surprised. "Randy has nothing to do with this. Why do you even ask?"

"Because Randy is Bubba, isn't he? The Bubba in your dream, the Bubba you knew as a child, knew and feared and hated."

"How did you know that?"

"It doesn't matter. But I think that he's more a part of this than you will admit, so I need to know why you hated him."

Alec looked around the room as events from his past circled about him on the walls, events projected dimly through his own dark lens, yet clear enough to remember because of their connection to the day that changed his life. "He killed my dog," Alec said. "It wasn't really my dog, but it could have been because he was as close as any stray dog can be to a person, and Randy knew how I felt about that dog. I thought the dog was run over by a car at first, but Randy bragged about it, how he killed it with a big rock, and he laughed like it was something to be proud of." Alec couldn't go on. Not about the dog. The walls had gone black, and he pushed back the emptiness with deep breaths. "I would stay away from Randy if I were you," Alec said.

Neva believed him. She had a reason for always believing what anyone told her, as long as it was even reasonably believable, and in this case, she had her own suspicions, something she had seen in Randy's eyes—a lack of emotion or conscience.

Before he left, Alec promised Neva that he would keep her informed about his plans, and Neva promised to keep an eye on Randy. That night, after dinner, Neva saw Alec and Emily walking down to the boathouse, much the same way she had walked through the sand down to the abandoned skiff that sheltered her memories, her thoughts, her sanity.

Jim was with me even after he was gone. Only I could see him. I wanted to be invisible like he was. I wanted to keep walking, right out into the water where the shrimp boats chugged off toward the horizon, to walk out into the depths of darkness and forgetfulness and peace. I wanted Jim to take my hand and guide me to wherever he was.

He talked me out of it, though. Jim wanted me to stay and fight, even after the bleeding stopped, even after two months had gone by and I still couldn't bleed. I sat under the skiff until the sun went down, and the great river of light flowed across the sky, and I finally understood what Jim meant—and what I had to do. There was nothing else but to bring it all out into the open, to tell Uncle Spencer—and my mother too.

● ● ●

There was nothing else to do but bring it all out into the open—to open Pandora's box and let all the fear and anger escape. Make them face what they were holding inside.

Krista played Emily's mother. Janeen was Emily's father. Emily was herself. Neva was the mediator, the referee to keep all the punches above the belt. The controller. That was the plan.

"What am I supposed to say?" Krista asked.

"Whatever you feel like. Why don't you start with why you left, and remember that you need to address Emily as if she were your daughter."

Krista looked at Emily and smirked.

"Why did you do it?" Janeen asked. "Why did you lie about it?"

Krista turned on Janeen as if she were out of line; then, she realized it was part of the play. "I wanted my freedom," Krista said. "I wanted to get the hell out and do my thing."

"Good for you," Emily said. "What about the rest of us? Did you think it was going to be easy for us?"

"I didn't care. Sometimes you have to look out for number one. Numero Uno. That's what life is all about."

"But I missed you," Emily said.

"I'm sorry, but like I said . . ."

"Oh, don't get me wrong," Emily cut her off. "I got over it. I quickly learned to hate you."

"Yeah, it wasn't fair," Janeen said.

"I missed having a mother," Emily said.

"You still had your father," Krista said.

"It's not the same. There were times when I wanted to share things with you, and you weren't there. A father's love is different. I missed having a mother's love."

"I took care of you when she left," Janeen said.

"Yeah, I know, but you didn't really love having us around. We were a burden. I could tell. You brought that woman to live with us. She really hated us."

"You had your sisters," Krista said.

"Yeah," Janeen said. "I thought you and your sisters were close."

"We were. They saved me, I guess, from the problems with our stepbrother."

"What problems?" Janeen asked.

"You know. Dean's mother found that letter I wrote, and she showed it to you. You got really mad, but you just didn't understand what happened and how I felt."

"What happened?" Krista asked quickly.

Emily paused enough for Neva to see the doubt in her change of expression, wondering if perhaps she had gone too far. "Do you feel up to talking about that?" Neva interjected.

"It's all right," Emily said. "My problems can't be any worse than anyone else's. I just don't want to bore anyone or make you think I'm feeling sorry for myself."

"No, it's okay," Krista urged. "Go ahead."

Neva narrowed her eyes at Krista. She was able to see clearly that Krista was gathering information, something to use when she needed it.

Emily sighed heavily. "I've always felt like a burden to everyone. My mother, my father, my sisters, even Marion English. My stepbrother was the only one who ever showed me any attention. Before I knew it, he was doing things that I knew were wrong, but he didn't hurt me. I thought he loved me. When Katie told me she wanted to take me away, I was too embarrassed to tell her, even when she told me the things he did to *her*. I had written some letters to Dean, and his mother found them and got real mad. I thought my father was going to kill me."

"Well, what did your father do when he found out?"

"Nothing. I remember one night Loretta had a big argument with him, and she told him she would kill him if he ever came near me. But I heard her ask him if he had ever touched me. The way she said it made me suspect that he had done something to her—you know, something sexual. We left shortly after that, and I never saw him again."

"What is left for you?" Neva asked, now addressing the group. "Where do you go when you find yourself out in the cold, alone with nowhere to turn for support? What we are talking about, of course, is sexual contact of any kind that causes a little voice in your head to tell you that something is not right about it. It's a heavy burden to carry around when you're left feeling that something happened. You felt that it was wrong, and you feel like it was your fault because you *let* it happen. Well, it is *not* your fault, and you cannot go on feeling guilty, punishing yourself for doing those things. Even if they made you feel good at the time. You need to stop seeking love in dangerous and punishing situations."

Janeen and Emily both silently gazed into their laps.

"That doesn't exactly pertain to you though, does it, Krista? You're different. I don't exactly know where to place you."

"What do you mean?" Krista snapped. "How could you even know how I feel, how any of us feel? You've never been there. You just sit there and make us play these stupid games. I'm beginning to think you get some demented pleasure out of hearing about our personal lives."

Neva breathed deeply and expelled all the anguish and anger. "You don't know where I have been, Krista, so don't assume that I am not empathetic. I was merely pointing out that you have had a different reaction to what has happened to you— different from Emily and Janeen. Where Emily and Janeen's reactions are turned inward, yours are turned outward. Your anger seems to take the form of revenge, toward your grandfather, toward Warren, and now perhaps toward me."

"I don't know what you're talking about," Krista said, suddenly stunned.

"I fell into your little trap, and I blamed Warren for something he didn't do. You knew that would happen. Isn't that right?"

"I don't know. Why don't you ask Emily?"

"Because it wasn't Emily's idea. It was *you* behind the curtain, wasn't it, watching me leave that night so you could put your plan into motion? You told Warren you would get even with him, and that's exactly what you did that night."

"No!" Krista screamed. "Why are you doing this?" Her face flushed with fear when Neva didn't respond. Tears pooled in her eyes. "So what if I did?" she asked. Her words were stiff and angry. "He had it coming. He had no right to punish me like he did."

"He had every right, Krista. That's his job. What you did was wrong, but it was the way you went about it that disturbs me. Anyone who has been in that position would never play a dirty trick like that on someone else, but you knew what it would do because you played that same trick on your grandfather, didn't you?"

"Is this game over?" Krista asked, getting up to leave.

"There are no more games," Neva said. "This is real. This is life. There are no more fake tears to shed while you tell your lies to get sympathy."

"But I do know!" Krista insisted. "All right," she said. "I lied about my grandfather. When he moved in, suddenly, it was like I didn't exist. I hated him for all the attention he got, and I hated him because I had to give up my room for him. You're going to send me back home, aren't you? I hate it there. You can't do that to me. It's not fair. If you send me back there, I'll ruin this place. I'll go to the police about Dr. Mueller, and this place will be shut down. Yeah, you see, I do know what it's like because right here under your nose, you're allowing it to happen."

"What on earth are you talking about?" Neva asked in disbelief.

Krista became very animated. "Don't tell me you didn't know about Dr. Mueller's physicals." She motioned two quotes in the air with her fingers. "A psychiatrist giving physicals? Yeah, that's normal. He says it's a physical, but I know better. I'm sure he gets his rocks off when he gives a breast exam. I bet he's not even a real doctor. And I'll tell! I'll tell it all!"

Krista broke free of her cage and ran from the room because she could see that they didn't believe her, and she didn't expect them to. Krista ran from the room because she had been humiliated for the last time. She ran from the room because she was crying, and this time they were real tears, and she was afraid because she had never known a sincere emotion like that before.

• • •

Alec and Emily ducked into the shed when Neva went by. She rounded the corner of the house and headed down the driveway in a hurry. There was a purpose in her walk, a blind determination. Neva didn't see them watching her.

"Where do you think she's going?" Alec asked.

"Probably to find Warren," Emily said. "His van has been behind Campbell's Grocery for the past two days. She realizes she was wrong about him."

"We were stupid to jump to conclusions."

"I think he loves her. He watches through the window whenever she leaves. He loves her, but he can't tell her. That's why he got drunk the night she went out with Dr. Mueller." Emily shook her head. "It's kind of sad because she doesn't see it."

When Neva was out of sight, they walked down to the boathouse. Alec opened the book he had brought.

"Do we have to study tonight?" Emily pleaded.

"I just want to show you something," Alec said.

Emily looked down at the page where the book lay open. "Shelley? We're not supposed to skip ahead."

"I know, but I thought you might like this one."

He read to her, and then, she read. They laughed at the words they couldn't pronounce and squinted at the words they did not know. They read until the sun went down, and it was too dark to read, and when they looked up through the broken window in the boathouse, they saw the stars spread out across the sky, flung like a warm breath into the cold air. A mist still remained like a wide river across the middle of the sky.

Alec pulled the sand dollar out of his pocket and held it up to view the star within. "Funny how all this seems so connected, like nothing ever dies. It just turns up somewhere else, in some other shape or a part of something different. Shelley's spirit lives on in his words, so we all must have some spirit or energy that lives on in something—even after we die."

Emily smiled with the feeling that everything was right in her life, and she placed her head on Alec's shoulder. He lit a small candle and placed it on the floor of the boathouse. With the light flickering in their eyes, Alec held Emily's face in the palms of his hands.

"I know about you and your past, and I don't care," he said. "What you were, it doesn't matter. I know you now, and I know that when I'm with you, nothing else exists but you and me. I'm ashamed I doubted you before."

Emily held his hands in hers and gazed into his eyes. "When you touch me," she said, "there is no past. Without your touch, there is no future." The night broke with two mournful hoots from an owl. Emily smiled. "There was a time I would have been frightened, but now, even with the night and all its strange noises all around me, I feel safe." Emily took the book and opened it to where they had been reading. She held it up to the candle and read.

"My soul is an enchanted boat,
Which, like a sleeping swan, doth float
Upon the silver waves of thy sweet singing;
And thine doth like an angel sit
Beside a helm conducting it,
Whilst all the winds with melody are ringing."

With a trembling hand, Alec cupped her cheek and leaned over to kiss her. Emily held her face up to his, and when the tenderness of her lips met his, a spark shot through his body, awakening all the senses he had only known before in words, what he had read and fantasized and kept hidden from the world because he had been afraid that it didn't exist without pain.

188

"The sound of your voice is like a key that unlocks my soul. It's greater than any freedom I have ever dreamed of. Knowing it's there, I'll never let anyone send me back to that place. I could never bear to be away from you, not now, not ever."

"We could run away," Emily said. "Remember what you said at the beach? We could just get on your motorcycle and go wherever it takes us. We could go to New Orleans. They would never find us there."

"I would go anywhere as long as I could be with you, but there's still one thing I have to do here."

Emily looked into his eyes and saw a fire, and she realized that something unsettled lay inside him, something she couldn't help him forget. "I'll wait for you," she said.

Part Three: House of Wind

Chapter Fifteen

They stood in the yard behind the house, waiting nervously, trying not to disturb anything. One of them looked back toward the house, where a watchful shadow stood in the thin, open space of a drawn curtain. The rain began to fall, the dispassionate rain, blowing in on the wind.

Large, scattered drops made odd, thumping sounds on the body as the men hurried to cover it with a tarp. When Detective Kelly arrived, the rain strengthened, unfurling over them like ocean waves. They quickly raised the tarp like a tent to allow Detective Kelly to examine the body. It lay awkwardly twisted in the rose garden, the fingers curled and stiff as if caught in an instant of surprise or shock, the eyes already a dusky gray, the jaw shifted with pallid lips left slightly agape. A yellow patina of death had settled on the skin, with the exception of a few dark freckles circling the neat little hole beneath the right ear. All the darkness had pooled against the brown earth where the left ear was torn away. Death had been quick, instantaneous.

Detective Kelly stood up and peered under a trembling umbrella toward the boathouse. He shook his head; he thought something like this was bound to happen, and now that it was in front of him, he could only think about how senseless it was. Detective Kelly knew he would need to talk to everyone and take them back to the beginning.

• • •

Warren

The motorcycle is the first thing I remember—Alec's motorcycle in the parking lot.

He had a black canvas saddlebag that he tied to the back on one side, so I wasn't surprised when he came out of the store. He pushed by me in the doorway, like he was in a hurry to get somewhere, but he looked pale, and he was holding his stomach like he was going to be sick. He stopped and took a deep breath, the way a diver gasps for air when he breaks the surface of the water.

I asked him if he was okay, and he just looked at me as if he didn't recognize me; then, he stumbled toward his motorcycle.

I told him he didn't look so good, that he shouldn't be riding a motorcycle if he was sick. I held the handlebar of the motorcycle so he wouldn't leave. He looked at me again and finally seemed to recognize me.

"I'm all right," he said. "I just got dizzy for a minute, and the sun was in my eyes." He laughed nervously, and his eyes turned sullen.

I knew I wasn't going to get anywhere with him as far as getting a straight answer, so I let go of the handlebar and watched him cross the street and ride up the driveway toward the house. That was when I entered the store.

I had been in Campbell's Market at least once a day since I started working at Morning House. After Krista tried to get me fired, I helped Duffy Campbell in the store, so I was familiar with the bell that rang when you entered the front door. When it didn't ring, I felt this unearthly silence that made me shiver. Duffy wasn't at the register, so I waited to see his face appear over one of the aisles or from behind the freezer door, all flushed and jolly like a ripe tomato, but he never appeared. I waited but heard nothing. I stopped at the front counter, where Duffy always kept a display of flowers in case someone wanted a last-minute purchase. Even a single rose, he would say with a chuckle, as a statement of affection or a make-up offering. I saw several stems left on the counter, as if they'd been picked through but not replaced. That was when I noticed the open cash register, and it looked empty.

I had this sinking feeling that Alec took the money, that he had been the thief all along, and this time he knocked over the roses reaching for the register—but I still didn't want to believe it. I walked toward the back of the store, glancing down each aisle in case Duffy was stocking the shelves.

I called out once, and there was no answer, so I went around the meat counter toward the door that led to the back of the store. I thought Duffy might be in the storeroom and couldn't hear. I called out again, but the only reply was the humming of the freezer motor. I backed out the door, and when I turned, my foot pushed something across the floor and under the counter. I could tell it was a knife because the handle was sticking out. I picked it up and noticed that the blade had blood on it. It was a long blade, with a smooth elliptical edge—a butcher knife.

Mentally, I searched for some logical explanation, that Duffy had been trimming meat and accidentally dropped the knife—or cut himself and left to get medical attention. That would explain why the store was left unattended, something Duffy would not ordinarily do. But there was still Alec's unexplained presence in the store.

I placed the knife on a wooden block next to the other knives and felt something sticky under my shoe. When I looked down, I saw a dark red smear. Blood was on the floor and the counter, too much blood for any reasonable explanation. My heart raced and radiated through a panic that told me I was following in footsteps that Alec had traced only moments before.

Suddenly, I saw it all, as if my mind had somehow blocked it out before. I saw bloody fingerprints on the counter, a bloody towel by the knives, and another smear of blood by the back door. I followed the trail of blood to the storeroom, which was surprisingly clean and cool—and smelled of spices. A feeling of dread crept into my throat, but I kept hoping I was wrong—that I wouldn't find anything, or there'd be a logical explanation. Then, I saw his feet sticking out from behind boxes of beer.

• • •

Neva

I was working at my desk that afternoon when I heard Alec drive up on his motorcycle. It wasn't unusual. It was the time he always got off work. The back door slammed, and someone bounded down the stairs. That's what drew me to the window. It was Emily, and she was happy, which made me feel good. The developing relationship between her and Alec was healthy.

There was a knock at my office door, and I looked up at Spinner, who stuck his head in.

"I'm sorry to interrupt, but I can't find Janeen. It's our turn to cook dinner. I tried her room, but she didn't come to the door. And I asked Krista if she's seen her, but she's being Krista. So she wasn't any help."

"Okay, I'll see if I can find her," I said. Then, the phone rang. Before I answered, I told Spinner to tell Krista I said to go in their room and see if Janeen's in there.

"Aye-Aye," Spinner said and bolted out the door.

When I answered the phone, Warren's voice sounded alarmed, and I immediately thought something had happened to Janeen. Instead, he told me about Campbell's Market. Still on the phone, I went back to the window and watched Alec and Emily walk down to the old boathouse on Mud Lake. They were holding hands, and Emily was carrying a small bouquet of flowers.

Alec couldn't have done it, I thought. *Alec's so much like Jim, and Jim could never do something like that.*

"Neva! Neva," Warren yelled. "Are you listening?"

"Yeah. Sorry. I'm here."

"Have you seen Alec?" he asked.

I couldn't bring myself to tell him that I was looking at Alec. There had to be some explanation. Warren was going to wait at Campbell's Market until the police arrived, so I figured I had some time to do some investigating of my own—and so what if my motives were protective rather than prosecutorial? That was my job. I was about to go talk to Alec when Spinner came running down the stairs in a panic.

• • •

Krista

I was watching videos in the dayroom when Spinner came in and asked me if I had seen Janeen. I told him no, and he left. I could hear Alec's motorcycle come down the drive beside the house, so I knew it must have been close to dinnertime; he always got back from work about that time. I remember hearing footsteps on the stairs. I thought it was Janeen because it was her and Spinner's turn to cook.

Spinner came back a few minutes later and said that Neva wanted me to help him look for Janeen.

"She just came down the stairs," I said.

"No, that was Emily," Spinner said.

"Well, go check our room. She's probably just studying,"

"I knocked, but she didn't answer," Spinner said. "Krista, I need you to go see if she's in there."

"Gah. Can't you see I'm busy? Get Neva to go check. Or go in there yourself. I don't care."

"Krista, you know the rules. Just check the damn room," he said, louder.

"I'm so sick of this shit. I can't ever get any peace in this shithole," I yelled.

But I did get up and head to our room. Spinner followed me. I stared at Spinner as I pushed the door open wide with a shrug, and I gave him a look that said, "Wasn't that real hard?" I expected him to come back with a smartass remark, but instead, he got this startled look on his face and rushed in the room.

Janeen was lying on the bed like she'd been knocked out. Seriously, I thought she was dead. Spinner tried to wake her up, but we could tell something was wrong. Spinner picked up something off the floor next to the bed and put it on the nightstand. He tried to wake her up again by shaking her. I just stood at the foot of the bed, watching him, unable to move, unable to take my hands away from my mouth.

Spinner turned back to me, and I think he was yelling, but I could barely hear him. It was the strangest thing, but all I could hear were letters like H and OD. Finally, I heard him say, "Go get Neva," but for some reason my feet wouldn't move, even though I knew he was frantic and angry with me.

He got up and ran out of the room. As I waited, I just watched Janeen lying there. I've never seen a dead person before. It was eerie. Her body was sort of twisted like how little kids fall asleep all limp and lifeless. Her mouth was open, and one arm was draped over the side of the bed. It was like she had fallen asleep in a drunken stupor.

I heard footsteps on the stairs. Neva hurried into the room. She stopped and took a deep breath to collect herself, waiting for me to tell her something, but I couldn't. I didn't even move when she brushed by me. Neva sat down beside Janeen. I tried to speak, but my voice would only come out in a whimper.

Neva touched Janeen's neck, then leaned over and placed her cheek next to Janeen's open mouth. Neva said she thought Janeen was still breathing, and I felt my heart leap. After a moment, Neva stood up and rubbed her forehead like she was trying to remember something. She started muttering, something about trying wake up Janeen.

She held out her hand to me, and my hand instinctively shot out. Neva said she didn't know if there was anything we could do, that she felt so helpless. We hugged each other, and I started to cry, and my words came out in sobbing breaths. I felt so terrible. I had no idea Janeen was going to do anything like this.

Neva tried to reassure me that none of us knew this was going to happen, that we didn't even know if Janeen had done this on purpose, that it could all have been just a big accident.

Spinner entered the room all out of breath. He stopped suddenly and walked slowly toward us. His eyes never moved from Janeen. He assured us that an ambulance was on the way. He asked how Janeen was. We all stood there and watched her, her breathing hardly noticeable, and her skin so pale and transparent.

"I wish there was something we could do while we wait for the ambulance," Spinner said.

Neva suddenly sprang into action, barking orders at us. She grabbed one of Janeen's arms, and Spinner grabbed the other one while I went to the bathroom to get a wet washcloth. They started walking her around the room and talking to her, almost shouting, trying to wake her up, and splashing water from the washcloth onto her face.

"What do you think was in the syringe?" Neva asked Spinner.

"Heroin, probably," Spinner said.

Neva brushed the hair out of Janeen's face. I had never noticed how fine and wispy her hair was. She looked like a fragile, broken doll.

I heard sirens wail in the distance, and Neva started to cry. It was a sad cry, with tears streaming down her cheeks, but her face looked peaceful, like she was thinking about something long ago and far away. She started muttering again about things falling apart and spinning out of control and not being able to stop them.

Spinner and I looked at each other because Neva was getting scary, and we didn't know what she was talking about. Neva wiped away the tears and took a deep breath. "You might as well know," she said. "Something terrible happened at Campbell's Market, and Alec might be involved."

I started shaking.

"Keep an eye on Alec, and be careful around him. And promise me you won't bring it up to him," Neva said.

• • •

Warren

It was just an impression, but Neva acted like she was hiding something. When I asked her over the phone if she had seen Alec, she said no, and I had just seen Alec drive up to the house only minutes before. Later, when I went to the house with the police officer, I saw the ambulance parked in front, and my first thought was that Alec had done something else. I hurried inside as the paramedics were bringing Janeen downstairs. As they placed her on a gurney and took her out to the ambulance, I was looking around for Alec, but I only saw Spinner and Krista, who followed the gurney outside. I guess Neva saw me looking around because her eyes shot me a worried look, and she shook her head as if she was giving me a signal.

The officer asked what happened, and Neva told him that it appeared to be a drug overdose. He asked other questions—where it happened, when they found her, and if they found any drugs. That's when Neva told him about the syringe.

"Did you find anything else, like a note?" the officer asked.

Neva put her hand on her forehead and ran her fingers back through her hair. I could tell she was oscillating between anger and worry. She gave the officer a piercing glare that seemed to admonish him for being so callous, but when she spoke, her voice was very calm and polite.

"I have no idea where Janeen got the drugs, but I know that she had no intention of harming herself. Janeen is just a mixed-up girl who has been used too many times by all the people she trusted. Perhaps your efforts would be better served by going after the suppliers. You can probably find them at any elementary school in the area."

The officer excused himself and went upstairs to collect the syringe, and when he was gone, Neva turned to me in panicked anger. I was beginning to think that she saved this side her personality just for my benefit.

She yelled in odd, whispered tones. "We can't let this get out of control. There has to be some mistake. We have to protect Alec. There's a reasonable explanation for all of this!"

I grabbed her by the arms because I thought she was the one who was actually losing control. "I know you know where Alec is. You lied to me on the phone. Protecting him could just make things worse."

She held her hand up, denying my accusation. She focused on my eyes, and I could feel her whole body relax.

Krista burst into the room and said the ambulance was leaving with Janeen.

"I have to go to the hospital," Neva said. "Can you stay here?"

"What good will that do? I don't know where *anyone* is," I said.

Krista smirked and said, "Emily is probably with Alec because she came downstairs earlier when Alec drove up on his motorcycle."

I just stared at Neva, hoping that she would come to her senses.

"I have to go," Neva said flightily and turned to leave.

"Someone murdered Duffy Campbell, and I *saw* Alec at the store!" I yelled. "The cops will want to talk to him. Immediately."

We all heard a noise come from the kitchen, and we turned to see Emily standing in the doorway, backing away, looking at us as if we had been plotting against her. I caught only a glimpse of her face, but it was enough to see horror and distrust just before she turned and ran.

When I reached the back door, I heard Emily calling to Alec to start his motorcycle. I think she was trying to reach him so they could ride off together, but I caught up with her at the edge of the driveway. As I grabbed her arm, she yelled at Alec to go on without her.

I handed Emily off to Neva, who had come up behind us. I started for

Alec with Emily yelling at me to leave him alone. Alec fishtailed in the gravel so I couldn't get close enough to grab him before he took off. He was headed down the driveway toward the street when the police car turned into the driveway from the front of the house. He was trying to block Alec, but Alec just swerved off the driveway into the trees and came back out across the drive and into the street.

Emily cried on Neva's shoulder, and through her sobs, I heard her say, "Alec couldn't have done that."

• • •

Detective Kelly

That kid could really ride a motorcycle. It was like he was born to it. We chased him all around Clear Lake. It was almost like he knew what we were going to do, and he was just toying with us, like he had something to prove. When he rode off into the trees at Morning House to avoid the patrol car that was trying to block him from leaving, I was standing outside Campbell's Market. I got in my car and was right on him when he pulled out onto the highway. Funny thing is, he didn't punch it right away. Instead, he looked back; then, as he shifted through the gears, the front end of the bike lifted up off the road. Oh yeah, he was having fun. I could tell he was laughing at us. He had made up his mind he was going to give us a run for our money.

He got out ahead of us pretty good going through El Lago, but I knew that when he reached Seabrook, he would have to slow down, and that would give us time to catch up. Our only hope was that he would turn right and head toward Kemah. If he went left toward La Porte, he would have been able to get ahead of us and disappear into Pasadena or Deer Park or even through the tunnel into Baytown—and we would have never found him.

I don't know how he was staying on the road because the wind was blowing us all over the place. We could see the rain coming in real fast too. I knew it would overtake us in Seabrook, and those clouds would bring on a darkness blacker than night. We only had about one hour of daylight left, even without the rain clouds moving in on us.

When he hit the dead end of the highway in Seabrook and turned right, I knew we had him. I got on the radio and told the dispatcher to call the drawbridge operator and have him raise the bridge right away. With that roadblock up, he would have nowhere else to go except right back at us—or into the water. He looked back at us again before he took off toward Kemah, and then, he did two more wheelies. He was really having fun, and he didn't want us to miss the show.

Right about then, I remembered this kid who tried to jump the Kemah drawbridge seven years before. I had just started on the force then, and this kid was the first coroner's case I worked. I really felt sorry for his sister, who stayed right there the whole day while we fished his body out of the channel.

We stayed with Alec all the way around that big curve in the road, and as the bridge came into view, I could see that it was still down. In my head, I cussed that operator, thinking he was asleep or maybe just giving our dispatcher a hard time. I could see the roadblock arm start to go down, and I expected Alec to start slowing down, but instead, he looked back at us and waved. I swear to God he had a grin on his face as big as a Cheshire cat. He punched it, and I knew he was going to try and jump the bridge. We had done just what he had wanted us to do all along. Not only did he want us to witness it, he wanted us to set it up for him, and that's exactly what we did.

There we were chasing after him, and as the bridge was going up, he was crouched real low on that motorcycle, moving like a bullet through the wind. It was like a neck-and-neck horse race that brings you out of your seat. He wasn't going to stop. I could tell that much. Something in my mind triggered that girl's face on that terrible day years ago as she waited for her brother, and I realized that she was Neva.

I was actually hoping that Alec would make it. The bridge was cranking up slowly, but there was not much time left before it got too high. For some unknown reason, the operator came out of the booth and stood on the bridge waving his arms. I guess he was trying to help by warning us, but Alec was too close by then. He would have had to dump the bike to keep from hitting the guy.

Alec kept going like he didn't even see the guy standing there. He passed the roadblock and looked up like he was checking all of his bearings. He crouched down again just as the operator leaped out of the way. And that was the end of the line for us. We skidded to a stop at the base of the bridge, just as Alec disappeared over the top.

● ● ●

Anna Gogarty

I didn't know who could be at the door so late, especially on such a stormy night. I nearly screamed when I looked through the window and saw Alec standing on the porch. He was soaking wet and shaking. By the look in his eyes, I could tell something was terribly wrong. When I opened the door, he came in, closed the door quickly behind him, and turned out the light.

"What's wrong?" I asked him.

"I can't go back there."

"You mean Morning House?" I asked, knowing that's what he meant. "Alec, what happened?"

All he said was, "You have to let me stay here tonight."

I'm his mother. What was I going to tell him? No? I was thrilled he had come home, that he had thought about coming to me when he was in trouble. "You can stay here as long as you want," I told him.

He seemed so grown up, so mature—a change I could see in the way he looked at me with his dark, troubled eyes and his clenched jaw. His hair was like the night, glistening with the rain. He was no longer my baby.

He was ready to handle true knowledge. It was the power of knowledge that brought him to me, as I had predicted. I told Dr. Mueller that something would happen—something that would change everything at Morning House. There was nothing he could do to stop it, and I knew the power would bring Alec back to me.

In a predictable head-shrink manner, Dr. Mueller asked why I believed in witchcraft.

"This is the only true power of the universe. The world is ruled by the devil," I told him. "Just look at all the evil, hate, and destruction. I don't care what anyone tells you about religious beliefs or what lies in the heart or any other holier than thou garbage. Everyone worships the devil in action. You can see it whenever anyone does something cruel. Why do you

201

think there are wars and murder? And what about people shooting each other the finger just because they disagree with you or because you pass too close on the freeway? And what about mind control? Have you ever watched commercials on television? Some of the biggest lies of all just so somebody can make a lot of money off people who believe the crap they're selling. That's what they're selling, not a product, just some lies about a product.

"And have you ever listened to politicians telling us what we want to hear just to get elected? Whoa, there's some people who sold their souls to the devil a long time ago. So why shouldn't this power be used for good? Why shouldn't I use it to achieve what I want?"

"You will never see Alec returned to your home as long as you believe that way," Dr. Mueller said.

I laughed in his face. I put a spell on him right then and there. His eyes got so big, I thought they were going to pop out of his head.

So anyway, I asked Alec, "How did you get here?"

That's when he told me about his motorcycle, so I helped him move his motorcycle into the garage so no one would see it on the side of the house. He went into the kitchen and sat down with his head in his hands. "They're going to send me back to the hospital," he said.

I was wrong after all. This was terrible. "They can't do that," I said. "I won't let them."

"They're looking for me right now," he said. "They chased me, but I got away. That's why I came here."

He told me that he jumped the Kemah drawbridge. It was a frightening story to hear him tell it. "A boy was killed trying to jump that bridge many years ago," I told him.

Of course, he knew. He talked about him as if he knew the boy, as if they were the best of friends. When he told me that the boy was Neva Bell's brother, her twin brother, it all began to make sense—why she had shown such an interest in Alec and why she was not willing to release him back to me.

I knew she would protect him, but I was right to believe that her intentions were selfish. That's why she had been in my dream, but she failed. My dream came true.

Alec came back to me just as I had dreamed, crossing the rainbow.

Somehow, I must have known that Alec was going to jump the Kemah drawbridge, and I must have known that boy who was killed there was Neva Bell's brother. Alec jumping that bridge gave Neva her brother back again. For her, her brother made it this time.

"Why were they chasing you?" I asked.

He slammed his fist on the table and yelled, "What difference does it make? They're always after people like me. Whatever I do is going to be wrong."

I tried to calm him and told him he was going to wake up Josh. Alec looked shocked. He had forgotten that he had a little brother, so I led him into the bedroom and showed him where Josh was sleeping. Josh looked so beautiful, even with his labored breathing.

As we stood there, April came into the room and didn't seem surprised that Alec was there. It was almost like he had always been with us.

"I wanted to give you two some time together," she said. She was so thoughtful. She placed her hand on Alec's arm and looked at Josh. "He looks like he could be your son," she whispered.

Alec said something that stunned me. "I don't think fatherhood will ever happen for me."

I asked him, "Why do you say that?"

He didn't answer. He just stared at Josh and said, "Don't let him sleep anywhere else. Promise me that."

"Alec . . ."

He held his hand up. "Josh looks like a good kid," Alec said. "I want you to keep him that way. Don't let him sleep with you," he said, and his voice sounded monotone.

The intonation of his voice accused me of doing horrible things to him in the past. Alec just didn't understand.

Right then, there was a knock at the front door. Alec turned and started for the back. "It's the police," he said.

I told him to wait, that he would be safer in the house. "That can't be the police anyway," I said. The knock was way too soft. I told him, "Whoever it is can't know you're here. If you're quiet, they'll never find out."

Alec and April stayed with the baby while I answered the door. It was Neva Bell, and she was looking for Alec. I spoke to her through the door, and she knew he was in the house because the porch was wet where he had been standing. She pleaded that she only wanted to help Alec, that she was alone, that no one had followed her.

Alec came into the room and said, "Let her in, Anna."

I frowned, hearing him calling me by my first name, and said, "I don't think it's a good idea. She's gonna try to trick you into going back to Morning House. You're home now, and you don't have to do what anyone else tells you to do, Baby. You can decide to stay, and there's nothing anybody can do about it, because there's no law against a child living with his own mother."

His voice was still cold when he said, "I've already made up my mind about what I'm going to do, but I still want to listen to her. I owe her that much."

Against my better judgment, I let her in.

Neva was polite, and when she saw Alec standing behind me, she let out a sigh of relief.

She wasn't mad. When she asked if he was all right, he just nodded that he was. She started tapping her fingers on her leg like she had something to say but didn't know how to say it. She was very nervous.

Finally, she started talking. "The detective told me that you jumped the Kemah drawbridge. I'm so glad you're okay. Alec, I'm really proud of you, and Jim would have been proud of you too."

Again, Alec just nodded.

Then, she said, "You were right when you said that a part of Jim would be jumping the bridge with you. I can feel that now."

"It seems so unimportant now," Alec said.

Neva shook her head. "No. It was very important. It shows what you can do when you put your mind to it. It was so important to face your fears and control your life, not run from it."

"It doesn't matter. Dr. Mueller will make sure I go back to the hospital, anyway."

April had been listening to all of this from the doorway at the back of the house. "There's something you're not telling us," she said to Neva.

"I don't think I should say anything. Alec, I think you should talk about it. It's the only way to deal with it and clear things up."

"Clear up what?" I asked. Now, I was getting upset and angry.

Alec was silent, but he nodded at Neva, so she agreed to say what she knew. She sat down and took a deep breath. She said it all very quickly like she didn't want us to dwell on any one part of it. "The owner of the market across the street from Morning House was murdered, and the police think Alec knows something about it. They wanted to talk to him, and that's why they were chasing him, so now they think he had something to do with the murder—that maybe he even did it."

Alec was just as shocked as I was. He was in such disbelief that he had to repeat what she said like he hadn't heard her right. Of course, he denied everything. He said he ran because he had taken some roses and some wine, that he meant to pay for them, but when he couldn't find the owner, he took them and put them in the saddlebag on his motorcycle. He was about to leave when he changed his mind and went back in the store to look for the owner. He walked to the back of the store, and that's when he saw some blood on the floor. He started feeling sick and left in a hurry. That was when he saw Warren outside the store. He never saw Duffy Campbell.

It finally dawned on me what was happening. "I was hoping you were our friend," I suddenly said to Neva. "I won't let you do this. Alec is here now, and he is going to stay here for as long as he wants."

Neva started pleading that we needed to trust her—that she *was* our friend but that Alec needed to go back and explain what happened.

"He can't," I said. "I won't allow it. Not now." I knew they wouldn't believe him after what he had done before.

Alec was looking straight at me and shaking his head. "I didn't murder anyone," he said. "Even if no one believes me. I have to prove it on my own. I can't let everyone else run my life anymore. I'm tired of everyone using me, and that means you too."

He broke my heart because he didn't know how I had changed.

"You've got to let me go," he said. "I'm sorry, but I had to tell you that. I think that's the real reason why I came back here tonight. I knew I had to get everything settled for my own peace of mind."

I knew what he was going to say before he said it. "Alec, don't . . ." He promised he would never tell.

Alec looked straight at Neva. "All these years, I've never told anyone this, not even the doctors. I tried to protect her, keeping our little secret.

My dad was a truck driver, and he was gone a lot. On nights when it was raining, Mom brought me into her bed because she was afraid of the rain."

"No, Alec, stop," I said. I just wanted to hold him because it settled me and made me feel safe. His voice was so cold, and it made it all sound so dirty. I was scared, and he said he was scared too. I only did it because I loved him, and I wanted to express that. "Alec, you don't understand. I was afraid and lonely, and I didn't want to bring some stranger into my bed and cheat on my husband."

Alec didn't even glance at me. His eyes remained focused on Neva. "What she did drove me crazy. I loved her, and I hated my father. I killed my dad to protect her, but in some strange way, I feel like I was forced to do it because there was no other way out. I've felt guilty for it ever since. I felt guilty for loving her, and I'm tired of feeling like that."

"Alec, no," was all that I could manage between my sobs.

"I can't go on anymore feeling like my life was stolen from me. I never had a chance to live a normal life."

He was saying such terrible, hateful things about me. I was thankful when we heard the footsteps on the front porch. We all froze, trying not to make a sound, waiting for the inevitable. Even so, I was still startled by the knock of the door.

Alec went to the window and cracked the blinds. He turned around and said, "It's Detective Kelly." Alec looked at Neva and said, "I trusted you. I can't believe you'd do this to me."

"I didn't. I haven't talked to anyone," she whispered.

"I don't believe you," he whispered back.

Neva followed him into the kitchen, asking him to wait, to let her prove she didn't lead the police to him. When she returned, there was another knock at the door. I was still frozen to the chair and shaking because I didn't know what to do. I whispered to Neva, "What are we going to do?" She said she didn't know but that I needed to get up—that I had to answer the door, that I owed Alec that much.

We lied and said that we were in the back of the house with the baby and that was why we didn't hear the knock at the door. We also lied, saying that we hadn't seen Alec that night.

We were just trying to stall, and that's when I looked around for April. Suddenly, she emerged from the back of the house wearing only a short, little teddy with her beautiful, long legs glistening in the dim light. Those big breasts of hers surged beneath the thin, transparent fabric. She smiled as she walked past us and out onto the front porch. I could hear her call out in a sweet voice to the other policemen who must have been waiting outside. My stomach leaped when I heard her say that she was going to open the garage so the policemen could stand inside and not get wet.

At first, I wanted to stop her because I knew that Alec was in the garage, but then, I realized what she was doing—she was providing a distraction for Alec, getting all those cops outside to watch her instead of what was about to happen. I heard the garage door go up, then a rumble in the garage and a sharp screeching noise.

We all realized that Alec had started up his motorcycle. We ran outside into the glaring darkness, where the steady downpour was broken by sparks and flashes of light. I caught only a glimpse of Alec hunched down over his motorcycle swerving out into the street, and I heard the policemen yelling at him to stop as loud echoes of gunfire exploded into the darkness.

● ● ●

Neva

Janeen was lying in a hospital bed, barely a whisper of a breath disturbing the sheets. She looked so peaceful and unencumbered, unaware that she was tethered intravenously to life, suspended on the brink of death through sheer will. I held her hand and thought how I must have looked the same after my odyssey seven years before.

It was a time I had hoped to forget, a time after my first life, which ended when Jim died. I started getting sick a lot, so my mother called Uncle Spencer for advice, even though I pleaded with her not to. It seemed that she just couldn't handle any more trauma on her own. Uncle Spencer picked us both up one day and took me to a clinic, where a doctor examined me. He listened to my lungs, took my blood pressure, probed into my ears and mouth, and told me to lie on my back while he put my feet in the stirrups, which were absolutely medieval.

The doctor reached inside me, and I felt this terrible pain like he was pulling me inside out. I wanted to kick him. The last thing he did was take some blood from my finger, then left me alone in the examination room. It was like being raped and dumped on the side of the road.

I waited for an eternity until my mother finally came back into the room. She had been crying. She stopped just inside the door and took a deep breath, which seemed to draw away all the air in the room. Then, she expelled all of her despair, leaving only anger. She didn't say a word. She just walked straight over to me and slapped my face. Then, she left the room.

If I had suspected for a moment that I was pregnant with Jim's baby, I think I would have kept it, but I knew I wasn't—that would have been impossible. I never got to ask Uncle Spencer why he told my mother that, why he broke his promise not to tell her about what Jim and I had done, why he apparently lied about it. When he dropped us off at home, he left, and I never saw him again.

The doctor told me I was pregnant, but that wasn't why I was crying. I had suspected that I was pregnant anyway. I cried because my mother slapped me and because I couldn't tell her the truth about her beloved brother. Uncle Spencer moved away—not because he failed to help me but because he couldn't face what he had done.

My mother disowned me and told me to leave the house so she wouldn't have to look at me ever again. She never believed me—that it wasn't Jim's child—and she said she would never forgive me. She never answered my letters. She hung up on me when I called her. She didn't come to see me in the hospital.

Deanna was the only one who visited me in the hospital. I don't know if Deanna was her real name. I met her on Montrose in Houston, where I ended up when I left home. Deanna saw this police officer stop to talk to me, and she came up and pretended to be my sister so he wouldn't hassle me about being out after curfew. She looked like she was older than she really was, which was only a year or two older than me.

Deanna lived with her boyfriend, Max, in an apartment not far from a strip joint called The Foxy Lady, where she worked. Max was the bartender and also announced the names of the strippers when they came out on the stage. Deanna was really pretty in the natural light of morning when she wasn't wearing any makeup. At first, I was afraid Max might try something with me, but he was a gentleman and actually put me at ease about what I had to do. He got me a job waiting tables at Foxy's, and he promised not to tell the boss that I was underage, since I was too young to be serving alcohol. They let me sleep on a fold out couch in their living room and told me to stay with them for as long as I wanted.

I was turned down at the neighborhood clinic because they needed a parent to sign the forms. Deanna pretended to be my sister again, but this time, it didn't work. The nurse said she would like to help me, but law required a parent's approval. Max said he had a friend who knocked up his girlfriend once, so he found out where they went. I was afraid to go through with it, but Deanna said she would stay with me through the whole thing.

We rented a motel room under the name of Mary Rose, and we waited until this woman who looked like she could have worked in a drug store as a cosmetic clerk showed up. She wore heavy perfume, and she kept calling me Honey. First, she wanted the money. She pulled some instruments out of the big handbag she carried. She had me lie on the floor on top of several towels. She moved fast, almost as fast as she talked. She was very pleasant, which distracted me from what she was doing. I was only able to endure the discomfort because Deanna was holding my hand the whole time. At one point, I thought I was going to be sick. Suddenly, it was over. The woman got up, wrapped her instruments in a towel, and put them into her handbag with the money. She wrapped another towel in a separate plastic bag, then stood up and said, "Good luck, Honey." I stared at the door and smelled the lingering scent of cheap perfume, and I began to cry.

When I tried to get up, I ruptured something inside and bled all over the floor. Deanna screamed when I collapsed. That was the last thing I heard until I woke up three days later in the hospital and saw Deanna smiling at me. I think Deanna was really an angel. Funny how religion becomes important and gives us hope when we need it.

That's what I was hoping for, that by holding Janeen's hand, I could give her some of my own life force. It didn't matter if she had done this intentionally, by accident, or unconsciously. This was not the way to end the trial of her life. If there was any hope of putting it all behind her, then maybe, just maybe she would be the one to succeed. I was trying to get this through to her when I thought I heard unintelligible muttering. Her lips were barely moving. I held my breath, waiting for her to speak, to move, to blink, anything that would be a sign that she was coming back, but there was nothing. It wasn't long after that when the nurse came in and said that visiting hours were over.

• • •

Janeen

Clean. That's how I felt. I stood in the rain, looking up into the falling drops and watching them as they came down fast and hit my face, but they didn't hurt. It felt good. I spread my arms out and let the water wash all over me. The rain was warm and gentle. It kind of scared me for a second that I was feeling so good because I didn't trust it, so I looked down at my feet and saw a pool of blood. I felt blood running down my legs. After a while, it stopped, and I stepped out of the pool and watched the rain wash it away.

I began walking because I had always wanted to walk in the rain. I felt so good, and I started skipping and dancing. I paid no attention to where I was going. I didn't care. Only the feeling mattered. When the rain stopped, I was in a forest, only it looked more like a grove of trees, just rows and rows of tall trees. The air smelled sweet, and I thought I heard music coming from high up in the branches. I even thought I heard a woman's voice singing softly. Not any particular song, just a beautiful, melodious songbird voice. It wasn't scary at all. I moved along a path, as if being guided by someone who was holding my hand, someone I couldn't see, and when I looked down, my feet weren't moving, but still I glided over the path.

The further I walked, the brighter it got, first with beams of sunlight breaking through the trees, then whole areas that seemed to be alive with shadows dancing on the ground. The tops of the trees moved in a wind that suddenly got stronger, so strong it tried to blow me back as I walked along the path. I walked toward this one really bright light at the end of the row of trees. As I got nearer, the light became blinding, and I had to squint, but I kept looking into it. The wind stopped, and everything was peaceful and quiet as a church. I was almost standing in the light, but I could see someone appear in the distance. I couldn't tell who it was, but this person was motioning to me and reaching out from very far away, and yet I could feel a touch on my hand.

Spinner was the first person I saw when I opened my eyes. He was so funny. He said, "Hey, kid, welcome back." I didn't know what he was talking about, but he was always kidding. I didn't know why he was in my room—it was against the rules—and I didn't want him to get into trouble. "Neva's going to catch you in here," I said. "You better go, and turn out the lights when you leave so I can go back to sleep."

He looked at me real funny and laughed. That's when I looked around and realized that I wasn't in my room. It was a small room with a curtain next to the bed; the light was real bright and hurt my eyes.

Spinner told me I was lucky to be here because I had really taken a hit. That was when I started to remember what I had done.

"I didn't mean to," I said. I pleaded with him not to tell.

"Too late, kid," he said. "They all know. No hiding anything now." He told me that Krista and Mr. Mac were outside, and he asked me if I wanted them to come in. I told him no. He sat down on the edge of the bed, and I reached out, and he took my hand in his. It felt good. I had done terrible things, and I wanted to forget. I wanted to run away. Maybe I *did* do it on purpose. Maybe I *did* try to kill myself. I told Spinner all this, and he said, "You know, kid, I think maybe I'm beginning to get the hang of this group home thing. I mean, it feels good being here with you."

I'll never forget him telling me that. I was feeling like the lowest, most terrible thing in the world, and what he said made me feel better. I told him to think of something that makes you sick, and whatever it is, I'm lower and more disgusting. All he asked for was a chance to prove that he could help me. He told me that he really liked me just the way I was. I was feeling so comfortable with Spinner that I confided some pretty dark secrets because I wanted him to know the truth.

"That time I passed out on the kitchen floor, I was having withdrawals, and somehow, Randy knew I was hooked. He said he knew a guy who could get me some stuff."

Spinner started to get angry and said he was going to kill Randy.

I said it wasn't all his fault. "I could have said no. I don't know why I allow myself to get into these things. Anyway, I didn't have any money to buy it. But Randy told me all I had to do was to come on to this guy at a gas station, and he could handle the rest. He said he would signal me when he was through. It sounded easy, so I did it, and the next thing I knew, Randy was taking the money out of the cash register. He said if I snitched him off, he would take me down with him. We did two more like that, and he used the money to buy the stuff from the guy he knew."

Somehow, Spinner knew about this guy, 'cause he asked me if the guy had blond hair and always called me Angel. He told me it didn't matter how he knew, that all that mattered was that they would never get to me again. Spinner was going to help me kick this thing, but that wasn't even the worst part. I was starting to feel tired, and I could barely keep my eyes open. Spinner told me I should rest, that he would get Krista to sit with me because he was going back to Morning House. There was something he had to do.

I begged him to be careful. I remember telling Spinner that Randy was dangerous. I wanted to tell him the rest—to confess all the awful things I had done, to feel as clean as I had felt in my dream, but I was so tired. God, I was tired.

• • •

Detective Kelly

After a lot of work, we had an arrest warrant for this Davy kid. Davy was a blond-haired kid who had been hanging out with Randy since they were in grade school. He wasn't very smart, so I don't think he realized how much information he gave us. After talking with us, he revealed that he and Randy were part of the trio who picked up Emily the night she was walking to Gilley's.

A clerk at one the markets they robbed recognized Davy, so we arrested Davy at his home without any problems. Davy claimed the last time he saw Randy was the day they drove to Morning House. Except he didn't call him Randy— he said Bubba was Randy's nickname, ever since elementary school.

Davy was waiting in his truck at Morning House when Emily came down the stairs, and he knew she was going to remember him sooner or later. Davy said she got this look in her eyes and kept watching him like she was trying to place where she'd seen him. Neva was with her, and Neva asked Davy what he was doing there. He was scared that she was going to call the cops, so he said he just showed up and was waiting on Bubba.

Davy realized from the look on Emily's face that she was piecing things together. He thought she was going to freak out. Neva started back toward the house to look for Randy. Davy called her a mother hen.

Emily stayed there, right at the front of his truck, and Davy knew it was coming to her. She was about to put two and two together, and all he wanted was to get the hell out of there before she remembered.

"What happened that night wasn't my idea," Davy said. "It just happened. We were all stoned, and Bubba saw her hitch'n a ride, so he let her in the van, laughing like he just struck gold. He kept telling us to give her more beer and light'n up more joints until she nearly passed out." She couldn't have known what was happening.

Davy was waiting in his truck when he heard a motorcycle. Emily headed out toward the driveway. Davy saw Alec in his rearview mirror, coming around the corner of the house, and he said he knew "shit was about to hit the fan." Davy knew that we were looking for Alec. He and Randy had seen the story on the front page of the paper about Duffy Campbell 's murder and how Alec had escaped by jumping the Kemah drawbridge. "When we saw that story in the newspaper, Bubba said we could pin it all on Alec," Davy said.

Davy actually had a conscience. I saw it all over his face, and it didn't take him long to give up Randy for everything.

"Bubba thought up a scheme to get some money," he said. "He said we could use a girl that he knew from Morning House to distract the clerk. He said it already worked for him once. The first night he stayed at Morning House, Bubba followed Emily to the store across the street and took the money from the register that night while she was in the back with the clerk. When he told me who Emily was, I didn't like that plan. I knew it'd come back on us for what we did before. So Bubba said he'd find another one of the girls in the house to do it. This other girl was willing to go along with it to get some dope. Her name was Janeen, but Bubba started calling her Angel because she did such a good job.

"She would go into the place first and make eyes at the clerk. When he took the bait, they'd go into the back of the store. She always kept him busy long enough for Bubba to go in and take the money from the register."

"And what was your role?" I asked Davy.

"Shit, man. I didn't do nothing. I just waited in the truck and drove 'em home after they were done."

"Wait," I said. "I thought Randy was using your motorcycle."

"Yeah, I mean sometimes he would. He'd just drive the motorcycle up into the back of my truck, and then, I'd take them home. I was just driving them. That's all."

"But you got a cut."

"Well, yeah. I mean, nobody was getting hurt. It was a pretty good scheme."

"Until someone *did* actually get hurt," I said.

"The first time went off without a hitch, but the second time, the clerk must have heard something and ran out in time to see Bubba riding away on my motorcycle. Bubba just rode down the street and right up into the back of my truck. We just rode off like nothing happened. When Alec got arrested for it, we were just lucky."

"But what about Campbell's market? What happened there?"

"I was waiting outside in my truck when I saw Angel run out of the store. She usually gets into my truck, but she ran across the street towards Morning House. I just sat there waiting, and it took a while for Bubba to come out. When he finally did, he was all out of breath, and he looked weird. He got in the truck and leaned back against the door and put his arm up on the seat. I saw blood on his shirt."

"What happened next?" I asked him.

"Well, he told me to drive him to my house, but I won't ever forget what he said after that."

"What'd he say, Davy?" I asked.

"Aww shit, man, if he finds out I'm talking to you about this, he'll kill me."

"He won't get that chance if we can arrest him, Davy. I've already explained this to you. You help us, and we'll help you. We've easily got you on rape and probably as an accomplice to murder. We can make your life a lot easier if you cooperate."

"Alright. Alright. When we were driving back to my house, Bubba said, 'I didn't realize it was so easy to kill a man. Now, Alec ain't got nothin' on me.' He said that the old man in the store didn't go for it with Angel. Bubba went in thinking he'd be in the back with Angel, but the old man was at the register, and Bubba tried to take the money anyway."

"What else did he say?" I asked.

214

"He said the old man pulled out a gun. Bubba said he wasn't going to let an old man get the jump on him, so he hit Duffy Campbell and took the gun away from him. Bubba said he was going to tie him up in the back of the store, but the old man started fighting for the gun. Bubba grabbed a knife off the counter and stabbed him."

"Anything else?" I prodded.

"Well, Bubba was bragging. He said the old man didn't die right away, so Bubba dragged him to the storeroom. He said the old man was pleading for his life, and Bubba shot him in the head just to see what it would look like." Tears formed in Davy's eyes. "I never wanted anyone to die. And shit, man, Bubba was laughing the whole time he was telling me all this. He's sick, man."

"So what about the day after the murder?" I asked.

"Well, Bubba told me to drive him back to Morning House. I was still in the truck when Alec rode up on his motorcycle. Emily ran over to him, and they talked a while. Then, Alec walked over. He told me to get out of the truck, and I tried to play it cool. I said, 'Is that any kinda hello?' I asked him 'Don't you remember me?'"

"So did he remember you?" I asked.

"Yeah. He remembered, but he was serious, and he looked pissed. I kept trying to be cool. I said, 'Bubba told me you're staying here, too,' but he told me to shut up and said, 'I never liked you, Davy, so stop acting like we were friends.' He was different from what I remembered. He used to be wimpy, but he got right up in my face like he wanted to fight."

"And what'd he say to you?"

"Well, he said, 'I know you're waiting for Bubba.' Then, he said, 'You two gonna go somewhere together, like Gilley's maybe?'"

"So that's when you realized that he knew about you—and what you and Randy had done to Emily."

"Yeah. I mean, I just wanted to get the hell out of there. Alec looked like he was about to foam at the mouth. And I tried to deny it. I said, 'I don't know what you're talking about. You're crazy, man,' but that must've really pissed him off because he grabbed me by the front of my shirt and shoved me up against the truck. He was yelling that he wasn't crazy. I shouldn't of ever got outta the damn truck."

"So did the two of you fight?" I asked.

"Well, I tried to push him back, but he hit me upside the head and knocked me down. I was laying in the dirt, and I thought Alec was going to hit me again, but I heard a car pull up next to my truck."

"Who was it?"

"It was that black kid that whipped Bubba. He was saying something about Bubba trying to kill somebody with some bad smack."

"And you were still laying in the driveway?"

"Yeah. Well, then, we heard a scream come from the house. They all ran back in the house, and I got back in my truck. I was about to get the hell out of Dodge, but before I could pull out, Bubba ran down the stairs, jumped in my truck, and told me to get the hell outta there."

"And the rest is history," I said. "I'm going to need you to write down your part in all of this just like you told me. Okay?" I stood up and patted him on the back. "You did good, Davy," I said. "You did good."

Davy's concession read as follows:

> I didn't want no part in killin' that old man or what happened to Angel or any of it. I admit what I did to that girl, but I didn't rape her. We shouldn't a done what we did 'cause she looked like she was sick, and when she tried to get up, I held her down, but I didn't do it with her. She got too sick, so we just left her in the parking lot at Gilley's.
>
> That was Bubba's idea too. It was kinda cruel leaving her there like that, but that was Bubba. He always had a mean streak, just did mean things for the hell of it. Once, he killed a dog just 'cause Alec liked the dog, and Bubba thought it would be funny. He has a real mean streak, I tell you. I'm glad I turned him in. It was worth it. All I ask is that you don't put me anywhere he's gonna be 'cause he'll kill me for sure.

• • •

Neva

I don't know why I did it. It was stupid, telling Randy to come into my

216

office. I just wanted to find out what was going on, why he didn't return to Morning House the night before. I wasn't expecting his reaction.

He walked around the room looking at everything as if biding his time until I was through talking; then, he turned to me and smiled smugly. He had the nerve to tell me that I had a problem, that I was too uptight. I was trying to restrain myself and simply told him that he didn't belong at Morning House any longer, that he was not ready to accept any help and may never be.

He came right out and said that he didn't want any help. He accused *me* of needing help. He was arguing like a six-year-old, with this "No, I don't, you do" comeback, so I knew right away that I wouldn't be able to reason with him.

He walked to the window and glanced down at the backyard, where his friend was waiting. Suddenly, I remembered that Emily was down there alone with that strange boy, and I suspected Randy was trying to distract me for some reason. Then, I heard a motorcycle, and Randy got a worried look on his face.

"What's wrong, Bubba?" I asked him.

His whole demeanor changed then. He glared at me. "Why'd you call me that?" he asked.

I said, "It's your name, isn't it? You're the Bubba who used to tease Alec because you knew he wouldn't fight back. You are the same Bubba who stands for everything Alec is afraid of becoming and who reminds him of what he used to be. You are the reason that Alec fights bullies like you— because he has something to prove, that he is not frail, he's just human, and there is nothing wrong with that."

All Randy said was, "Why should I care about Alec?"

He was so smug, I wanted to slap his face. I told Randy that I wanted him to understand the difference between him and Alec, to know that there would be no hope in this world for him unless one day he realized that he needed to change and that he was going to need help to do that. I just made him angrier. He accused me of playing favorites with Alec, that I thought Alec was perfect.

"You'll see soon enough it isn't true," he said. "There's evidence, and sooner or later, the cops will find it, and it will show that your precious little Alec is really a murderer."

He went on to accuse Alec of being the thief all along—and using Janeen to help him. I knew Randy couldn't be trusted, and when he said that, I knew that he had done it all, and now he was setting up Alec to take the blame. I didn't know how he did it, but I knew I was facing a dangerous kid. Worst of all, he knew I didn't believe him. He had said too much, and he realized it. I told him to go up to his room and wait for someone to come and take him back to juvenile hall.

He looked at me with this horrid smile and said, "No, you and me are going to do something else."

He walked over to my desk and moved the back of his hand down my hair real slow. I stood up and told him to get out of my office, but he was almost on top of me, and he pushed me back into the chair. He pulled a knife out of his pocket and opened up what looked like a very long blade.

I said, "Randy, please think about what you are doing." I knew these words were useless. He wanted to hurt me and humiliate me. My only hope was to catch him off guard. I wanted to scream, but I couldn't, and part of me feared that this would send him over the edge.

Then, he said, "Take your clothes off."

I don't know where it came from or even exactly what I did—it was all so instinctive. I think I was going to pretend to cooperate; then, suddenly, I kicked upward as hard as I could, and luckily, I caught him in the right spot. He doubled over with a moan and went down to one knee.

I started to run, but he grabbed my ankle, and I fell to the floor. This time, I did scream. I knew it was loud, and it gave me a great deal of energy. I turned over and kicked at him again, this time hitting him in the shoulder. He hardly moved. I kicked again and again, and he just started laughing. That's when Spinner and Alec burst into the room and charged toward us.

I tried to warn them, but I was too late. I tried to tell them about the knife, but they had already moved by me, and Randy was rising up from the floor to meet them. Alec kicked Randy in the face, snapping his head back. Then, Spinner pushed by Alec as if he wanted Alec out of the way. He was on top of Randy in one fluid motion, and they were both going down to the floor. It looked like Randy punched Spinner in the chest, and Spinner didn't even feel it. He just kept hitting Randy in the face again and again, and then, he suddenly stopped and leaned back against the desk.

Randy got up, still holding the knife, and backed out the door, saying, "It's his fault. He should have showed me more respect."

Alec knelt down, and Spinner slipped into his arms. The front of his shirt was already red, and his breathing was labored and liquid. I called for help, and we tried to keep him calm. For a moment, he seemed stable, like he was going to be okay. He tried to talk, only his voice was slipping and seemed to be someone else's voice.

"Oh God," he said, looking up as if he had just remembered something. His voice was sputtering and full of blood. "This ain't happening. This can't be how it ends. I don't . . . I . . ."

Alec kept saying, "Hold on, brother," over and over again until he choked on the tears in the words.

I couldn't find the right words to give Spinner the comfort he needed. There were too many tears, or maybe the shock silenced the words and the understanding we all needed on that bright Saturday morning as Spinner slipped away.

● ● ●

Krista

I was the only one upstairs when Alec and Emily came back that night. The floor creaked just like that first night I saw Emily sneaking out. They were in the hallway just outside her door. They didn't say a word when they saw me. Words seemed useless.

I asked if they were going to stay. Alec just shook his head and said that too much had happened. I couldn't blame them. I felt the same way. I told them I was going home in the morning if my parents would still have me.

A door opened downstairs, and Neva started up the staircase. Mr. Mac had gone to the hospital to be with Janeen, so I knew that Neva was the only one in the house besides me. Alec and Emily looked at me, and I could tell that they were wondering what I would say. I could see the fear in their faces, the fear of being discovered, of having their plans ruined. I motioned toward the room, and they went inside. I was standing in front of the door when Neva saw me. She seemed startled.

"Are you all right?" she asked.

"I couldn't sleep," I explained. I asked her if there was any word about Janeen, and she said there was nothing to worry about. Janeen was just resting. No one had told Janeen about Spinner yet.

Neva looked around. She was nervous, preoccupied. She said that she couldn't sleep, so she had come up to get some of Spinner's things together. I asked if she needed some help, and I was glad when she said no because I still wanted to talk to Alec and Emily. "I'll be in my room," I said.

She smiled and waited for me to go to my room; then, she went to Alec's room. She was in there a long time. I was afraid to open the door to peek, but then, finally, I heard her hurry back down the staircase. When her door closed downstairs, I went next door to Emily's room, and we were once again left in silence, a disturbing longing to make things right, to change what could no longer be undone.

Emily thanked me, and I guess I had this puzzled look on my face, so she told me that she thought I was going to tell Neva that they were here. "It doesn't seem to be important anymore," I said.

I took her hands and told her I was sorry for all that I had done, that I wished I could make up for everything. Her hands were so cold and trembled in mine like she was afraid. Suddenly, I was afraid too. I put my arms around her, and as we held each other, I felt her forgiveness.

She asked me if I would take care of Janeen and make sure she got better. "Of course, I will," I said.

Emily smiled. It was a funny, serene smile, and she said, "You were right about Dr. Mueller. I know you weren't lying about him, and I have a feeling that things will get worked out when we are gone."

"I wish you would stay," I pleaded.

"We can't," Alec said. It was like they had to catch a plane and they were in a hurry. They had just come back to pick up some things, and he hoped I didn't have any bad feelings about them.

"Of course, I don't," I said. Then, I asked where they were going, and Alec only said that it was a secret place. They wouldn't really know until they got there.

As I hugged Alec, I began to cry; then, I told them that they had better hurry. When Alec told me goodbye, I knew it was final. I would never see them again.

• • •

Neva

The rain started up again, not long after what had happened to Spinner, and it stopped just as suddenly during the night, leaving the musty smell of damp leaves outside my open window. Alec said he changed his mind about turning himself in. Promises didn't matter anymore. No one could promise him anything that would make him believe that his life would get any better. He left before the police arrived, and Emily insisted on going with him. Krista and I were the only ones left in the house that night. Warren had gone to the hospital to stay with Janeen in case she woke up again. We were all trying to salvage what was left.

I kept thinking about what Randy had said about Alec and how the police were going to find the evidence. What evidence? The police had already searched Alec's room once and didn't find anything. But that was before Randy came back. When I saw Randy, he was just coming down the stairs. I thought he had gone up to his own room because he was leaving. Then, it occurred to me that he had gone up to Alec's room, not to get something but to leave something behind. Whatever that was had to be the evidence that would implicate Alec in Duffy Campbell's murder.

I didn't know what I was looking for, but I knew it was there and that I had to find it before the police came back the next day. As I went up the stairs, I was startled to find Krista standing on the landing. She looked lost and frightened. I didn't want her to know what I was doing, so I told her I couldn't sleep and that I was going to gather some of Spinner's things. I was glad she didn't insist on helping me. We were all feeling so lost.

I went into Alec's and Spinner's room and looked through everything—dresser drawers, desk drawers, closets, and even under the bed. I was sitting on the floor, trying to think of where Randy would have hidden something so the police would find it but not think it was too obvious. It had to be somewhere they would have overlooked during the first search. Not knowing what I was looking for made it even harder. I thought that perhaps I was wrong, that whatever it was might still be over at Campbell's Market. I was about to leave and grabbed the side of the bed to pull myself up off the floor, and my hand slipped between the mattress and the box spring. My fingers touched the tip of something hard, and for a second, I was frozen there. I moved my hand in slowly around it, and I knew right away that I had found what I was looking for. I pulled it out and held it, staring at it, thinking that I never knew that guns were so heavy.

Feeling that it was something I had to hide even from myself, I hurried downstairs and put it in my desk drawer. My initial plan was to turn it in the next day, but I knew I would have to report where I had found it. This would still look bad for Alec, so somehow, I would have to explain why the obvious wasn't true. I took the gun from my desk and wrapped it in a towel, went outside to the garden, and buried it next to the house. I thought I heard something, but when I turned, no one was there. The wind was beginning to pick up again, rustling the leaves in the trees and throwing their shadows about on the ground. Through a break in the clouds, the sky was clear and full of stars. Down the hill, the boathouse appeared to float in soft, surreal moonlight. I went back inside and cleaned up, then went to bed, but I couldn't sleep.

Morning came slowly, but when it arrived, it was brilliant and blustery. At breakfast, Krista told me she was worried that Alec and Emily were in trouble. I asked her if she knew something, and she admitted that they had come back during the night. She wanted to make amends for everything she had done. This was why she didn't tell me. They wanted time to get away, far enough away so no one could talk them into returning. I understood. I couldn't get mad at her. We all wanted time to change our reality and make it clear again.

I asked Krista if they said where they were going. She hesitated, so I reassured her that I wasn't going to chase after them. I just wanted to stay in touch with them to make sure they were safe. She said she didn't know. They only said they were going to a secret place. When she said that, I dropped my coffee cup on the floor, which startled both of us because I didn't even realize I had lost my grip.

The sinking feeling I felt came with regrets that I had told Alec about the secret place Jim and I had. I also told him about my vision of him and Emily walking hand and hand down to the old boathouse on Mud Lake. I ran out the back door and through the gardens, stopping only when I reached the edge of the grass near the boathouse. Through the blowing wind, I could hear the mournful creaking of the boards as the boathouse rocked in the waves, and I could feel my own labored breathing.

Krista came up behind me and cried because she didn't understand. I took her by the shoulders and told her to wait, nearly shouting to hear my own voice over the fierce wind that was blowing all around us. When I was sure she wouldn't move, I opened the door to the boathouse and stepped inside, praying that it would be empty.

I saw an image on the floor of the boathouse. Instinctively, I closed my eyes, thinking my worst fears had come true, and when I opened them again, the image was gone, and I heard an odd sound escape from my lips with a mixture of fear and elation.

There were neatly arranged blankets, a bed for newlyweds, with one pillow where their heads had lain together. Only one red rose rested on the pillow. Off to the side was an empty bottle of wine, a small seashell—the kind where you can hear the sea when you hold it up to your ear—a beautifully intact sand dollar, and a book of Japanese poems with an envelope addressed to me and marking the page of a poem titled "Seventh Day, Seventh Month."

Before I opened the envelope, I went back outside and told Krista everything was all right. I instructed her to go back to the house to pack. After she returned to the house, I went back inside the boathouse and opened the envelope. Inside were several notes. I thought I had remained unusually calm during this crisis, but as I tried to read the notes, I had trouble focusing on the words, and I realized that my hands were shaking, and my eyes were filled with tears.

Dear Neva,

Please forgive us if we have hurt you, but try to understand that we have reached this decision together, neither forcing the other. For the first time, we have determined our own destinies. We leave knowing that we will be together to create another life, beyond this one, in a place where this life, with all its sadness and fear, is forgotten.

Alec and Emily

Alec had enclosed the card with the picture of the white bird and the words by Martin Buber, the ones that had been framed on my desk, the ones I had given him when he arrived at Morning House. During the time I had known him, they had been his first and his last.

> *Here on the earth's brink*
> *I have for a time*
> *Miraculously settled my life*

How precariously we all sit on this earth. There was a second note written by Emily and attached to the first. It was a more disturbing note and made me tremble as I read it.

Dear Neva,

Please do not be upset with Krista. She told you the truth about Dr. Mueller. I was afraid to say anything at the time because I was ashamed after you helped me understand why I was the way I was.

Krista was able to resist him because she's stronger, but I thought I needed him, and his attention felt good, so I gave in. I only understood what real love was when I discovered Alec's kindness. When I told Dr. Mueller about my love for Alec, he said that Alec was going back to the hospital because he was dangerous, and I should be careful of him.

Dr. Mueller gave me some pills when I told him I was depressed. He didn't know I wasn't taking them. What we have done has nothing to do with Dr. Mueller, but I don't think he really cares about helping people the way you do. I hope you don't take all this personally. Please believe us when we say that we are happy now, at last.

Emily

I could not help but take it personally, but I didn't take it the way Emily thought. As I stood in the boathouse, I noticed another piece of paper tucked in a fold of the blanket. It was another poem, scribbled in Alec's handwriting, and it made me think that, even then, Jim was talking through Alec.

The Kiss
Our hands entwined,
Our wedded souls,
Give promised kiss
Eternal breath.

So kiss me now,
My love, and dream.
Your kiss brings peace
And restful sleep.

Reading these notes did not allay my fears. These were suicide notes, and I suspected that Alec and Emily had intended to carry out what I initially feared. What had stopped them, and where were they now? My brain ached with confusion. When I left the boathouse, I headed back up the hill toward the house. In the whirling fury of dust and leaves, I saw Warren and Dr. Mueller walking toward me.

Krista was still inside the house. I walked right up to Warren and told him to go the boathouse. He seemed to understand. I asked Dr. Mueller to stay with me, that I had something to show him. He just looked at me coldly. My Uncle Spencer's smile was no longer on his face, and in its place was the lie that Uncle Spencer had told my mother, the lie he told to protect himself, the lie that it was Jim's baby I carried and not his.

Then, Dr. Mueller said, "There is no need. Morning House will be closed. I'm sure you understand." That was it. It was so simple. He was so smug. I knew that next would come all the lies to protect himself.

"I know more than you realize," I told him.

He said something that I now believe was the trigger that destroyed my sanity. He said there was no need for me to be there any longer, that he held me responsible for what happened at Morning House, and that it would never be erased from my record.

I felt a rush of heat flow into my head and burn my eyes. I took a deep breath. I don't know how long it was before I actually was able to speak, but when I could, I told him that I wanted to show him something before I left. I was perfectly calm again. I explained that he was right about my dream, that I *did* lose my religion, but I also lost my love, my passion, my family, and my dignity. I lost my whole life; I had not resolved any of it, and I was not at peace.

"You don't look well, Neva," I heard him say. "You should go inside and lie down."

I pulled away from him, tore my arm away from his grasp, and although I felt violated and angry, my voice was very calm. "Stay away from me." I told him that he was the vulture all along, circling above us all, waiting to destroy us, and he watched me as I backed away from him. I turned and walked back to the house, back to where I had buried the gun.

He must have thought I was going inside, because when I pulled it from the ground and turned around, he was facing the boathouse, talking with Warren. I remember wondering why Warren was speaking with Uncle Spencer, and I envied Alec that he had settled affairs with his mother while he had the chance.

They did not even have the decency to turn around when I approached them. There was no need. What I had to do was more for my own benefit—and the benefit of others. The wind was blowing around us so fast it seemed that time was moving in a deafening frenzy, but I could move only in slow motion. I was thinking that I wanted him to pay for what he had done, but suddenly, I felt very heavy, and I couldn't raise my hands because something was holding them at my sides. Even if I didn't do it, I wanted to. The wind was so loud in my ears, I didn't hear another sound, but I knew it was over.

● ● ●

Warren

I had come back up from the boathouse just before it happened. I don't remember feeling much. I was still numb because of Spinner's death, and after seeing the scene in the boathouse and wondering what might happen to Alec and Emily, I was thinking that if I allowed myself to feel, then I would crack. So much had happened in such a short time. It was like a tornado had dipped down out of the sky, and in the blink of an eye, it had changed the face of the land and drawn into its vacuum all emotion, leaving only emptiness.

Dr. Mueller was standing at the edge of the rose garden, and when I approached, he said the police were on their way. I thought he meant because of Alec and Emily. I thought Neva had told him. I didn't know about the gun, so I didn't know that the police were coming out to look for it. The first I knew about the gun was when I saw it in Neva's hand.

She was walking toward us, and she wasn't holding the gun like she was afraid of it. She looked very uncomfortable with it but oddly determined, like someone else was controlling her movements. I remember looking at the gun, hanging there at her side, and looking at her eyes, which were sort of glazed over but staring ahead at something like she knew where she was going and why. Dr. Mueller was saying something about closing Morning House, but I wasn't paying any attention to him because I was thinking Neva might be feeling guilty about what had happened, that she might think that somehow it was her fault, that she had caused this tornado to drop out of the sky and suck up all reason and understanding.

There wasn't time to figure it out. I just reacted. I lunged toward her and grabbed her hands, holding as tight as I could, thinking that it wasn't worth it, whatever she was going to do. I knew that much from firsthand experience, that sometimes there aren't any acceptable answers to the pain that can drive us mad. I grabbed the gun from her. I know it was in my hands. I felt her release it, but it still went off. I don't know how. I'm not that familiar with guns. It just did.

Her eyes were still glazed over, but then, they looked down like she was relaxed. She muttered something about it all being over, and I thought she meant that she wasn't going to fight me anymore. When I turned, I saw that she was looking down at Dr. Mueller.

It didn't really hit me then what happened. I was more concerned for Neva, so I took her inside where we could wait. It was only later, when the police arrived and I went back outside, that it all became very real. The rain was beginning to fall then, and you could tell it was going to be a big one, so the police officers who were waiting placed a tarp unceremoniously over the body as if to preserve some dignity and decorum to this surreal scene. None of us meant for this to happen, not any of it.

Part Four:
Time is a
Foolish
Fancy

Chapter Sixteen

She ran down the hall, just a step ahead of them, laughing gaily, her dark hair bouncing, her white nightgown rustling against her legs. It was a game of chase, a child's game, she thought, until they caught her. She squirmed in the grasp of hard, thick hands on her slender arms.

"Come on, now," one of them insisted, "you have a visitor."

"No!" she screamed, twisting angrily. But they just gripped her harder still and pulled her back down the hall to her room.

She saw him waiting at the door. With immodest curiosity, she watched him, forgetting the two attendants even as they took her in. When they loosened their grips, she shook herself free, and when they left, she was better. That was her game.

"They want me to leave the door open," he said.

"I don't care," she snapped. She was pouting now.

"It's good to see you, Neva." Warren's voice was anxious and heavy. He had to clear his throat, and he was embarrassed when she turned quickly and narrowed her eyes at him.

"I don't know if I can trust you," Neva said. After a moment, as if playing with him, she added, "I used to think I could tell, but I was wrong." She turned away and stared silently out the window.

"Perhaps this is a bad time," Warren said.

Neva remained silent, and he waited, uncomfortably.

"Lovers," Neva said finally. "They should have been, could have been, were meant to be . . . were. Perfect. And as any perfect love, tragic."

Warren was confused.

Neva closed her eyes and put her hands to her breast dramatically. "Oh, Heaven, what is your price for one more hour?"

Warren started to ask Neva what she meant, but he realized she was not addressing him. At least, not directly. Neva began again, and Warren stepped closer to make sure he heard her correctly.

"I had this dream of Alec and Emily. She was sitting in his lap, perched like a flickering candle. They were sitting on a wicker chair, not that it matters the type of chair, as far as I can figure. The room had black walls. They were just sitting. They gave off a glow, a perfect flame, bright and clear. But it burned for such a short time. Then, the room was in total darkness, with only a faint silhouette of their image remaining. They were like those tiny flickers of purple light—the kind you see beneath your eyelids when your eyes grow tired—so faint and ephemeral. She was his Raymonda, and he was her Jean de Brienne. He came to take her out of the darkness, but it was useless because darkness was their world, you see. What comes at you in darkness takes you by surprise. They couldn't help what happened, not any of it."

Warren looked around for a place to sit, hoping to draw Neva away from the window. He started to sit at the corner of the bed, then pulled the chair away from the desk and sat facing the chair next to her. Neva paid no attention. She was gazing at the stooped little man raking leaves in the courtyard.

"Do you want to talk about what happened?" Warren asked.

Neva smiled, and her eyes flared for a brief moment. Then, she closed her eyes and breathed deeply. "It's going to rain," Neva said. "I can smell it." With her eyes still closed, she laughed briefly, as if discarding the connection between her senses and her thoughts. "It's just a memory, of course. The air is translucent and tremulous, and everything is so still, as if in hiding. It's amazing how the calm before a storm smells so fresh and clean."

Neva began to speak softly. Warren thought she was talking to someone in the courtyard before he realized she was reciting a poem. Warren thought he recognized it, but he couldn't remember where he had heard it.

"We lie one against the other,
Tangled together like painted
Clouds on a screen, then,
Thighs enlaced, heads together
On the pillow, we sing softly
To the full moon and watch time pass.
The declining moon marks the hours.
Suddenly, we are seized by grief and fear.
Three o'clock in the morning
Has gone by, but we cannot
Get enough of one another. Insatiable
Passion, night swift as the shuttle
In the loom. Oh, Heaven, what is
Your price for one more hour?"

"That's beautiful," Warren said. "I could never recite poetry."

Neva turned and looked directly at him, but he could tell she was far away, that the poem had triggered something, or perhaps it was her way of being able to tell him what she had been thinking about for a long time. Warren waited silently as her enigmatic smile emerged. In her dark eyes was that same sparkle of gypsy intrigue that caused him to fall in love with her the first time he saw her at Morning House.

"'Seventh Day, Seventh Month,'" Neva said. "That day, I didn't read it. It was marked with an envelope, but I didn't read it until later, and only then did I realize that the day was the seventh of July."

Suddenly, Warren remembered where he had seen the poem. "Did you want to talk about it?" he asked.

Neva looked surprised that he had asked, almost angry. "If you have ever loved or wanted love, even to be with someone again for just one night, then you already know about the poem."

Neva didn't realize how she had hurt Warren, how she had assumed that something he had kept hidden all this time wasn't even there. "The title, 'Seventh Day, Seventh Month,' what does it mean?" he asked.

"According to an ancient Chinese myth, the god of heaven arranged the marriage of his granddaughter, Tian Sun, the weaver maid, with Qian Niu, the ox herder, who lived on the west bank of the river Han. Their marriage was so joyous and filled with pleasure that Tian Sun neglected her duty, which was to weave the cloth of heaven. This angered her grandfather, who ordered her back across the river, where she toiled day after day weaving clouds. But her desire remained too great, so on the seventh night of the seventh month of every year, Tian Sun would steal across the river Han on a bridge of magpies to sleep with her beloved Qian Niu for one night. The poem was written in the thirteenth century, but it is hard to believe that it is about anyone but Alec and Emily."

There was a rumbling in the sky, and Neva pulled back the edge of the curtain for a better look through the thick, shatterproof glass.

"Thunder," she said.

"It sounds far away," Warren said. "I had hoped we would be able to go for a walk."

They heard another far-off rumble, and as Neva listened, she recited another poem.

"Thunder. My heart trembles.
I lift my head from my pillow and listen.
It is not a chariot."

Neva was more animated as she continued, moving her hands about her face like a ballerina. "I found that in Alec's book. I memorized it last week on my birthday. I am thirty now." An embarrassed laugh escaped softly from her lips, and Neva turned her head so that Warren noticed the sleek lines of her neck. He wished he could paint her portrait. "I have nothing to do now but listen to the world," she said. "When you are imprisoned, this is all you have, until you are able to free your spirit. I listen to the thoughts of others and repeat them because this is what they want to hear. They want to hear me tell them what they already know. Then, they will think I am cured. I used to be the same way. Now, I just talk, but I don't let on. I listen to the sound of my own voice. It has grown raspy and filled with the fluttering of wings. It is an old woman's voice. And I listen to my own thoughts, what I can remember."

"I want to listen, Neva. I don't want to judge."

After a long silence, Neva said, "It all took place in such a short time, that summer."

232

"I remember."

She looked puzzled, then shrewd, as if she knew something he didn't. "It was Spinner who called Alec a cowboy, and of course, it makes sense. You see, Alec was Altair, the cowboy, and Emily was Vega, the weaver girl." Neva noticed his bewilderment, then added as an explanation, "They are the stars of the summer triangle. The Milky Way flows between them like a river of light. It is the Western version of the Chinese myth." Tilting her head, she said, "Don't you find that odd?"

Neva turned back to the window when Warren did not answer.

The little man was making his way back toward the building, abandoning the piles of leaves he had raked into little islands, like a small model archipelago rising out of a sea of green waves. "It's beginning to rain now," Neva said.

"The walk can wait until another time," Warren said, hoping that she would not dissuade him.

"Rain reminds me of death." Neva paused. Then, she turned toward Warren sharply. "Why did you come here?" she asked.

"To stay in touch. To see you. To see if you have been able to work through what happened."

"I would rather talk about pleasant things like the ocean or the shrimp boats in Kemah. I remember how they glided through the water like birds with their trawler beams wingward, casting dark shadows over slender curls of white keelfoam. The boats talked to me, you know, through the clanks and gurgles of their engines. I used to stand on the shore in the early morning and wave goodbye. The smell of the ocean was always strong in the early morning, and when the boats were gone, I could hear the creaks and groans of the wharf planks, and the mournful echoes of seagulls lolling overhead. It was very peaceful. That was my first life. We lived in Seabrook then. My father was an engineer for NASA. I was seventeen when he died. My mother only lived for tennis and soap operas. At least I still had Jim. Jim was my twin brother, and we were inseparable."

"When Jim was gone, there was no one else left for me. I would sit on the boat docks in Kemah, hoping to find adventure, a reason for living in the shrimpers that sputtered in and out of their slips as sure as the sun rose and set. That was when my definition of God changed, because I knew that that much grief could not be part of a divine plan. I miss the sea. I miss the way it talked to me and helped me to forget all that had happened. Its loneliness was frightening, its solitude comforting. The sighing waves, like a constant cradlesong, used to lull me to sleep, and only then would I forget my own loneliness, and sometimes I would be with Jim again. Do you believe in the hereafter?"

"I believe it's possible, and I guess we will all find out the truth soon enough." Warren laughed awkwardly, hoping that a light air of laughter would elevate her spirits.

"I believe God only protects us in the hereafter," Neva said. She didn't look at Warren or wait for him to respond. Her mind continued in its own state of free association. "For now, my life has been reduced to this room and the parking lot beyond with its monument, a single elm tree. Even the birds ignore it, and the gardener curses it when he rakes the leaves into those lovely piles of orange vermilion. He doesn't realize that he is scraping away the color from my palette, and no one here will tell him. The reach of the building is a red brick pier, blocking my view of the sunsets. I am denied life's wondrous pleasures, and there is no one to describe them to me the way a mother describes the world to her child. Everyone who works here accepts life as commonplace. They listen to me and wait for me to decide that I am no longer insane. In the meantime, I have my books and my Mozart and, of course, the poetry. Jim liked poetry, and so did Alec. Poetry is a religion for those looking for answers."

Neva moved away from the window and sat down with her arms on the chair rests. She stared at Warren like a great sphinx for a long time before she began again.

"This is my third life. My first life was with Jim. My second life was at Morning House. I had no life in between. I guess you really can't call this living either. They won't allow me to decorate my room the way I would like, to reflect my personality. I wanted flowers, but they won't consider wallpaper. They won't even paint over this awful yellow. They say I could be leaving, but they won't say when. It's only an excuse. None of the rooms are permanent. They want us to be normal, but they won't allow even the most basic element of human dignity—to extend one's identity to a sense of belonging. What is normal anyway? Psychiatry sucks!"

Neva laughed, then looked away, the laugh still lingering silently on her lips. Warren just listened.

"I'm beginning to sound like Spinner now. He didn't like being at Morning House, but he hated the thought of going back to Gatesville. That's why he cooperated. That's what he said anyway, but I always suspected that underneath his cynicism he was crying out for help, just like the others. But he couldn't show it, of course, not on the surface. No chinks in his armor. So he talked everything down. 'The system taketh, and the system giveth away,' he used to say. He joked about it, but he had our inadequacies pegged."

"I never gave any of them enough credit," Warren said.

Neva smiled at him as if she suddenly remembered what he had done for her; then, an irony of sadness broke through the smile. "We all seemed to be chasing dreams and running from nightmares. The faster we ran, the closer our enemies got."

Warren thought about simple acts of what he considered negative human behavior. Acts of theft or self-abuse that come from desperation, and the senseless acts of violence or arrogance that made him sick, that made him feel good about what he did, about playing even a small part in bringing peace to victims, and even some change, however small, in the behaviors which could turn their lives upside down. Then, Warren thought about what happened to Neva.

"I want to understand," he said. "I think you deserve that. I think there was a reason for what happened to you, what made you feel you needed to do something."

"I didn't want anyone to die because of me."

The rain fell harder, spattering on the walkway, and they both looked toward the window of this prison, his and hers, each in their own way. Warren realized that their lives had become sad and perfunctory, that there was a certain safety in Neva's rambling, but there was also an ironic sense of clarity.

In the moments of silence between them lingered an immeasurable sense of guilt. So they continued to talk about what happened because Neva sensed that Warren was there to help, and as she took them back to that summer, he knew that somewhere in her words lay the truth. When they had finished and the rain had stopped, the earth seemed to breathe a deep sigh.

"They believe the place is haunted now." Warren laughed. "The neighborhood kids call it the House of Mourning and sometimes just The Morgue. They dare each other to sneak in through the boarded-up windows and sleep overnight. Some even say they have seen the ghosts who live there."

"Ghosts?" Neva asked, with a slight smile of remembrance.

"They've been seen walking between the house and the boathouse. Some claim to have seen a candle burning in the boathouse."

"Where did you hear this?"

"I was eating at Jimmy Walker's in Kemah, and I happened to notice the new bridge, the one they are building to replace the drawbridge. The waiter didn't know me. He just started talking."

"A new bridge," Neva said. "That's progress." She was looking out the window again, this time at the remnants of patchy clouds and the big elm tinseled with broken sunlight. Time and distance had taken her far from Morning House, but Neva still felt its presence. "We all learn from our mistakes," she said.

"I did some checking on the others," Warren said. "Krista is back with her family, trying hard to make it work this time. She even gave me a hug when we said goodbye. Janeen finally got into a foster home, a good family. I think she'll make it with them. She seems happy, as happy as can be, considering. We talked mostly about Spinner. She cried, of course, but she was talking about the good times, so there was a lot of laughter mixed with her tears. I went to Spinner's funeral and spoke with his grandmother. I think she appreciated hearing the stories and what a good heart he had."

Warren stood and moved toward the door.

"It's not good to dwell on the past forever," he said. "We all have to learn how to move on." After a moment, knowing there was no other way to say it, Warren concluded, "There is still no word of Alec and Emily."

Neva remained by the window until Warren asked if she would like to go for that walk now that the rain had stopped; then, she went with him, not because there was a reason to, but only because there was no reason to stay. Neva was beginning to enjoy the bluebonnets that flourished along the roadside near the fence. She stopped as a stiff breeze crossed their path, and she watched the bluebonnets dance, rejoicing in the warmth brought by the rain. Soon, they would be gone, until next summer.

"There are some things we cannot move away from," Neva said. "They stay with us forever and return like the seasons to remind us that we are mortal, that sadness is as much a part of life as joy."

"As long as you don't let it overwhelm you," Warren said. "You of all people should know that."

"What I did was wrong."

"You were cleared of that. Detective Kelly saw to that."

"*You* saw to that. We both know the truth."

"Detective Kelly was no fool. He knew it had to end if there was going to be any healing."

"What's funny is that the better understanding I have, the more confused and depressed I become about what happened. It's like I am trapped in this space between sanity and insanity. I know exactly what's happening, but I can't do anything to change it."

"Dr. Mueller had ruined many lives. You were just reacting to that."

"No. During those weeks, I wrote down what was happening to me. I have gone over it again and again in my mind, and I know now that I transferred to Dr. Mueller all the hate I harbored for my uncle, and now I must live with the anguish of that."

"What happened was an accident. I will always believe that you would never have pulled that trigger."

Neva was quiet for a long time, turning her face into a shower of sunlight that slipped from behind the trees. She seemed refreshed by it. "I have to believe that Alec and Emily are in a better place now," she said finally. "That somewhere they still are lovers. Anna Gogarty was right about that after all. Our souls will find in some Brontean hereafter what we are not allowed to have in this conscious life. We live in a kissproof world. Alec knew that, and he did what he felt he had to do. I am so envious of Alec and Emily. My own soul still aches for Jim, but all I can do is dream. It doesn't help."

They walked on awhile in silence, and Warren wanted to tell her how he had loved her and how he had been so jealous of Dr. Mueller because he thought they were becoming lovers, but he didn't.

"How do you cleanse the spirit?" Neva asked. "How do you start anew when the very reason for your being has been destroyed?"

"I don't know that it is ever completely possible," Warren said. "I believe that each person must somehow find a way. I know you are right, that the past is never forgotten, but we must learn to live with it, hold on dearly to the good memories and somehow channel it all into something productive."

Warren wanted to hold Neva, but he knew it wasn't the right thing to do. He thought he noticed a sparkle in her eyes and smiled, knowing that this time it was not the sunlight.

"I know that one day you will heal," Warren said, "and move on from this place. You're the strongest person I know, Neva, and I am glad to be your friend."

Neva thanked him for coming by to see her, then used his shoulders to pull herself up to kiss him on the cheek. "You see," she said, "There are some spots I can reach on my own." She asked him if he could stay longer. Neva was being so polite and sweet, throwing him off his guard, that Warren felt bad when he inadvertently glanced at his watch, so he told her that perhaps he could stay for one more hour.

"The river runs eternal," Neva said, laughing. "But sometimes the price for one more hour is too great."

Thank you so much for reading *Kissproof World*. If you've enjoyed the book, we would be grateful if you would post a review on the bookseller's website. Just a few words is all it takes!

Also by William West

The Ascension of Mary
2021 American Writing Awards Finalist

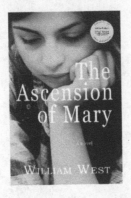

"Utterly unique, exquisitely crafted and quietly powerful."
—NetGalley Reviewer

"West draws the reader in through excellent storytelling and intricate settings. The book is perfectly complex in the layers of stories that weave together the past and present, allowing the reader to feel more connected to the story. The narrations add depth to each character and gives a better understanding of their struggles with loss, and the relationships that are building between them. The author brings up important topics like racism and grief, while highlighting the value of love. From the beginning to the end, this book is a page-turner."
—Sublime Book Review